flipping the pages until the final twist that will leave you reeling. Grey skillfully and lovingly plays within the rules of the genre while also bringing a fresh voice and perspective to the *And Then There Were None* premise that will delight not just Agatha Christie fans but fans of tense, clever, and goose bump–inducing stories as well. Clear your calendar for the day, because this is a one-sitting read!"

—Brianna Labuskes, bestselling
author of *A Familiar Sight*

"*Knives Out* meets Lucy Foley's *The Hunting Party* in this tense locked-room mystery. Be wary of invitations where everyone could be a suspect."

—Georgina Cross, author of *One Night,*
Nanny Needed, and *The Stepdaughter*

"Readers who were raised on a steady diet of Agatha Christie will find much to love in *She Left*—the intriguing cast of suspects, the red herrings scattered through the story, and the sleuth who has to put it all together to get herself to safety. Grey's story is a satisfying riff on the classic mystery story structure that will keep readers guessing until the end."

—Eva Jurczyk, author of *The Department*
of Rare Books and Special Collections

"In *She Left,* Stacie Grey combines a clever setup with all the excitement of a classic whodunit, complete with a compelling cast of characters (and suspects). The tension grabbed me from the first page and ratcheted up relentlessly with each scene."

—Elle Grawl, author of *One of Those Faces* and *What Still Burns*

"*She Left* by Stacie Grey, with its sharp writing, a cunning locked-room setting, and eerie atmosphere, reads like a modern-day Agatha Christie and has all the hallmarks of a can't-put-it-down thriller."

—Ashley Tate, author of *Twenty-Seven Minutes*

"Immersive and hypnotizing, *She Left* is the effortless summer read that will enthrall you from the first chapter. Suspense and mystery lovers will find each character to be convincingly suspicious and the decades-past crime to be full of compelling unanswered questions. Start this in the morning, because Grey's taut writing will drive you to finish this book in one sitting."

—Elle Marr, Amazon Charts bestselling author of *The Alone Time* and *The Family Bones*

PRAISE FOR STACIE GREY

SHE HAD ENOUGH

"In Stacie Grey's *She Had Enough,* a massive earthquake provides the perfect cover for a cold-blooded crime. Grey delivers a taut, atmospheric thriller where the deepest fault lines lie between friends."

—Daniel G. Miller, *USA Today* bestselling author of *The Orphanage by the Lake*

"The fault line pressure beneath the earth is nothing compared to the trembling rubble of secrets and lies above. In the aftermath of a San Francisco earthquake, the hairline fractures prove as difficult to navigate as the gaping ruptures. Facades are skewed, paths bent, and people displaced, as Stacie Grey keeps us hanging by our fingernails until the final chapter."

—KD Aldyn, author of *Sister, Butcher, Sister*

SHE DIDN'T STAND A CHANCE

"The brutal desert heat meets a cold-blooded killer in this taut mystery from Stacie Grey. A Palm Springs setting, rich people behaving badly, and the laugh-out-loud family dysfunction made this a winner for me. I couldn't put this book down."

—Joshua Moehling, *USA Today* bestselling author of *And There He Kept Her* and *Where the Dead Sleep*

"For *She Didn't Stand a Chance*'s engaging outsider, Gertie, the inhospitable and deadly desert is nothing compared to the suspects trapped with her at her dead father's estate. Clever, atmospheric, and sizzling with suspense, this book is an addictive binge."

—Heather Chavez, author of *Before She Finds Me* and *What We'll Burn Last*

"In *She Didn't Stand a Chance,* Stacie Grey combines classic mystery elements (a sprawling family comprised of wealthy misfits, a shocking will, members of 'the help' who know more than they should) with a contemporary setting and effervescent tone. The result is a freshly contemporary mystery I inhaled as though it were a beloved Agatha Christie novel. Extra points for featuring an architectural monstrosity of a dwelling, too… Begin this one at your own risk! You're not going to want to stop."

—Kemper Donovan, *USA Today* bestselling author of *Loose Lips* and *The Busy Body*

SHE LEFT

"Deliciously twisty—Agatha Christie would be spellbound."

—M. M. Chouinard, *USA Today* bestselling author of *The Dancing Girls*

"In this engrossing mystery, a vividly drawn cast of characters, claustrophobic setting, and propulsive pacing will keep you

ALSO BY STACIE GREY

She Left

She Didn't Stand a Chance

She Had Enough

A NOVEL

STACIE GREY

Published by Poisoned Pen Press, an imprint of Sourcebooks
1935 Brookdale RD, Naperville, IL 60563-2773
(630) 961-3900
sourcebooks.com

Library of Congress Cataloging-in-Publication Data

Names: Grey, Stacie author
Title: She had enough : a novel / Stacie Grey.
Description: Naperville, IL : Poisoned Pen Press, 2026.
Identifiers: LCCN 2026003663 | trade paperback | epub
Subjects: LCGFT: Thrillers (Fiction) | Novels
Classification: LCC PS3602.A85347 S535 2026
LC record available at https://lccn.loc.gov/2026003663

Printed and bound in the United States of America.
CR 10 9 8 7 6 5 4 3 2 1

For Cameron, with all my love

1

Mallory's wineglass tilted perilously, nearly crashing before she could recover it. She took a moment to rearrange the sharing plates crowding the too-small table so it wouldn't happen again and had a sip before going on.

"So then he says, 'That's why girls like you die alone surrounded by cats.' And I'm like, *Don't threaten me with a good time.*"

The other women laughed, and Mallory started to relax. *The only consolation for never being able to think of a comeback in the moment,* she thought, *was sharing it with friends after the fact.*

"Why are men?" Rachel said. "Honestly, I'm *this close* to deleting the apps and going to live in the woods."

"I don't know how you guys do it. I'd go crazy in a week." Kendra shook her head.

Rachel looked across the top of her cocktail glass at her. "Says the married lady. We can't all find our dream guy at freshman orientation. We're just out here doing the best we can with what's available."

Laughter again, and the conversation lapsed as the busboy approached to refill their water glasses. There were six of them around the table—Mallory, Lourdes, Rachel, Sonali, Kendra, and Caitlin. They had all gone to college together, and Mallory had known most of them for years. The only exception was Caitlin, who was a few years younger and a friend of Kendra and Rachel's.

"Speaking of impossible things, how's the house hunt going, Lourdes?" Mallory asked. Two weeks earlier, their group text had been filled with the craziest San Francisco real estate listings Lourdes had come across, but recently the stream had dried up. So it wasn't a surprise when her friend sighed.

"'Impossible' is the word. We put in an offer on a three-bedroom in Dogpatch that went for two hundred thousand over asking. I don't know, maybe we'll try again in the summer. February isn't a great time for house searching."

Mallory nodded and tried to keep her expression sympathetic. The truth was, Lourdes worked in finance and her boyfriend was on the partner track at a big law firm, and even on Mallory's quite decent programmer's salary, she couldn't even begin to contemplate the houses they were looking at.

Not everyone saw the question from the same angle.

"Dogpatch? Oh god, I couldn't live there. You might as well move to Oakland." The horror in Kendra's tone was so strong that Mallory actually laughed out loud. But it was Caitlin, who had been mostly silent so far, who took up the defense.

"I like the neighborhood," she said, so softly it was hard to hear her over the restaurant's sound system. "A girl I used to work with has her art studio there, and there are some nice coffee shops."

"And then you go back home to Sea Cliff," Kendra snarked and then looked like she immediately regretted it. Mallory knew why—in a separate text during the planning for the dinner, Kendra said she was inviting Caitlin because her mother had died recently. (She hadn't mentioned that Caitlin lived in one of San Francisco's fanciest neighborhoods.)

"Anyway," Kendra hurriedly went on. "What's everyone's dream feature in a house? I don't want to think about reality anyway. I'm holding out for an infinity pool."

"In SF? I think I'd go for something I could use more than three times a year," said Lourdes. "Give me one of those giant stoves and separate standing freezer. Never gonna run out of Totino's again."

"Pfft, that's thinking small." Rachel was gesturing with her fork, a sure sign she was on a roll. "Everyone's got a fancy kitchen. What I want is one of those Japanese bathtubs that keeps the water at the perfect temperature."

That got a laugh from Sonali. "Is that a thing? I'm holding out for a Sub-Zero makeup fridge."

The atmosphere was thawing, and Mallory felt relieved. It was the first time they had gotten together in months, and the conversation had started off strained and awkward. Sonali had been in a weird mood, which hadn't helped—she was usually the one to kick things off with her characteristic oversharing. But for most of the evening she had rivaled Caitlin for silence.

Mallory had been feeling isolated lately—it was too easy to

split her time between work and streaming shows, commuting between her desk and the couch on the days she wasn't in the office. The occasional dates, like the one earlier that week, were no break. Even when they weren't disastrous, they just felt like another project, a box to check in Mallory's Big Adulthood Plan.

So, as much as she had been tempted to cancel at the last minute and spend another Saturday evening in her pajamas, Mallory was glad she had come.

"Speaking of luxury," Kendra said to Lourdes. "How was Tahoe? That cabin looked amazing."

"The cabin was really nice," Lourdes agreed. "The part where Emil's stepbrother busted his knee because he thought he could do a black diamond run his first time on a snowboard? Not so great. And of course Emil's stepmom thought we should all go stay in some Motel 6 by the hospital to keep him company. Like, lady, that is a grown-ass man, and I don't get enough vacation as it is. Anyway, that was a fun conversation. Especially since we were paying for the cabin."

"Stepparents are the worst," Caitlin said, with feeling.

Rachel opened her mouth then shut it again and frowned down at her plate like she was thinking something she didn't want to say.

Sonali must have noticed the awkwardness, and she leaned forward and nodded sympathetically. "Family issues are so hard," she said. "We have these people in our lives we didn't choose, and we're stuck with them."

Mallory was as impressed by Sonali's ability to come up with the right thing to say as she was surprised when Caitlin laughed.

"You could say that. Definitely, you could say that," she said.

Even Sonali didn't seem to know how to respond, and the group fell silent as everyone at the table suddenly became more interested in their dinner.

The restaurant was one Mallory hadn't been to before. It described itself as serving "global California cuisine," which seemed to mean they put gochujang in the hummus and preserved lemon on the chicken salad. But somehow it all worked, and now there was only the last tamari-glazed Brussels sprout sitting on its sharing plate, daring someone to take it.

Mallory wasn't falling for that this time. She set her napkin next to her plate, pushed back her chair, and gestured at her glass.

"I'll be right back," she said. "If anyone asks, I'll see the dessert menu and have another sauv blanc."

To her surprise, Caitlin stood up too. "Me too," she said. "Not the wine part. I think I saw a bathroom sign by the bar."

The women's room was small, with only two stalls. When Mallory came out, she found Caitlin already at the sinks, fiddling with an ornate lipstick tube—gold colored and set with brightly colored bits of glass.

"That's really pretty; what brand is it?" Mallory asked.

Caitlin was less than two feet away from her, but she jumped like she had been startled.

"Oh, this? It's not—it was my mother's. You put the lipstick in as an insert."

"Oh, cool." Looking closer, Mallory realized Caitlin had been crying. That shouldn't be surprising, Mallory reminded herself—grief was unpredictable. Guessing the other woman wanted some time to collect herself, she got her own lipstick out and started applying it.

"Have you lived in the city long?" she asked, keeping an eye on Caitlin in the mirror while she blotted her lips.

"Most of my life. We were in San Jose when I was little, but after my mom's job took off, we moved up here." She sniffed a couple of times and then turned to look fully at Mallory. "You're a computer programmer, right? That's what my mom was too."

"Really? That's cool. I bet things were different in her time. Not saying it's easy now, but some of the stories you hear…"

"Oh yeah." Caitlin nodded vigorously. "She was tough, though. No one could get anything over on her."

Mallory caught Caitlin's eye in the mirror and smiled. "I'm sorry I didn't get a chance to meet her. She sounds like she was quite a person."

"She was." Caitlin looked back down at her hands, and Mallory gave her a moment.

They made a funny pair in the reflection—at five foot two, Mallory barely came past Caitlin's shoulder, and the black jeans and blouse that were her going-out default made her look like Caitlin's personal assistant or butler. Caitlin was dressed in an emerald green coatdress over silvery tights and boots with "Prada" on the buckles, but Mallory couldn't bring herself to be jealous. Caitlin was only a couple of years younger than her, but she seemed like a kid—sad and scared.

Scared? Mallory thought. *Why did I think that?*

But now that she had seen it, she couldn't shake the impression. Behind the red patches under Caitlin's eyes and trembling mouth, there was a hunted look.

Mallory barely knew this girl, and she had no business probing into her personal life. But maybe it was the wine she had with dinner or the unspoken community of the ladies' room that made her feel like she needed to say something.

"Are you okay? Can I help with anything?"

Caitlin drew a sharp breath, and for a moment, her eyes met Mallory's in the mirror. There was something there—Confusion? Indecision?—but then it was gone. Caitlin dropped her gaze down to the clutch in her hands.

"Actually, would you mind holding on to this for me?" Caitlin held out the lipstick. "The latch on this bag keeps slipping, and I'm afraid it's going to fall out."

"Oh, sure, no problem." Mallory made an elaborate show of opening her own purse to cover for her embarrassment. Zero points for perception, as usual. Still, she did offer, so she took the lipstick tube and tucked it into an interior pocket.

"Don't let me forget to give this back to you," she said. "I guess you'd hate to lose it."

"Oh yes, definitely," Caitlin said.

2

Dessert was three kinds of cheesecake and six spoons. Everyone but Sonali had at least one more drink, and the conversation split into smaller groups with Rachel, Mallory, and Lourdes arguing over the essential components of a burrito, while Kendra, Sonali, and Caitlin talked about their preferred routes for getting around the city.

The restaurant was empty, and the staff was clearing the tables when they finally got up to leave.

“Who’s up for the club?” Kendra asked as they reached the curb. The February night was chilly but clear, and her breath coiled around the restaurant’s lights.

Lourdes was the first to beg off. “We’ve got brunch with Emil’s cousins tomorrow,” she said.

“And I’ve got work to catch up before a meeting on Monday,” Sonali added. “This is already later than I meant to be out.”

“What happened to Caitlin?” Rachel asked.

“She left while we were doing the check,” said Sonali. “She said something about being tired.”

Mallory wondered about that. But all she said was, "That makes all of us. Sorry, Kendra, I think we're officially old. Thirty-four is the new sixty."

Kendra sighed dramatically. "Fine. But one of these days I'm going to remind you guys what fun feels like."

"Next time," Mallory said, as the others started down the street to the parking lot. "I promise."

Exhausted by an evening's worth of social interaction, Mallory opted for a driverless taxi and settled into the back as invisible hands steered her out into traffic. It wasn't until they were passing Golden Gate Park that she remembered Caitlin's lipstick, still in her purse.

Oh well, she thought. *I can get it back to her later.*

It was after eleven and the house was dark, but the lingering smell of pot told Mallory her landlady, Joan, had been out for her nightly joint in the backyard. The smoke gave her a headache, but she wasn't going to complain—the odds she would find another apartment she could afford were slim to none, and aside from smelling like burning roadkill every evening, it was a great place to live.

Joan had owned the house, and its downstairs in-law unit, since she and her husband moved there in the eighties. He was long gone—dead or divorced; Mallory had never asked—but Joan had stayed on, painting brightly colored landscapes she sold through a friend's gallery. Mallory didn't know where Joan's money came from, but there must have been enough of it, because she hadn't raised the rent on the basement one-bedroom apartment where Mallory lived once in five years.

Despite the smell, Mallory lingered for a moment outside her door, enjoying the night. It was a clear night in February, a welcome break in the rainy season, and even the cold was worth savoring.

Mallory leaned against the picnic table and looked up at the stars. Sky shine from the city lights blotted most of them out, but even this many were a rare sight, with no clouds overhead. She lived on the west side of the city, where there were no hills to separate her neighborhood from the ocean, and the fog was a regular presence. So any view of the sky was a treat, even if the only constellation Mallory could identify was Orion and a neighbor's nighttime car maintenance provided an uninspiring soundtrack.

But it was the sound of meowing that finally drew her inside, where her two cats were waiting impatiently. Mallory checked their food and water while Celine (tortoiseshell with very strong opinions) and Mariah (tabby regularly startled by her own tail) wound around her feet.

There was nothing more Mallory needed to do, but she was reluctant to go to bed. She had been telling the truth when she said she was tired, but now she was fully awake and on edge for reasons she couldn't place. Some of it was her normal reaction to spending too much time around other people—next would be the part where she went through everything she had said and done and wondered if she needed to clarify or apologize.

But that wasn't the heart of the problem, and it didn't take long for her to admit the conversation with Caitlin was on her mind. Had she been wrong about the fear? Mallory didn't think so, but she had no experience with the kind of grief that came with the loss of a parent. Caitlin's words and actions had seemed unusual, but Mallory didn't know her well—how could she be sure that wasn't just how she was? Plenty of people thought Mallory was strange when they first met her.

She wandered around the apartment, tidying up while she thought. The space wasn't large, but she still managed to make a mess, and as she was gathering some bills that somehow ended up under her desk, she thought she heard something in the kitchen. Going to see what it was, she looked at her laptop screen and happened to notice the time, 11:42.

There was a thump, like something had hit the house, and Mallory stumbled. She had barely caught herself when it started.

The earthquake rolled through the building, throwing Mallory to the floor. She saw her books and her computer fall around her, and the television had started to tip over when the lights went out, and she could only hear it smash on the floor.

She crawled under the table, dragging the chairs into a fortress as the walls tipped one way and then the other, and the roar of the earth was punctuated by the sound of breaking glass. From the kitchen, she could hear the cabinet doors swinging open and the crashing of plates and glasses falling out. Her eyes started to adjust to the darkness, and she saw metal bowl roll past her and spin like a top.

The table slid along the vinyl floor, squeezing Mallory in between it and the chairs, and a heavy object fell on top of it. The tabletop creaked but didn't crack, and Mallory gave silent thanks for the strength of Ikea particleboard.

Something touched her elbow, and she looked over to find Celine crouched next to her, while Mariah's yellow eyes glowed from under the desk.

"Oh, hell no," Mallory said.

3

Mallory did not die alone with her cats. The shaking felt like it went on forever, but when it stopped, she looked at her watch. Eleven forty-five. Less than three minutes had passed.

She slowly released the breath she didn't realize she had been holding when her phone sprang to life with a screaming alarm. EARTHQUAKE WARNING the screen announced. Mallory wouldn't have thought she was able to laugh, but it turned out she could.

She stayed under the table as the first aftershock hit, shaking what was left of her possessions like something was trying to work them through a sieve. A few minutes later, there was another, and then when she was thinking about getting up, one more. They finally grew less frequent, and her knees were aching from kneeling on the hard floor. Mallory pushed her way through the chairs and got unsteadily to her feet.

For a moment Mallory only looked around, unsure of what to think or do. The cats were okay, at least—Mariah had come out from under the desk and was washing her paws, and Celine was batting around some earbuds that had fallen on the floor. Mallory was relieved, but she didn't think she was going to be able to achieve that level of normalcy for a while. She had lived most of her life in California and had been through plenty of earthquakes, but this one was different. She had never experienced anything so violent, and her first instinct was to reach for her phone to look for information. But the signal was down to one bar and nothing would load.

She sent a text to her parents, safe in their new home in Virginia, to let them know she was all right, and then she turned it off to save the battery and tried to take stock of her situation.

The room was dark, but the moonlight that filtered through the window gave an idea of the damage. The small flat-screen TV that had been there when she moved in had fallen off its stand, as had everything on the bookshelves. All of her houseplants were also on the floor, with some of their pots smashed, and it wasn't until she tried to scoop one up to put it in a temporary bowl that she realized that one of the reasons the light was getting in so well was because the windows were broken; the glass had mixed with the potting soil.

Mallory went to wash the shallow cuts on her hands, but after a moment of running, the tap sputtered and would only drip. She cleaned herself as well as she could with a dish towel and found the Band-Aids mostly by luck. Her flashlight was on a shelf in the kitchen, and she was able to get a good look at the room. That was when she noticed the cracks in the wall.

The walls of her apartment made up the foundation of the

building above, and Mallory had always thought they were sturdy. She hoped that was still true, but the three long cracks that ran from the ceiling to the floor weren't reassuring.

Mallory decided to go outside.

It took a minute to get the cats into their carrier, and by the time Mallory got outdoors, there were voices coming from the direction of the street. Leaving the carrier covered with a blanket and far enough from the building to be safe, she went to investigate.

Despite living in the apartment for half a decade, Mallory had never gotten to know her neighbors. Some of them she recognized by sight, like the older Asian woman across the street who was often out tending the roses in her front yard, or the middle-aged white couple who took turns walking their hyperactive border collies around the block. But she knew none of their names, and she doubted anyone knew hers.

Except for Joan, of course. Her landlady was loudly present, asking names of everyone she didn't know and hugging everyone she did. As soon as she saw Mallory, she made a beeline toward her.

"You're okay?" Joan asked but didn't wait for an answer. "That was a hell of a quake, wasn't it? Harry thinks it could have been a nine."

Mallory didn't know who Harry was, but she thought he might be right. Looking around, she could see that Joan's house had been lucky—other buildings on the block had sustained a lot more damage. Roof tiles had slid to the ground from one, a duplex was askew on its foundation, and down the block one building had lost its entire facade.

"Is anybody hurt?" Mallory asked. "Can we get help?"

"No casualties so far," said a man wearing a headlamp and a high-visibility vest who walked past them. "Which is good, because I don't think help is coming."

He didn't sound like he was joking. As Mallory looked around, she understood what he meant.

The power was out as far as she could see, and the sound of distant sirens filled the air. Her neighborhood was at the foot of the hills that made up most of the city, so the view beyond them was blocked, but what was most striking was what Mallory didn't see. The sky shine from the city lights had always been in the view in that direction, and now the horizon was completely dark.

"The power must be out all over the city," she said. She was mostly talking to herself, but Joan answered.

"Seems like it. I tried calling my friend Andy who lives in the Castro, and I couldn't even get through. He works for the mayor's office, so I thought he might know something, and he has a landline. But all I got was a bunch of beeping before it disconnected."

"Do you think there are fires?" Mallory asked. She was thinking about what she knew of the 1906 earthquake, when half the city burned, and about the way the water hadn't come out of the tap.

"Probably," Joan said. "All those gas lines, some of them are bound to break."

She sounded surprisingly calm about the idea. Mallory wished she could feel the same. The truth was, her immediate situation wasn't too hazardous. She was out of the building, and there was nothing at risk of falling on her; there were no fires she could see, and she didn't smell gas. The night was chilly but not dangerously cold, and if any of the people there posed a threat, they weren't showing it.

But that safety could be temporary, and Mallory didn't know what she could do if it changed. She had about half a tank of gas in her car, but where could she go? How far would she get? Even here, there was debris in the street—what if she got further and found the way completely blocked? San Francisco was at the top of a peninsula, after all, and she didn't think the chances of getting across the bridges to the north or the east were good.

That left the route to the south, through the tech-heavy cities of the peninsula, toward the South Bay valleys and beyond. Mallory didn't know what she would find if she tried to go that way, but she did know that right now, tens of thousands of people across the city were having the same thought, and she didn't see how getting stuck in the world's biggest traffic jam was going to improve her situation.

The people around her must have felt the same, or they knew more than she did, because no one else was going either. A helicopter passed overhead, sweeping a spotlight over them. A few people waved, and Mallory hoped for some sort of announcement, but the aircraft passed on with no response.

"I heard you were asking about fires?" The man with the headlamp had come back, carrying a bundle of blankets under his arm. He had tilted the light up so that she could see his face—an Asian guy about her own age. Mallory recognized him as being from the same house as the old woman with the roses—probably his grandmother.

"There are at least three large fires on right now, but none of them are threatening us," he went on, shifting the blanket bundle so it was more secure. "One near Fisherman's Wharf, a small one in Chinatown, and an explosion in the Mission that started at least four related fires. But the prevailing winds are from the west, so we should be fine. As long as there isn't anything brewing down in someone's basement or a gas line explosion or something."

"I guess we can hope," said Mallory. "Are you with the fire department?"

"No, I'm just prepared. I've got two emergency band radios, and I've been able to pick up some fire department communications on my CB. I'm Harry, by the way."

Since his hands were occupied, Mallory nodded her greeting. "Mallory. Thanks for the information." She looked past him to the house with the roses. "Is your home okay?"

"I think so. I'll get a better look in the morning, but we had a structural engineer come out two years ago to bring everything up to date."

"Oh. That sounds like a good idea." The way he said it, Mallory was reminded of college conversations with guys who had very detailed ideas about everything, but under the circumstances, she couldn't really argue with this one.

"It's a good thing, too," Harry went on. "I think I can convince Grandma to stay outside tonight, because there's so much going on, but that's not going to last. Anyway, I'd better get her these blankets before she starts a fire."

With that, he was gone, before Mallory could ask if his

grandmother was a firebug or just liked to stay warm, and she was left to think about what she was going to do for the night herself.

She wasn't tired anymore. The adrenaline that had struck with the quake had subsided, but what it left behind was a feeling of unease, like she was caught in a dream where everything was familiar, but also not. Sleep would have to come eventually, but she couldn't imagine how.

When it did, it wouldn't be in her bed, not with those cracks in the wall and the creeping fear of another earthquake that might finish what the first one started. She looked around to see if anyone else shared her feelings, but aside from the strangeness of the setting, it looked like they were holding a block party. People were chatting, even laughing, meeting neighbors for the first time, and corralling children. Outfits ranged from going-out clothes, like Mallory was still wearing, to pajamas.

Mallory wanted to walk up to some of them, to grab that guy who had just slapped his friend on the back and shout, *Don't you know what is happening?* But she didn't, because she had it together just enough to recognize that she was having a reaction to the shock, and also, who was she to judge? Standing there with her arms crossed, like someone at a party they couldn't wait to leave—she must look like she didn't care at all.

In truth, she was cold, worried, and unsure of how to start a conversation with anything other than *Do you think we're going to die?* So she hung back and said nothing until Joan came back and handed her a bowl of ice cream.

"Might as well eat it; it's going to melt!" her landlord said as she produced a pair of spoons from her pocket. "Food is bound to get weird soon, so we should enjoy it while we can."

It had been only a few hours since dinner, and Mallory wasn't hungry, but she didn't feel like she had a choice.

"What do you think is going to happen now?" she asked, as she ate the half-melted rocky road, chasing walnuts around the bottom of the bowl.

"That's a damn good question," Joan said. "Right now, I'm happy to just stay put and be grateful I've got a home that's still standing."

"There are a couple of cracks on the back wall," Mallory said, but that didn't seem to concern Joan, at least not right away.

"Nothing's perfect," she said, then thought for a minute. "Still, I guess we should stay outside for a while. I've got some tents."

Caitlin

How could I have been so stupid?

Caitlin leaned forward, gripping the steering wheel as she raced through the city streets, blinking back tears. Everything was clear now, but how much damage had she done? She had been so completely convinced. If it wasn't for one little word, one mistake, she would have gone along with it to the end.

It had been absolutely crazy to give Mallory the lipstick. Caitlin barely knew her—she had probably turned around and told the rest of them about it as soon as Caitlin was out of the room, and then it would have all been for nothing.

If only I had kept my cool, gone through with the handoff as planned, she wouldn't suspect anything. But by now she knows. She must know.

That would have been the right thing to do. If she hadn't given away that she knew, she would have been safe. But that would have been too much, to betray her mom like that.

She shouldn't have given it to Mallory; she should have thrown it off the bridge.

Caitlin parked her car in the garage, checking the mirror as she pulled in to see if anyone was following her. But the street was quiet, not even a light in the tower across the street where her neighbor was always watching what was going on.

Ann might have seen something. I should ask her.

But she would ask over the phone, or email, or something else she could do from far away. Caitlin wasn't sure where she was going to go, but it would be somewhere it wouldn't be easy to find her. Hawaii was too obvious. Maybe Fiji? Or she could just take off driving, see how far she could get.

The house was dark and quiet. Caitlin didn't turn on any lights on her way to her room. No point in advertising where she was. It meant it took her longer to do what she needed to, and she wasn't even sure what clothes she was packing, but that didn't matter. If she needed anything, she could buy it wherever she ended up.

Gimli hated his carrier, so she left him until the end. He had gone into hiding as soon as she got her suitcase out, and she knew she would find him under the drying rack in the laundry room, so she let him stay there until she was ready to go.

Caitlin needed to hurry, but she kept remembering things she couldn't leave behind. She didn't know how long she was going to be gone, or what might happen before she came back, and anything she left in the house wouldn't be safe. So she packed up every computer that might have important information, every document she could get her hands on. If they were going to try and take what wasn't theirs, Caitlin wasn't going to give it up without a fight.

It was after eleven by the time she was sure she had everything. Nothing had happened—Caitlin was looking out of the windows every few minutes, but no one approached the house. What if it had all been a misunderstanding? Caitlin checked her phone, but there were no messages, no missed calls.

Maybe she thinks I just freaked out and need some space.

And maybe she did. But she could get that space at a pet-friendly resort in Nevada, or wherever.

Caitlin had her last bag in hand, and she was about to reach under her mattress for her diary, the last thing she wouldn't leave without, when another thought occurred to her.

Mom's diary.

She was sure Charlie hadn't found it. She had caught him looking just that week, trying the bottoms of all the bookshelves. Caitlin wasn't even sure what he thought was in it that he wanted, but she couldn't let him find it. Not after what he did.

The problem was even she wasn't sure where it was hidden. There had been a lot of renovations to the house over the years, and her mom had loved a secret compartment. It would take forever to go through all the options, but Caitlin thought she knew where to start.

Her stepfather would have had plenty of opportunities to search the main bedroom in the last several months, as he hung on like the parasite he was. But he hadn't understood her mother any more than he had loved her, and anyway, he was pretty dumb.

Deborah had liked to write in her diary first thing in the morning, when she had had the chance to sleep on the events of the day before, and she had a bay window with a seat put in, where she could sit and look out at the Golden Gate, watching from the ocean side as the sun rose over the bridge.

Caitlin crouched down next to it, running her fingers over the wood to look for a hidden latch. Finding nothing, she climbed up on the seat, searching the bookshelves on either side. She felt it shake under her feet. Caitlin looked down, confused. The builders who had done the work were supposed to be top quality; was this thing really that unstable?

Then the entire house swung out from under her. Caitlin tried to keep her balance, but her foot missed the edge of the seat, and she tumbled forward.

Her head hit a corner on the bookshelf, and everything went black.

4

Mallory helped Joan set up the tents in the backyard. While they were working, another aftershock hit, strong enough to make Mallory stumble and drop the hammer. Panicked shouts and curses came from the street, and even Joan stopped what she was doing and stared nervously at the roof. But nothing more happened, and eventually she exhaled.

"This old Earth of ours," she said to Mallory. "She's a real mother, isn't she?"

There were two more aftershocks that night, neither serious, but they kept Mallory from relaxing. Around sunrise the waves of exhaustion were so strong that she gave in, crawled into her sleeping bag, and fell asleep, with Mariah curled up at her feet and Celine breathing into her face.

She woke to bright sunshine and the sound of helicopters. Emerging from the tent, Mallory looked up to see one after another pass overhead—police, military, Coast Guard, and uncountable numbers of small aircraft, some with news station logos, circling so low she could see the cameras.

There were voices coming from the street, so Mallory headed toward them, hoping someone there would know more about what was going on.

What she found was a repeat of the scene from the previous night, with the same people wearing the same clothes. There was a slightly more organized feeling to this gathering—someone had set a folding table on the sidewalk, stocked with perishable foods, and a radio sat on the end of it, relaying emergency messages.

But most of the information came in the form of rumors, shared along with the tubs of yogurt and cartons of orange juice.

"I heard someone tried to cross Golden Gate Park in a Cybertruck and got stuck in the bison paddock."

"What happened to the bison?"

"No idea. Burgers?"

"Somebody said the navy was going to bring a carrier and park it at Pier 39."

"I heard they're using ferries to get people over to Treasure Island and flying them out from there."

"How? There hasn't been a working runway there for years."

"All I know is nobody's getting out by the roads," said a voice close to Mallory.

It was Harry, the young man from the night before. He had traded his headlamp for a helmet to go with his fluorescent vest, and he was holding a sandwich, piled high with lettuce and lunch meat between slices of white bread.

"How do you know?" Mallory asked. "Was it on the radio?"

"Yes, and I went to see for myself," Harry said. "You don't have to go far. Nineteenth is totally stopped all the way to the park. And people are running out of gas in the backup, which makes it worse. Anyone should have known that would happen."

His attitude was irritating, but Harry was her best source of information, so she saved her snark. "Have you heard anything more about the fires? Or when they might get the power back on?"

Harry shook his head. "Last I heard they had the fire in the Financial District under control, but two of the ones in the Mission had merged. But as far as the power, no, I don't think we're getting that back soon. Or water, and definitely not gas. It's going to take weeks before they can even start."

That wasn't what Mallory wanted to hear, but it was what she had suspected. "I guess we're on our own, then," she said. "At least it's dry."

"For now." Optimism was clearly not in the cards for her new friend. "The weather service says a cold front is moving in."

Mallory looked to the west, but there was nothing in the sky but a scattering of white clouds. "I hope it's not too bad," she said. "If we're stuck outside, it's going to be hard to stay warm."

Harry nodded. "I've got a generator, but I don't want to use it while there's still a risk of gas leaks. That's why I wouldn't let them do a barbecue for the food. My detector isn't getting anything, but better safe than blown up."

"Good point." It hadn't occurred to Mallory that a gas leak

detector was something that existed, let alone that she might want one, but now she regretted not being better prepared.

"How do you have all this?" she asked Harry. "Have you been through an earthquake before?"

"Not really. I was a little kid during the Loma Prieta, but I don't remember it. I like reading about this stuff, and the more I learned about it, the more I wanted to get ready. We've known for a long time that something like this was going to happen."

He sounded pleased with himself, and why not? He wasn't the one standing there after a major disaster with no idea what to do.

"If we can't get out, where are we supposed to go? I mean, things are okay here for now, but..." Mallory didn't want to say she was thinking about the temporary latrine she had helped Joan set up in the corner of the yard the night before, with a bucket, a shovel, and some sheets on a clothesline, so she trailed off and then mumbled, "You know, we're going to need stuff eventually."

"The nearest shelter is at Kezar Stadium, but I'm not sure how well supplied it is. Anyway, it doesn't matter for me. Grandma won't leave, no matter what. She says it's all fine, and people are overreacting." A look of embarrassment washed over his face, and Mallory thought she understood what his deal was. Not a smug survivalist finally getting a chance to exercise his obsession, but a harried grandson, aware of his limited options.

Or maybe, she thought as he began explaining liquefaction zones, *a little bit of both.*

"Thanks, that's good to know," she interrupted as soon as she had a chance. “I’m going to go see if Joan needs help with anything, but I appreciate the info.”

“Any time. I have a solar charger for my radios, so I’ll be able to stay connected. And I’ve got a good supply of water purification tablets. Let me know if you need any.”

“Thanks,” Mallory said again. “I’ll keep that in mind.”

5

Eventually, more information started trickling in. The earthquake had hit to the north, on the San Andreas fault, and had been about an eight on the Richter scale. Destruction in Bolinas, the town closest to the epicenter, was nearly complete, and part of the Golden Gate Bridge had collapsed.

The damage in the city had been worst along the flat stretches that bordered the bay, where the marshes had been filled in to make new land and many buildings floated on top of them, unconnected to bedrock. There were reports of entire neighborhoods reduced to rubble and million-dollar homes leaning at forty-degree angles, but it was hard to know how much of that was true and how much was embellishment by the news media, breathlessly thrilled by the stories of devastation.

Mallory walked from one end of the block to the other, looking along the long cross streets that went uphill toward the center of the city and down to the ocean, but going no further than the corner. For the first twenty-four hours, there had been persistent tsunami warnings on Harry's emergency radio, and even though those had subsided, she didn't feel comfortable getting any closer to the glittering Pacific.

While she was standing there, Mallory's phone pinged. The signal had been unreliable since the earthquake, and she hadn't managed to get more than a few messages to and from her family, but now the screen was full of texts.

The last thread was in response to the group chat from planning the dinner.

Sonali: Are you guys okay? My building was damaged. They're not even letting us back in to get our stuff.

Rachel: Everything is fine here. We don't have power or water, but the building management set up a generator. They're bringing water bottles later.

Lourdes: No power here either. We're going to go tonight to try to make it to Emil's dad's place in Santa Barbara.

Caitlin: i'm fine

Kendra: I'm okay, but Mark fell down the stairs and tore his Achilles. We've been trying to get in at the hospital since last night. It's a total nightmare.

Mallory added her own update to the thread and watched the dots cycle for a long time before it went through. There was comfort in knowing they were all going through this together, if separately.

She scrolled up, back to the texts they had been sending before the dinner. Lourdes had gotten there early and was waiting at the bar, Kendra couldn't find parking, and Rachel had made a joke about the time in college when they were meeting at Chevy's, but Kendra showed up at Chili's instead.

Ordinary messages, the sort her phone history was full of. Mallory smiled as she read them, feeling good that she had friends like this—people who could reach out to each other after a disaster.

It was the timestamps that caught her attention. Her phone showed how long ago a text was sent, up to two days. But the times on the texts were in hours, not days.

Mallory stared at the numbers like she had trouble understanding them. It couldn't possibly have been less than twenty-four hours ago that she had been sitting in the restaurant, calculating how much of the dessert she could eat without being weird. Obviously, it was. But it seemed so wrong that she scrolled up and down a few times, to be sure.

It hadn't been an entirely normal evening, of course. There was that odd conversation with Caitlin in the bathroom, which was probably what Mallory would have been dwelling on if she didn't have so many other things on her mind. She wondered if she should reach out to Caitlin, to make sure she really was okay, whatever her text said.

But then another aftershock hit, literally shaking her out of the idea. Mallory had started to get used to them—it was like being on a boat, where the floor beneath you was never really stable. But they brought her back to the fact that this was not normal life, and it wasn't going to be for a long time.

Whatever had been bothering Caitlin that night had probably faded into unimportance, like everything else.

6

On Monday morning it started to rain. Lightly at first, like the fog was getting heavier, but by noon the fat drops were coming down thick and fast, and the wind made a joke of Mallory's tent stakes. Cold, wet, and miserable, she tried to wait it out in her car, but as the hours passed and the cats got more agitated, she finally gave up and went into the house.

She entered cautiously, worried her footfalls might bring the whole place down. But aside from the mess, there was very little that was different. The floor even creaked in the same places, and the cracks in the walls were only as deep as the plaster, exposing undamaged masonry underneath.

Mallory gave one of the walls a little push to test it, and immediately felt silly. If she thought she could move it with her own strength, then she had no business being in here, and if not then what was the point? But there was comfort in the feeling of solid resistance when she tried.

She spent the first hour going around the house, cleaning

up broken glass. The power was still out, so the vacuum cleaner wasn't an option, but she had a little dust buster that had just enough battery to get most of the glittery shards.

Once she was as sure as she could be that the floor was safe, she released the cats from their carrier, where they had been yowling with increasing intensity. Mariah shot straight under the couch, while Celine did a complete tour, like she was inspecting for structural stability, before settling down next to her food dish and staring meaningfully at Mallory.

After that, there wasn't much to do. A truck had come around first thing in the morning, distributing bottles of water and telling them where they could get them refilled, and her habit of stocking up on canned soups and vegetables meant she wouldn't go hungry. So, with her immediate needs taken care of, Mallory thought about the future.

She was going to have to leave, obviously. Her immediate family lived on the other side of the country, and it wouldn't be easy to get there with her cats. Neither her parents nor her sister had room for her anyway, though she knew they would have tried. But a simpler solution had come from her mother's cousin, who lived in Fresno, well out of the range of the earthquake damage, and had offered to take her in. So Mallory started packing, with an eye to moving to the Central Valley, who knew when and for how long.

Mallory spent the first couple of hours sorting out the things she couldn't leave behind—her laptops and papers, essential clothes and toiletries, supplies for the cats. Then the extras:

favorite books, the shoes she had spent too much on and worn once but still loved, the fuzzy blanket she had kept on her bed since high school. When she took a break for dinner (tomato soup, only barely edible cold), she was getting close to what would fit in her car.

There was no hope of finding somewhere to store the remainder of her stuff. She wasn't even sure Joan would let her leave it until she got back, when or if that ever was. But she could only deal with the problem in front of her, so Mallory packed up the things she was leaving as well as she could, until exhaustion got to her and she tumbled into bed.

—

At first Mallory thought it was an aftershock that woke her. But as she lay in bed, waiting to see if there would be another one, she realized that wasn't it. Someone else was in the apartment.

They were trying to move quietly, but the old floors had too many spots that creaked. Every time they stepped on one, the intruder stopped, probably listening to see if Mallory had woken up.

What will they do if they know I have?

Mallory had gone to sleep fully dressed, in case she had to make a quick evacuation—she had even brought her purse and put it next to the bed—and she was glad for it now. Whatever she was going to do, at least it wouldn't be in a *Blue's Clues* nightshirt.

She eased herself up into a sitting position and tried to plan. There was only one door out of the apartment, and the other person was between her and it. She could take her chances with the element of surprise—try to run past them and hope that they were more interested in stealing things than stopping her. But that was risky. The intruder might be armed, and they almost certainly were larger than Mallory—most people were. Even if they hadn't come with violence in mind, being surprised like that could make someone dangerous.

The bedroom had a window, but it was small and tended to stick. Mallory could get out that way if she had to, but it would be time-consuming and noisy, and the process would leave her vulnerable.

Her other option was to stay where she was and try to secure the room. The bedroom door had no lock, and none of her furniture was very heavy, but if the intruder was only taking this opportunity to grab whatever they could find, maybe they wouldn't bother fighting their way in.

And if they were intent on getting to her, then Mallory probably didn't have much hope anyway.

She crept across the room, relying on her experience to know where she could step noiselessly. From what she could hear, the intruder was in the living room—it sounded like they were digging through the boxes Mallory had packed to leave behind. That was strange—if you were going to rob a place, why not take advantage of the fact that things had been packed up for you to carry out, and sort through them later? But maybe they were only looking to see if there was anything of value (there wasn't) so they didn't waste their time.

Whatever the reason, what mattered was that the person was far enough away that Mallory was able to close the bedroom door before they would have had a chance to get to her. She could do that quietly, but her next step was to drag her dresser across to block it, and once she did that, there was no question they would know she was there and awake.

Mallory leaned against the veneered plywood and waited to see what would happen. She had her phone, but calling 911 wasn't going to do much good. The police had a lot more on their minds than small-scale housebreaking.

Still, she gripped the phone with one hand and used the other to brace herself on the dresser. She knew that if it came down to it, nothing was going to keep out someone who was determined to get in. The door was light and hollow—easy enough to punch through even without a weapon—and the dresser only had the weight of her clothes and her own pitiful strength behind it. The best she could hope was that they wouldn't want to deal with any resistance and would just take whatever they found in the rest of the apartment and go.

There was no question that the intruder was aware of Mallory's presence now. When she was moving the dresser, she had noticed a sudden stop in the noise from the living room, and as she settled in behind it, she heard footsteps getting closer. She held her breath, but they didn't even hesitate near the door. The steps were quick and light—it wasn't a large person, at least—and they passed the bedroom like they were afraid Mallory would come out and catch them.

There was no danger of that, of course, but she was curious. The hallway was short, with only a small closet and one other room, and the latter was where the intruder went. Leaning forward to listen, Mallory caught the sound of sneaker soles on the tile floor, and cupboards opening. They were moving faster now, with no regard for noise, and only spent a few minutes before the footsteps retreated back down the hall and out the front door.

Mallory stayed where she was, tense and exhausted. The house fell silent and stayed that way, but she wasn't going to risk looking out. Whatever there was to see could wait until morning.

That didn't stop her from wondering. About why, of all the houses on her street, a solo housebreaker would pick her basement apartment, or why they didn't just grab the electronics in the living room and go.

And what did they think they were going to find in the bathroom?

7

Mallory woke up around dawn to the sound of claws scratching the bottom of the door. She must have been dreaming—something about a demon—but the monster meowed, and the spell was broken.

"I'm coming," Mallory said as she moved the dresser. She was still shaken by her experience, but there was no clearer sign that the house was empty than the cats being out. They had both started their lives as strays, and though they were comfortable with Mallory, they would vanish if anyone else was around.

Still, Mallory felt bad about doing nothing to protect them, and she was relieved to see both furry faces waiting for her when she opened the door. She gave them some extra food as an apology and then went to see the damage.

To her surprise, it wasn't that bad. Several of the boxes she had packed had been emptied, their contents scattered across the floor, but nothing was obviously missing—even her laptops were where she had left them—her personal one on the kitchen table and her work one on her desk in the living room. Confused, she continued to explore, trying to make sense of the invasion.

Though her computer was untouched, the desk she reserved for working from home had been turned inside out. The drawers sat partway open, their contents spilled onto the floor, and her containers for pens and paper clips had been emptied. Even the paper drawer in the printer had been pulled out, with the paper lifted up like someone had looked underneath it.

The kitchen had been less thoroughly searched, but it was clear they had been in there as well. Again, the drawers had been gone through, and again nothing was obviously missing. Even Mallory's small collection of alcohol was intact—if she had been looting somewhere at that point, she thought that was what she would have gone for first.

That gave her an idea, so she left the kitchen and headed for the bathroom. It had occurred to her that the intruder might have been looking for prescription medications, of which Mallory had very few, but the medicine cabinet was untouched, her allergy medicine and even the leftover pain pills from she when she had her wisdom teeth out exactly where they had been.

In fact, most of the disturbance was to her makeup collection, which was the weirdest part of all. The lipsticks she had lined up by color and the eyeliners she kept in a commemorative mug were all spilled across the counter, and the drawer that held her eyeshadows along with a million moisturizer samples had been dumped out onto the bath mat.

She scooped up the scattered palettes and dumped them

back into the drawer. It was probably pointless to try and understand the person's motivations. Not everyone was rational, and she guessed she had found one of the other kind. She knew she should be grateful the damage wasn't worse, and that she hadn't been threatened herself, but she didn't feel happy about any part of the experience.

And after all, if she was dealing with an irrational person, how could she be sure they wouldn't come back the next time they had a brain wave? Or that another, more focused thief wouldn't show up instead?

Outside, she hunted around the yard, looking for clues to how they had gotten in. It wasn't hard to figure out—the house was the last one on the block, and its yard was separated from the sidewalk by a fence. The lock on the gate had never been that sturdy, and the earthquake must have knocked it askew, because now it didn't latch at all. From there, it would be easy to reach through the broken window and open the front door, and there was nothing Mallory could do to fix any of that right now or in the near future.

She looked over at the cats, who had finished their food and followed her outside.

"It's time to get out of here."

—

Mallory finished packing her car as the sun came up, and then went to find her landlady. Joan was understanding and shocked when she heard about the break-in.

"You should have called me. I would have come down there and told them off. All this trouble, and they've got to go around messing with people's homes? Unacceptable."

"I'm just relieved they didn't do anything worse than messing with my stuff," Mallory said, glad she hadn't called her landlady for help. Mallory had a very clear image of how Joan would have come charging in, ready to tell the housebreaker how they weren't living up to her standards. What would have happened after that, Mallory was less sure of.

"Anyway, I don't think I'm comfortable staying," she added. "I can't take all my stuff, though, and I don't think I'm going to find a storage place right now..."

"Oh, don't worry about that," Joan waved away her concerns. "It's not like I'm going to find anyone else to rent it to. I'll be heading out soon to stay with some friends up in Mendocino. We can figure out everything once we're all settled."

"Thanks, that makes me feel a lot better." And it did. The knot that had been sitting in Mallory's stomach loosened slightly, and she found herself breathing easier. Not because she had been that concerned about what was going to happen to her thrift store plates and one nice chair, but there was something to the kindness of it, and Joan's general attitude did a lot for her own mindset.

Mallory took a deep breath and looked up at the sky, where the morning sun was coming through a break in the clouds.

"Anyway, I'd better get moving if I'm going to go today," she said. "I don't know how long it's going to take me to get out of the city, and I don't want to be stuck in my car in the dark."

Joan nodded. "Good point. Well, be safe out there, and tell the cats I said goodbye. Who knows, maybe this whole thing will have blown over in a couple of weeks."

"Maybe," Mallory answered, but she wasn't convinced.

8

Mallory meant to leave right away, but she had one more interruption before she could get on the road.

"Hey!" Harry said, crossing the street as she was loading up the cat carrier. "I heard you had a break-in last night?"

Mallory didn't know how he could have known that, but she confirmed it was true.

"That's too bad. I thought we'd have at least a week before the looting. So you're leaving?"

He sounded wistful, and it made Mallory oddly sad. It had only been three days, but their little neighborhood had started to feel like a community, and she felt like she was betraying that by going. But her neighbor clearly didn't share that philosophy.

"You're making a good decision to go now," he said. "They've started to clear the roads to the south, so you'll be able to get out before everyone else realizes."

That was the most encouraging thing Mallory had heard so far. "What about you? Are you going too?"

It must have been the wrong thing to ask, because her neighbor looked suddenly uncomfortable.

"I have to stay. Grandma won't go anywhere; she keeps saying they're going to take the house."

"Who's they?"

Harry sighed deeply. "I don't ask."

"Oh. I'm sorry." Mallory didn't ask him to elaborate—she had elderly relatives too.

"Anyway, we'll be okay. But you should go. Traffic will be pretty bad by midmorning."

"Right, thanks." The feeling Mallory had experienced earlier returned, and as much as she knew she needed to go, she was reluctant to turn her back on the relative safety of the neighborhood. So she temporized for a moment longer.

"I hope I can get back soon," she said. "It's nice of my relative to take me in, but I can't stay with her forever. And I'm leaving a lot of my things here."

"I can keep an eye on your place, make sure no one else tries to break in," Harry said, and immediately Mallory felt bad for bringing it up.

"No, please don't. It's just stuff." It was time to go, and Mallory took a deep breath. "Lots of people have lost more. I'll come back, and whatever is here then, I can work with it."

Harry nodded, and Mallory hoped he understood her point.

"How long do you think you'll be gone?"

"I wish I knew."

—

Harry had only been partially right about the roads being opened. The traffic down Nineteenth Avenue was heavy, but at least it was moving, and National Guard soldiers directed traffic and supplied fuel to stopped vehicles. But it was still a traffic jam like Mallory had never seen. She crawled on, with the cats getting more and more agitated in their carrier, until she decided it was less trouble to let them out, since they couldn't cause a high-speed crash if she was only going three miles an hour.

The slow progress gave Mallory plenty of time to examine the damage. Her route took her along the western edge of the city, which had fewer tall buildings and more new construction than the downtown area, but it hadn't been spared. Broken windows were everywhere—some covered hastily with plastic—and there was occasionally more serious harm, like collapsed chimneys or a restaurant sign that had come down and taken the outdoor tables with it. She didn't see any active fires, but a few houses had burned. The rain streaked the soot down their walls and those windows no one had bothered to cover.

It took most of the morning for Mallory to get out of San Francisco. By the time she passed the sign welcoming her to Daly City, all of her regrets about leaving were gone, replaced by a profound desire to never see the license plate of the car in front of her again. She had expected to be funneled onto the freeway at some point, but one of the Guardsmen who were directing the traffic explained why that wasn't happening. There were dozens of small bridges she had never been aware of, over the creeks and culverts that ran to the bay, and diverting around the damaged ones took her on a route that she didn't think she would ever be able to replicate.

But she was moving, and the farther south she drove, the less the damage. By the time Mallory made it to San Jose, she saw working traffic lights and her phone had full signal. But she was still a long way from where she had a bed to sleep in, and even though she had gotten an emergency refill in San Carlos, the needle on the gas gauge was getting close to the red. So she pushed on, finally joining 101 down through the endless farmland, where the earthquake hadn't done much because there was nothing to knock over.

Near the turnoff for the route through the hills to the Central Valley, she stopped at a gas station that advertised having supplies. As she was filling up her rationed amount, Mallory fished through her purse to see if she had enough cash to splurge on a Coke and some Cheez-Its to sustain her until she got to somewhere that would take credit cards. Poking in the side pocket of the bag, her fingers hit some sort of lumpy cylinder. Curious, Mallory pulled it out to see what it was.

She stared at Caitlin's lipstick for a while before she remembered. The broken handbag clasp, Caitlin's mother's lipstick tube.

She's going to want this back, Mallory thought. *I'll get in touch with her once I'm settled.*

9

SIX MONTHS LATER

Mallory stepped out of the car and took a deep breath. The August fog washed over her, and she spent a moment appreciating it. When she had left Fresno that morning, the temperature was a hundred degrees in the shade, and she had never been so happy as when she came over the hills and saw the gray bank of cloud enveloping the bay.

"Ah," she said. "Summer."

"You made it! How was the drive?" Joan must have been watching through the front window, because she was out the door almost before Mallory finished parking.

"A lot easier than getting out," Mallory said, resigning herself to the inevitable hug. She added, "I'm so glad to be back. Fresno really isn't my jam."

"Is it anyone's?" Joan said and then waved that away. "No, I'm sure there are people who love it. And I'm glad they're happy. But you can't beat the city. I liked Mendocino fine, but you would not believe what passes for Thai food up there."

Joan talked on, about her time with her friends up north and her battles with her insurance company, as Mallory unloaded her luggage. She was grateful that her landlord had taken her back after all this time, at the same rent she had been paying before, even though with the shortage of habitable buildings in the city, she could have charged a lot more. But it had been a long day of driving, and Mallory really just wanted to use what was left of her energy to get the apartment into a good enough state for her to have a microwaved pizza and some beer and go to bed.

There were going to be a few steps before she could get there, though. Some of them were literal, as Joan led her around the building and pointed out the changes.

"So at first the insurance people said I had to replace all the windows, even the ones that were fine. But I said no, and my friend Dora who works for the state said that's not right, so eventually we got it settled..."

Joan went on, diving into the minutiae of the negotiations that had been consuming her time since the earthquake had gone from being an immediate disaster to a long slog through bureaucracy. Mallory's attention wandered, from the backyard that hadn't recovered yet from being a campsite, to trying to guess which of the neighboring houses were still unoccupied. She missed most of what Joan was saying, until a phrase brought her back to the conversation.

"But after the second break-in, I didn't mind that."

"I'm sorry," Mallory said. "The second break-in? There was another one after I left?"

"Two more," said Joan. "That's right, I wasn't counting the one when you were here. Yes, twice after that, someone got into the apartment. Made a real mess. Finally, I got new locks put on all the doors and windows and the gate, and that seems like it took care of it."

"I had no idea. Did a lot of houses in the neighborhood get broken into?"

"Not so much, no." Joan gave her a sideways look. "A couple of the places that were standing empty had people go through them, and the Marcons had an issue with some squatters. But there's something about that apartment that seems to be drawing a lot of attention. I don't suppose you have any idea what that's about?"

"No, I swear I don't." It was the absolute truth, though Mallory wouldn't have blamed Joan for not believing her. She searched her mind, trying to think of some reason why a one-bedroom apartment might have been so tempting to thieves.

"Could they have gotten it mixed up with somewhere else?" Mallory asked. "Maybe there's another house around here where they have a safe or a valuable wine collection?"

"That's a possibility," Joan agreed. "Still, you think they'd have figured it out after the first time. Anyway, you should be okay. There hasn't been any trouble for a couple of months now."

"That's good," Mallory said, but her mind was still on the mystery of the repeated home invasions. An idea occurred to her—improbable, but not out of the question. "You know those videos about buried treasure being turned up by the earthquake—I wonder if one of those could have been sending people here. Did anyone see who did it? Was it the same person every time?"

"Huh. That's a thought. I know the ones you mean; my cousin keeps sending them to me. She likes the ones about an alien spaceship under the Presidio that tried to take off and caused the quake. Anyway, I'm not sure about anybody seeing them directly, but Harry across the street has had a bunch of cameras going, and he mentioned he might have gotten a shot of them. You should ask him."

"I will. Anyway, I had better take a look around now, make sure there are no surprises." Mallory had meant that as her cue to start going, but the older woman didn't take the hint.

"Good idea. Gummy?" Joan held out a brightly colored bag decorated with sketches of marijuana leaves.

Mallory looked at it in surprise.

"No thanks, not right now. I thought edibles weren't your thing?"

In fact, she had listened several times as Joan had held forth about how the corporate cannabis industry was the source of a variety of evils. But her landlady shrugged off the inconsistency.

"They still aren't, but I'm not doing any open flames these days. They started turning the gas back on last month, and they say it's only going to places where the lines have been fully checked, but who believes that? I'm not going to get myself blown up for a joint."

"Makes sense." That was a risk Mallory hadn't even considered when she decided to return, and she would rather not have thought about it now. But her suitcase was getting heavy, the cats were complaining about being stuck in their box, and gas leaks or not, she needed to get moving.

"Thanks again for having me back," she said. "I'd love to catch up some more later, but it sounds like I've got a major cleanup job to do, and I think I'd better get started."

Joan laughed. "Do you ever. Good luck, and let me know if you need any extra trash bags."

Mallory entered the apartment expecting the worst. And at first, it seemed like she had found it. All of the boxes she had packed and then repacked before leaving had been tipped over, their contents spread across the living room floor, and the drawers in her desk were pulled out and emptied again. The kitchen had been similarly ransacked, with even the bags of rice and flour she had left in the cupboard emptied across the counter and spilling onto the floor.

But it was in the bedroom that the invader had really gone to town. Mallory had only been able to take about half her clothes with her, and she had been thinking about donating the rest when she got back, because anything she could live without for six months was probably something she didn't need. That was going to be an easier decision now, because they had been spread out across the floor, and a crack in the window had let in just enough water for them to be thoroughly speckled with mold.

Mallory spent a minute taking in the scene. Then, with a deep sigh, she turned back to the kitchen to see if the thief had left her any garbage bags.

She was hauling out the third load when there was a knock on the gate. Mallory was generally wary of unexpected visitors, but the distraction was welcome. She might have accepted a survey taker, or even a Mormon, but it was only her neighbor Harry, holding a plate of lemon bars and looking helpful.

"Welcome back," he said. "My mom sent these. She's been hoping more people would return to the neighborhood."

"Thanks, I'm glad to be back." Mallory took the pastries and looked around awkwardly. "Let me see if I can find something to put these on so I can give you the plate back. Things are a bit of a mess here right now."

Harry waved off her concern. "Don't worry about it. Grandpa's been going to all the yard sales, and he keeps buying them. I think that might be the real reason Mom's been baking for everyone." As he talked, he looked past Mallory to the apartment, his eyes growing wide as he took in the wreckage of her possessions. "Wow, they really did a number here, didn't they? I'm sorry about the break-ins. I tried to keep an eye on things, but there was a lot going on."

"That's okay, really. They didn't even take anything, as far as I can tell. Just left me with a big mess to clean up." The conversation with Joan was still on Mallory's mind, and it occurred to her that Harry might be able to confirm it. "Is it true that nobody else's house was broken into? I guess everyone must have thought I was up to something here, but I'm really not."

Harry looked uncomfortable. "There has been some talking. Because, yeah, you hear about looting, but nobody else around here seems to be having the same problem with people breaking in as you have. And if they haven't taken anything..." He trailed off, confused. "That seems weird."

"Tell me about it. Honestly, if I knew what they wanted, I'd probably give it to them at this point." She remembered another thing that Joan had mentioned and added, "It would help if I had any idea about who was breaking in. Joan said you might have some footage of them?"

"I do. It's not great, but it's something. The camera is set up on the front door of our house, so it only has a partial view, but I did get a shot of someone coming in at least once. Do you want me to send it to you?"

"Sure, thanks." Mallory gave him her email and then laughed. "Who knows, maybe it's someone I know."

"Could be," Harry replied seriously, and then another thing occurred to him. "Do you want a Taser? I have an extra."

"I'm sorry?"

"I just thought, you know, in case. My mom wouldn't let me buy a gun for self-defense, so we compromised, and I got some Tasers. It's pretty easy to use. I can show you."

"I don't think..." Mallory began, but then she had a second thought. Something weird was going on, and if the break-ins weren't random, maybe she should take her own safety more seriously. "You know, actually, I'd appreciate that. I'm kind of busy with cleaning right now—can I come by later?"

"Sure, any time."

He left, and Mallory found herself alone with a plate of lemon bars and a rising sense of dread. When her home had been invaded for the first time, it had been terrifying but not hard to understand. While she was away, the news was filled with horror stories of San Francisco descending into chaos, and she had gotten the impression that her experience was one of many. But now that she was here, looking at the results of a robbery with no theft, and hearing that her small apartment had been targeted three times while the other houses had been left alone, Mallory was left feeling very exposed and very confused.

Lourdes

The condo was empty when Lourdes got home. She had enough reasons to be upset about that, but for the moment she was relieved. She had some preparations to make, and they were going to be a lot easier if she didn't have to worry about Emil seeing her computer screen from over her shoulder.

There was no way of knowing when he was going to be back, but still Lourdes hesitated until she finally got her nerve up and opened a new tab. She had put this off for too long, and she couldn't delay it anymore.

It wasn't that hard once she got going. None of what she had to do was actually that difficult; it was just the fact that doing it meant she had made a choice. From this point, she had to give up any hope of taking another path forward. But what was she hoping for, really? Life wasn't ever going to go back to the way it had been, in so many ways.

Lourdes got up to get a bottle of water from the refrigerator and brought it over to the sofa, sipping as she logged in. She opened her phone to get the 2FA code, and her eyes dropped to the text beneath it. It was Mallory, announcing she was finally leaving the Central Valley and coming back to town, suggesting with her characteristic vagueness that they should "get together sometime." Lourdes stared at it for a moment and then responded with a place and time. That would get one thing off her list at least.

The bubbles in the water got to her, and Lourdes allowed herself a belch. Emil would have been disgusted, but he wasn't there to complain right now. She needed to take advantage of that, to do some other things he would have disapproved of even more. But for the moment she just wanted to sit, to let the water do its work against the throbbing in her head, and think about what she had to do.

It wasn't going to be nice. But the necessary things rarely were.

10

They broke in three times? And they didn't take anything?"

"Not as far as I can tell."

Lourdes picked up her coffee cup and considered Mallory from over the rim.

"That's weird," she said. "Are you sure you didn't leave the door open or something? Maybe it was just someone taking advantage of the opportunity."

"I did not leave anything open," Mallory said, annoyed. Though she did have to add, "Nothing seems to have happened since Joan put on the new locks."

"Hmm."

Lourdes took in this new information, and Mallory let her think it over while she sipped her own latte. To say she hadn't slept well the night before would be an understatement, but nothing had happened. Still, she had been jittery and unsettled all day, and when Lourdes texted, Mallory jumped at the chance to get out of the house. She hadn't seen any of her friends since the quake, and just the sight of Lourdes on the other side of the table felt like a welcome return to normalcy.

Not that anything was normal, of course.

"Maybe it's not about you at all," Lourdes suggested. "The earthquake messed with a lot of people around here, pushed some of them over the edge. Maybe one of them got an idea about your apartment, and now they're trying to get in because they think they live there or something."

"Oh sure, just a crazy person with a fixation on my home. What could go wrong?"

"Well, what are you going to do about it? You could move."

The thought had occurred to Mallory, particularly between two and four in the morning, but she shook her head. "To where? I don't know if you've had a look at the rental market lately, but it's not great. My mom's cousin was nice to take me in for as long as she did, but she's redoing her kitchen, and she needs the spare room for storage. And what's the point of running away when I don't know what I'm running from? I might have the same problem anywhere."

"I guess so," Lourdes said, but she didn't sound convinced. Mallory knew better than to try to make her understand. Lourdes was one of her best friends and had been for fifteen years, ever since they met in a history class and bonded over their shared love of Greek mythology. But Lourdes's family was rich, and her response to any problem was to solve it with money. She had gotten better over the years, but it still wasn't easy for her to understand not everyone had the same options as she did.

"Anyway," Mallory went on. "Nothing has happened for more than a month, so maybe it's over. I'll look into getting an alarm system, but first I need to spend some time cleaning up."

"What about your work?"

Lourdes's job regularly had her putting in ten-hour days, and though Mallory worked hard, she got the sense her friend didn't think she could ever be successful without doing the same. But as much as Mallory liked her job, she wasn't about to let it consume her, and she knew when it was time for a break.

"I'm taking the rest of the week off to get settled in. My boss is okay with it—since I was able to get out of the city, I was one of the first people back online after the quake, and I was kind of holding things together while everyone else was dealing with their families and stuff," she said and then took another sip of her latte. "Anyway, I've been talking about myself nonstop. How are things with you?"

"Okay, I guess." Lourdes sighed and leaned back in her chair. The coffee shop had been her recommendation, and Mallory could see why—it suited her perfectly. Opened since the earthquake, in a space that used to be part of a large grocery store, it had high ceilings and walls of windows and industrial decor that stood in contrast to the tall-backed wing chairs with their velvet upholstery. Lourdes had chosen one in a soft dove gray, which must have been hell to keep clean but did work very nicely as a background for her glossy black hair.

"Just okay?" Mallory asked.

"Well, the earthquake's been rough on everyone. And I know, I don't have anything to complain about compared to most people.

But it's still—" She let out a deep puff of breath, fluttering her bangs. "It's still a lot."

Mallory couldn't argue with that, but she noticed her friend was avoiding giving any details on what was actually bothering her. "What's a lot?" she asked. "Is your boss doing her crap again?"

"Tina? No, her kid's school was too damaged to reopen, and she's been busy trying to keep him from being sent to the consolidated school in SoMa. You can imagine how she feels about that."

Mallory could imagine. "So, not work. Then what is it?"

"Oh, well, you know, it just sounds so dumb to be complaining when I have it so good. I mean, we got one of the helicopter trips out of the city, even before you left, I think. And we spent that whole month at Emil's mother's place in Hawaii, working by the pool."

"Must be nice to be rich."

"It definitely is." Lourdes laughed and then shrugged. "What can I say? It's not like there was anything useful I could have done here. Might as well get my rich ass out of town and let the help go to the people who needed it. But I'm back now, and it couldn't have come soon enough. I think I put on ten pounds worth of short rib plate lunches."

"Lourdes Meihui Yang, you are not about to complain about your weight. I won't allow it."

Mallory knew that when her friend was stressed, her insecurities about her figure came out. She had developed the practice of shutting it down, because if Lourdes started to wallow in her feelings, they would only get worse.

Lourdes knew it too. "Oh god, I'm doing it again, aren't I? Sorry, I'm sorry, you're right. Anyway, why don't you come and stay with us? We'll set up the guest bedroom, and you can help me pick out new tile for the kitchen."

"I can't. I've got my cats, and you know how allergic Emil is. Besides, I'll be fine. Didn't I spend senior year watching every slasher film ever made? If anyone knows what to do when a lunatic comes at her with a knife, it's me."

Lourdes didn't look convinced, but she did crack a smile. "Okay, well, don't scare the postman. Seriously, though, if you change your mind, let me know. We can board Emil for a couple of weeks."

They both laughed, but they were interrupted by a siren. It was only an ambulance passing the coffee shop, but there was a sudden hush across the room and a collective intake of breath.

Mallory laughed again, more unsteadily this time. "I guess we all aren't really over it yet, are we?"

Lourdes smiled, but she didn't laugh.

"No," she said. "Not quite."

11

Lourdes had driven herself, and Mallory had come on the bus, so they parted at the coffee shop door. As she was walking the three blocks to the bus stop, Mallory realized that Lourdes had never actually said what was bothering her. She reached for her phone to make a note to ask her other friends if they knew anything and at the same time as another hand was reaching into her bag.

Mallory tried to yank the purse closer to her body, but the other person had hold of the straps, and they were pulling too.

The thief was wearing an oversized black hoodie, with their face covered by ski goggles and a paper surgical mask. They were bigger than Mallory, but not by much.

They might have been stronger than her too, but Mallory was suddenly overcome by a burst of fury, like all the anger and fear and frustration of the last six months boiled over and poured out of her.

"No!" she shouted, feeling like she was screaming from the bottom of her soul. "You aren't going to take it!"

She hooked her arm over the top of the tote and leaned down, putting the full weight of her body against the hold the other person had on the straps. That might not have been enough, but the thief was wearing thin cotton gloves, which gave them no traction on the smooth leather. It slid out of their hands, and Mallory tumbled forward, knocking her head into their stomach as she fell to the ground.

By the time she got up, her assailant was gone, and a small crowd had gathered.

"Are you okay?" asked the man who helped her to her feet. "I saw them coming up behind you, but I wasn't able to get out of the shop in time." He gestured behind him to a tattoo shop where a customer was leaning out the door, a fresh bandage over her arm.

"But it seems like you did all right on your own," he went on. "Sorry, this neighborhood isn't really like that usually."

"I believe you," Mallory said. "I've been having some bad luck lately."

Mallory opted for an Uber to get home. The driver wasn't a talker, and she was so grateful that she didn't even mind that he had clearly put on the easy listening station as soon as he saw her.

As Adele crooned from the speakers, Mallory tried to get her thoughts together. She might have simply been the target of an opportunistic purse snatcher, but she'd had enough of theories that involved bad luck and coincidences.

But the alternative was that she was being specifically targeted, and that made even less sense. The Uber driver hadn't been entirely wrong in his choice of music—Mallory's life up to this point had been about as bland and unexciting as a person could get. Her family was on the other side of the country, her job involved writing customer management software, mainly for the food service industry, and her personal vices tended toward canned cocktails and fancy chocolates.

She'd had what she thought was a normal number of bad dates and lousy ex-boyfriends, but she couldn't think of any of them who might be a threat to her.

In fact, she spent the entire ride going over it, and Mallory couldn't think of any reason why she would be a target.

It was only when the driver was pulling up to the house that another problem occurred to her. She had left home several hours earlier, walked to the light rail stop, and gone to the bank and the library before she met Lourdes at the café. If someone was targeting her, how had they known where she was? Mallory didn't consider herself the most observant person in the world, but she thought she would have noticed if a masked figure had been stalking her for half the day.

Forgetting the question of why someone was pursuing her, how were they doing it?

Standing at the curb, Mallory took a long look up and down the block. It was far enough into the afternoon that the fog had lifted, so the view ran far enough to see anyone in the area, even if it was still bone-chillingly cold.

There were no cars coming, and no one was lingering on the sidewalk. Of the houses themselves, about half were clearly occupied—others were either under construction or tagged with ominous-looking notices on their doors. But no faces peered out of the dark windows, and there was no movement in the overgrown shrubbery.

Three blocks away was a major cross street, where traffic passed at its normal speed. The only pedestrians were a man walking his dog away from her and a woman who crossed the intersection, pushing a stroller and tugging a toddler behind her. None of them looked like they could possibly be tracking Mallory, unless there was some sort of crime syndicate after her. In which case, she thought she might as well give up, because she knew her limits.

But Mallory knew a few other things as well, which was why when she got inside, the first thing she did was to dump the entire contents of her purse out on the table.

She couldn't see how someone would have been following her in person all day. But the old-fashioned ways of tracking weren't all that was available, and it was the more modern alternatives that Mallory was considering now.

Her best guess was that someone had slipped a wireless tracker into her bag, one that didn't have the kind of security features to let her phone know it was there. Why anyone would do that was a question for another time, or possibly not, because as much as she looked, Mallory couldn't find anything that matched that description among her belongings.

She shifted through the crumpled receipts and almost-empty tissue packs, squeezing and folding anything that might be hiding a small piece of electronics. But there was nothing in the bag that she hadn't put there herself, and she was about to give up on the idea when she saw the lipstick.

It was silly to think that Caitlin would have been setting her up for some unknown hijinks, but Mallory had looked everywhere else, so for the sake of completeness she opened the tube.

The substance inside was red, but it wasn't lipstick. There was something familiar about the shade, though, and when she dug in a fingernail it had a firm, waxy texture. Twisting the base pushed it out, and Mallory finally recognized the lump in her hand. It was the kind of red wax that came on tiny cheeses, the stuff she used to turn into little balls and roll across the high school lunch table.

More confused than ever, Mallory set the wax on the table and looked at it. It had been formed into a cylinder, about half the size of the lipstick that should have been in the tube. She had some experience with these things, and she was fairly sure it was slightly larger than you could get from one piece of cheese. That might mean Caitlin had been doing more snacking, or it might be that there was something inside. Betting on the latter, Mallory began to dig through the wax and soon hit plastic and metal.

Once she had the wax completely cleared away, Mallory examined what she had. The thing that had been hidden inside the lipstick tube was small, about the size of the last joint of her ring finger, half in black plastic and the rest made up by a standard USB-C connector. There was a series of letters and numbers printed on the plastic, but no other identifying marks.

Mallory stared at it, dumbfounded. It wasn't any kind of tracker, she was sure of that. Her best guess was that it was some sort of hardware key, but that didn't narrow it down much. There were plenty of things that used keys like this, from wireless keyboards to bank passwords. Without the other end of the connection, it was as useless to her as if it had been another piece of wax.

And she couldn't imagine why Caitlin passed it to her. This item, whatever its purpose, was clearly something important—no one would go to that kind of trouble to hide a random office supply.

So Caitlin had brought it with her to the dinner, probably intentionally, because Mallory remembered the clutch, which she had claimed had a broken clasp, and it had been fairly small. And then what? Just chose someone at random to hand it off to? Or was it the setup for a joke that never had a chance to pay off? Caitlin wouldn't have known the earthquake was going to happen, of course. Maybe one of the other women had gotten her to give Mallory the lipstick for a punch line later.

That sounded like the sort of thing Kendra would do, honestly, but Mallory hesitated to believe it. She was thinking about that first break-in, the way they had gone through her desk area and bathroom, and the strength in those hands trying to take her bag. None of that was anyone's idea of a joke.

There was one person who could clear this up, and Mallory picked up her phone to ask her. She started to compose a text that laid out the details of what she had found, but a second thought stopped her. Consumed with her own problems, she hadn't been thinking much about Caitlin, but now the memories came flooding back, of the way she had looked in that bathroom, the trapped expression and the fear.

Mallory deleted the text and hit the phone icon.

12

Five failure-to-connects later, Mallory gave up. The earthquake had been hard on telecommunications; even now it wasn't uncommon to find a disconnected number. She sent a text anyway, carefully vague this time, in case Caitlin had another way of getting her messages. Then she stared at her phone for a while, unsure what to do next.

She was worried. Mallory reminded herself that not reaching a person after one try was hardly a reason to panic. And, after all, she didn't even know Caitlin very well. She knew other people who did, though, and possibly one of them would be able to fill her in—that Caitlin's phone had been crushed by debris, or she had taken the opportunity to leave the country or something. She should ask before she jumped to conclusions.

But what would she say? Anyone Mallory was going to contact would know her well enough to know she didn't randomly seek out people to chat. She could try to explain why she was looking for their friend, but something about that felt wrong. Caitlin had given her that lipstick in private, away from everyone else at the table. Mallory didn't know why, but not knowing was all the more reason not to share it. That she couldn't imagine suspecting her friends of anything didn't matter; what mattered was that she didn't want to betray a confidence.

It's not a secret if somebody else knows.

That had come from her grandmother, admonishing Mallory after she had been involved in some wholly avoidable middle-school drama. There were flaws in that philosophy, she was well aware, but for now she thought she would take the advice.

And besides, how could she even tell the story without sounding completely insane?

Ultimately, Mallory settled on a plan that was so simple, she was embarrassed she didn't think of it in the first place. She had been happy when Lourdes suggested they meet up; after everything that had happened, it was a relief to see a familiar face.

So she fired off texts to the other three women she had last seen on the night of the earthquake, with a question about reaching Caitlin as an afterthought at the end of each message.

Twenty minutes later, she had tentative plans to meet up with Sonali, Rachel, and Kendra within the next week, a follow-up with Lourdes, and no more information about Caitlin's whereabouts than when she started. Rachel thought she had heard something about her leaving town but couldn't say for where, and Kendra mentioned she'd also tried to get in touch with Caitlin to ask about a contractor she had hired in the past but had never heard back.

None of that was surprising—everyone was busy, and all their lives had been disrupted beyond recognition. Mallory knew that, and she reminded herself of it several times. But she kept looking back at the hardware key, sitting innocently on the table with fragments of red wax still stuck to it.

Something was going on here.

Her next thought was to try emailing Caitlin, which she did. While she had her account open, she noticed that she had three new messages, all from an address she didn't recognize, and all with attachments. The subject lines appeared to be automated—a string of letters and numbers, with a forwarding prefix. Assuming spam, Mallory nearly deleted them unopened when curiosity stopped her.

Hi Mallory,

Here are the videos from the camera by our front door from when the person broke into your place. I only have the second two because our power wasn't on the first time. I'm sorry the quality isn't very good, but I hope they help!

Harry

In all the excitement, Mallory had completely forgotten her neighbor had promised to send her the videos. More interested than ever, she opened the first attachment.

Harry hadn't been modest about the quality. Actually, that wasn't entirely true—the video itself was no worse than any others she had seen. But it wasn't nearly good enough to get a clear look at a person on the other side of the street. All Mallory was able to tell about them was that they weren't particularly tall or exceptionally short, and their build was on the slighter side. They were dressed all in black, with a hoodie and a mask, just like her attempted purse snatcher. No sunglasses, probably because it was night, but no matter how much Mallory squinted, she couldn't make out enough of the face to even tell if it was a man or a woman.

The section of video was short, covering just the time from when the figure came into frame, stopped in front of the house to look around for anyone who was watching, and then vanished around the corner to the gate that led into the backyard, where the door to Mallory's apartment was. They made no attempt to get into the main house.

Looking again, Mallory realized the subject lines of the emails were timestamps, and the next one was from about twenty minutes later on the same night. It was even shorter than the first one and showed only the same figure emerging from the gate, looking around again, and then leaving quickly in the direction they had come from.

Mallory paused the clip at the point when they were standing on the sidewalk, trying to see if there was anything she could glean from the image. If the person had taken anything, it couldn't have been much, because their hands were empty and they had no bag or backpack. That matched her impression that nothing was missing, but it wasn't comforting. She hadn't been holding out much hope that she had been the victim of a normal crime, but what she saw here settled it. That wasn't an opportunistic housebreaker looking for an easy score—whoever was wearing that black hoodie had come to her home on purpose and left when they didn't find what they were looking for.

And then they had come back. There was a third message in the inbox, this with the longest video of the three. Not because the invasion had lasted longer—exactly the opposite. The figure arrived at the sidewalk and turned the corner, but this time they came back less than a minute later. Judging by the date on the video, Mallory guessed this would have been after Joan installed the new locks to replace the damaged one. That was encouraging. If her stalker could be thwarted by a well-locked gate, then she couldn't be up against any kind of master criminal.

She paused the video again when the figure was on the sidewalk, but she was still unable to make out any details. Mallory couldn't be sure it was the same person, but the general appearance was similar, and more than anything, she wasn't willing to believe there were two of them.

And if her theory was right, they knew she had the lipstick, or at least what had been inside of it. And they wanted it. The questions of how and why, respectively, would have to wait. What Mallory needed to decide right now was, what was she going to do with it?

Her first instinct was to put it down the garbage disposal. Whatever this thing was, it didn't start out as her problem, and it could stay that way. That didn't solve the issue of the intruder, but maybe Mallory could put a sign on the door, informing them their target was gone.

She didn't do that for a couple of reasons. One was curiosity: If she ended this episode here, there was a chance she would never find out what it had all been about, and the thought of that was almost more than Mallory could bear.

But also, more seriously, there was the question of Caitlin. Mallory hadn't known the other woman well, and she had no reason to be loyal to her. But she was the source of the mystery, and as far as Mallory could tell, no one had seen her since the earthquake. That was enough on its own for Mallory to put off destroying the hardware key—she needed to at least give Caitlin a chance to explain herself.

But what to do with it in the meantime?

Mallory's apartment was small and short on secret compartments. She thought about taking it to the bank and getting a safe deposit box, but that seemed too obvious, and the key to the box would just be another thing for someone to try to steal from her.

In the end she settled on a solution that was almost idiotic in its simplicity. One of the first things Mallory had unpacked when she got back was what she called her "schlumping sweater," an old cardigan made of sweatshirt material that she put on whenever she was cold and not expecting to see anyone. It was ugly, worn-out, and supremely comfortable, but more critically, it had a hem that was starting to come undone. Mallory had thought of learning enough about sewing to fix it, but now she had another idea.

The hem was about as wide as the hardware key, which Mallory was able to squeeze in through the gap in the stitching and slide along until it was secure.

Pleased with herself, Mallory held the sweater up and examined her handiwork. There was a small lump where the key was hidden, but it was no different from all the other lumps in the hem, and she was fairly confident that, if someone was looking for a valuable thing hidden in her apartment, they wouldn't start there.

13

By morning, Mallory still hadn't heard from Caitlin. She had spent another sleepless night listening closely to every sound in case it turned into footsteps, and it was time to get this thing solved.

Caitlin's home was in Sea Cliff, a place Mallory didn't go often. It wasn't very welcoming to outsiders, and there was little reason to visit unless you were heading for Land's End or wanted to show out-of-town relatives what twenty million dollars of real estate looked like.

As the name implied, the neighborhood was on the side of the city that ended at the Pacific, which offered amazing views when it wasn't wrapping the city in fog. That was the case this morning, and it would be for the rest of August. But once September rolled around, the residents would be able to look out their windows at the crashing waves and the iconic orange lines of the Golden Gate Bridge and remind themselves why they spent so much to live here.

Some of the most valuable houses were poised over the cliffs that dropped straight down to the crashing waves. Caitlin's house was one of these, and Mallory stopped for a moment to ogle it before approaching.

Most of the houses in the neighborhood dated back to the 1920s and '30s, at least in their general outlines. Caitlin's was in the Spanish style that was popular at the time, with arched doorways, tiled roofs, and decorative details pressed into their stucco exteriors. But there were signs that more modern spending had been at work, in the new picture windows and fresh paint, to say nothing of the extensive security camera systems that decorated every exterior.

Mallory found the place intimidating. She knew plenty of people who were richer than her, and for the most part it wasn't an issue. But there was a difference when it was a close friend, versus someone who might be wondering why you were showing up on their doorstep.

But none of this had been Mallory's idea, and if Caitlin was going to give her a mysterious not-lipstick, then she could deal with an unexpected visitor.

Or, at least, she could if she was there. The house was surrounded by a tall hedge with a gate at the front. There was no lock, so Mallory pushed it open and went on through.

Beyond the gate, the garden was badly overgrown, with patches of ragged, dry grass scattered between the landscaped shrubs and dandelions going to seed at the edge of the front walk. It looked like a place no one had been taking care of for a while, and that dimmed Mallory's hopes.

The house itself didn't make her more optimistic. As Mallory drew closer, she noticed that both sides of the door had the red paint marks that the building inspectors used to indicate earthquake-damaged houses. A piece of paper had been stuck to the door at one point and torn down, leaving only a corner under a strip of blue tape.

She could have given up and left, but it seemed silly to come this far and not at least knock on the door. So she did and was surprised when she heard footsteps inside.

They came to the door, but it didn't open.

"I'm not buying anything," said a man's voice from the other side. "And if you're from the city, you can talk to my lawyer."

It wasn't a warm welcome, but it was a start. Mallory leaned over so she was visible through the window next to the door and gave a little wave.

"I'm a friend of Caitlin's," she called, hoping her voice would carry through the glass. "I'm trying to find her."

There was a rattle of chains and the thunk of a dead bolt, and the door opened a crack. A man peered out—probably in his sixties, though a combination of a facelift and fillers made it hard to say. His hair was bleached almost white, and he had a skinny black mustache that looked like he had drawn it on with an eyeliner pencil.

He looked Mallory up and down in a way that made her flinch then opened the door the rest of the way.

There was another step up to the house from where Mallory was standing, but even so, the man didn't exactly tower over her. Mallory put him at about five foot five, and from the way he raised himself up on his toes, she suspected if he was wearing shoes they would have had lifts. Despite being barefoot, he was dressed like he was expecting someone—even in Sea Cliff, pristine white chinos and a butter-yellow cashmere sweater seemed like overkill for hanging out around the house.

He gave her a predatory smile, baring teeth that were gleaming white and didn't quite fit in his mouth.

"One of Caitlin's friends? Well, I guess so. What's your name, hon?"

"Mallory," she said, biting back the impulse to share her last name. "I was hanging out with Caitlin the night before the earthquake. I'm trying to get reconnected with everyone, but I haven't been able to reach her."

"So you decided to stop by. Well, isn't that nice?" The man's face clouded over with a sour expression, but he must have thought the better of whatever he was going to say, because he pursed his lips and then held out his hand. "Charlie Williams. I'm Caitlin's stepfather. Unfortunately, I can't connect you with her right now. I was away when the quake happened, and by the time I got back, she had left. Sent a text saying she was heading up north somewhere, and that's the last I've heard from her."

"Oh." Mallory hadn't expected to hit a dead end so quickly. "You don't have any idea who she might be with, or where she would have gone?"

"No, and believe me, if I did I'd be on my way there right now. This goddamn house is her responsibility, and she left me here with the city breathing down my neck and no funds to fix it. Just because she got all the money doesn't mean she just gets to do whatever the hell she wants, and you can tell her that for me."

"Um, okay," Mallory said. She didn't bother pointing out that talking to Caitlin was what she was not doing at the moment.

He went on. "Also, if you find her, you can tell her I'm not taking care of her damn cat either. That thing can go straight off the cliff, for all I care."

"She left her cat behind?" That didn't sound right. Caitlin hadn't spoken much at dinner after they got back from the bathroom, but the one time she had become animated was when the conversation had turned to pets. Mallory didn't remember the cat's name, but she could recall very clearly the way Caitlin had talked about him, his favorite pillows in the windows, and the way he would only eat a certain food.

"Yeah, like I'm some kind of servant who's going to take care of it. Anyway, if the cops have their way, I'll be out of here, and it's none of my business what happens to that thing."

"I can take it," Mallory said without thinking. She had no business bringing another cat into her household, but there was no way she could leave it with this man.

Which made her wonder even more why Caitlin would.

"You want to?" Charlie seemed honestly surprised that anyone might care for an animal, and for a moment he looked suspicious. But then another thought seemed to occur to him, and a calculating look passed over his face. "Yeah, well, she probably would raise hell if she got back and he was gone. Okay, come on in, and we'll see if we can catch the little bastard."

14

In the end, catching the cat wasn't very hard. Mallory found canned food on a shelf in the giant marble-lined kitchen, and a pair of empty dishes next to the laundry sink. The can wasn't all the way open before a gray longhaired cat appeared, winding itself around Mallory's ankles and purring like an engine.

Charlie looked like he was expecting her to just pick the cat up and go, but it was so clearly hungry that Mallory let it eat before she did anything else.

She filled up the water dish and looked around for a crate. The dishes had been set up in what seemed to be a utility room, with serious-looking washers and dryers next to the sink, and beyond that a row of cabinets. What she didn't see was anything she could use to transport a cat, and she said so.

"Oh, yeah, I guess you can't just put them on a leash, can you? I've never had much luck doing that with pussy, anyway." Caitlin's stepfather grinned at her, and Mallory fought the urge to retch. He went on. "I think Caitlin keeps that stuff upstairs; I'll go have a look."

There was no way Mallory was going with him, so she stayed behind and stroked the cat's fur while he ate. It seemed appreciated—the purring increased until by the time he was finished he sounded like an airplane ready for takeoff. She stopped when he finished the food, but that was clearly unacceptable, and the cat butted her hand until she resumed.

The cat's fur was matted and dull, and Mallory wondered how long it had taken to get this way. She didn't imagine Caitlin would have allowed it, any more than she would have voluntarily left her pet alone with her creep of a stepfather. Mallory's concern was mounting. If Caitlin had left the area, it couldn't have been on a whim—she would have to have been running from something and too afraid to contact anyone. And if she hadn't...

As she petted the cat and worried about what could have happened to Caitlin, Mallory let her gaze drift around the room. It was on the cliff side of the house, with a window that probably would have an amazing view on a less foggy day. Even now, Mallory thought she could see some glimpses of water through the gray, and she left the cat to go get a closer look.

That was when she noticed the cracks.

There were two major ones, running the height of the wall on either side of the window and meeting at the ceiling. Dozens of smaller cracks spidered off those disappearing into the wall and down through the floor. And, unlike at Mallory's apartment, it was clear the damage here was more than surface deep. Now that she was looking, Mallory could see daylight through the larger cracks, and she became aware that part of the wall was at an angle to the rest.

She stepped back instinctively, like she expected the house to crumble around her, and almost tripped over the cat. Finished with his food, he came to wind around her ankles again, purring and butting his head against her leg.

"Huh. Well, he seems to like you okay." Charlie came back into the room carrying a pet crate and a bag that was overflowing with cat toys. "This isn't all his stuff, but it should be enough to get you started. There's a litter box too, but it's not very nice, you know? You can take it if you want."

"That's okay. I've got an extra one." Mallory could only imagine what the litter was going to look like after this much time under Charlie's lack of care, and she wasn't about to hang around to clean it.

Also not hanging around was the cat. At the first sight of the crate, he had shot straight toward the gap under the cabinets, and Mallory barely managed to grab him before he vanished. It wasn't pretty, but she managed to get him out and stuffed into the crate with only minor damage to herself, while Caitlin's stepfather looked on with amusement.

"Nice job," he said. "I could never handle that damn thing. He's better off with you, anyway."

Mallory agreed for different reasons. And now it wasn't just the way the man had neglected the animal that was worrying her.

Looking back at the damaged wall, she asked, "Are you sure it's safe, staying here?" Mallory thought it was obvious she was talking about the stability of the house, but Charlie seemed to misunderstand her.

"As safe as anywhere in this hellhole of a city. But I'm not worried. I keep a semiautomatic handgun next to my bed, and that baby is going to take care of me."

"Oh, okay." Mallory didn't know what she could add to that, and she didn't want to spend any more time here. She hoisted the crate with the furiously yowling cat and said, "I should probably get going. He doesn't sound like he likes it in there. If you hear from Caitlin, can you let her know I have him?"

"Sure, no problem." Charlie made it sound like he was doing her a favor and smiled condescendingly as Mallory squeezed past him on her way out of the laundry room. "You girls, always worried about something."

"Yes, well, sorry to bother you. Thanks for finding the stuff." Gripping the crate in one hand and the bag with the toys and food in the other, she made it to the entrance before Charlie could think of anything else and managed to open the door without having to ask for his help.

More than ever, Mallory was sure she needed to find Caitlin, but she wasn't going to do that here.

Sonali

Nothing was in the right place and everything hurt. Sonali looked at her living room furniture and sighed then got up to move the couch again.

She hated her new apartment. Not that there was anything specifically bad—everything about it was fine. That was what was wrong. Her old place had had windows that rattled, a kitchen that was installed in the eighties, and the smallest closet known to humanity. But there had also been towering ceilings and real wood floors and an arched window that looked out over her busy neighborhood street.

The new place had none of that. It was a neutral box in a tower full of neutral boxes, with decent water pressure and nothing else to recommend it. But Sonali wasn't going to be able to move back to her old home soon, or maybe ever, and this was what she had to make do with.

She was lucky to have found a place at all. Her job in corporate accounting paid well, but the way rents had gone up since the earthquake, this was at the limit of what she could afford. So she was having to look for ways to economize, like not hiring anyone to help her move in or assemble the new furniture she had just gotten delivered.

It should have been something she could manage on her own, but she still wasn't back to a hundred percent. That was why, after a minute of trying to drag the couch to a new position, she changed her mind and sat down on it where it was. She was getting together with people later, and she couldn't let them see she was in pain. It was going to be her first big test, seeing them in person, and Sonali hoped she would be able to pull it off. If she couldn't...well, that didn't matter. She would.

15

Mallory was back on the sidewalk before she realized she had never learned the cat's name. Not that she expected it to come when called, but it didn't seem right, and she resolved to find out from one of her friends.

As it happened, that wasn't necessary. She had just finished loading the cat and his belongings into the back seat of her car when an older woman who had been working in the garden of one of the houses across the street waved her over.

"Is that Gimli you've got there?" she called as Mallory crossed to meet her.

"I guess so—he's Caitlin's cat. Is that his name?"

The woman nodded vigorously. "That's him. I'm so glad someone is taking care of him. I've been giving him some food when he comes around, but I couldn't take him in because of my dog. He's very excitable." As if to illustrate her point, there was a flurry of barking from inside the house, and a small black dog threw itself repeatedly at the picture window.

"Marty, hush!" the woman said, then turned back to Mallory. "Are you a friend of Caitlin's?"

Mallory's hopes lifted a bit. After the reception she had gotten at the house, she wasn't sure she was going to get anything out of this trip except the scratches on her arms, but Caitlin's neighbor seemed friendly and genuinely interested. "Yes—I saw her just before the earthquake, but I haven't been able to get in touch with her since then. Have you seen her at all?"

"No, and I have to admit I've been getting worried." The woman pulled off her gardening glove and held out her hand. "I'm Ann, by the way. We've lived here for the last forty years. I remember when Caitlin and her mother moved in across the street. She was just a teenager, but she always cared so much about her animals. I couldn't imagine what would have possessed her to leave Gimli with that man."

"I was wondering that too," Mallory said. "I didn't have the impression that Caitlin got along very well with her stepfather."

Ann snorted. "That's because she had some sense. More than her mother, poor thing. Brilliant woman, but she didn't have the best taste in men. To be honest, when Caitlin wasn't around after the earthquake, I thought she just couldn't stand living in a house with him anymore. But she wouldn't leave her cat behind. And after what happened to her mother, I've been worried."

"What did happen? I know her mother died recently. Had she been sick?"

Ann snorted. "No, and don't let anyone tell you otherwise.

She also wasn't drinking or doing anything else that would cause a healthy sixty-year-old woman to fall in her bathroom and hit her head so hard she never woke up."

"I had no idea," Mallory said. "You think someone might have...done something to her?" Mallory shivered, for reasons that had nothing to do with the cool air. She had started this hunt with vague concerns at the back of her mind, but now there seemed to be suggestions of violence everywhere she looked. Still, Mallory couldn't bring herself to say it out loud. It was just too strange, to be standing on one of the fanciest streets in the city with the fog swirling around her, talking scandal with a stranger while her friend's cat wailed in the background.

Ann must have felt the awkwardness too, because she backpedaled as delicately as she could.

"Well, my husband says I think a lot of things. The police seemed satisfied, and they spent plenty of time here. But..." Her momentary restraint failed, and Ann leaned conspiratorially across the fence. "Deborah, that's Caitlin's mother, she did a lot of traveling for her work. And let's just say, when she and Caitlin were away, there were a number of repeat visitors to the house. I never got a good look at a face, but Charles certainly had a lot of female friends. I tried to tell poor Deb, but she wouldn't hear it. She was so sure she had gotten it right this time."

Ann sounded indignant, but it just made Mallory sad. She had never met Caitlin's mother, but she felt bad for the woman, married to someone like Charlie with the neighbors talking behind her back. But she did see why there would have been some questions about her sudden death. Enough so that Mallory couldn't help asking questions of her own.

"I'm surprised the police didn't suspect Charlie. I thought it was pretty common to look at the husband when a woman dies suddenly."

Ann sniffed. "*Allegedly,* he was in LA, playing records in front of a thousand people when it happened."

"Oh."

"It was probably more like twenty. But anyway, I guess it was good enough for the police. And Caitlin was out at a pottery class—she was the one who found Deb when she got home. So she was all alone in the house. Allegedly."

That was a lot of alleging, and Mallory didn't know what to do with it. She also wasn't sure how it could connect to Caitlin's absence, or her own problems, but she didn't like any of it. There were too many things that were wrong or didn't make sense, and even the earthquake couldn't account for them.

While they had been speaking, Gimli's yowls had gotten progressively more insistent, until finally he made a noise that sounded like it came from the very depths of hell.

"I should probably get going," Mallory said. "I don't think he's very happy in there."

That was nothing like how unhappy her cats were going to be when they found out they were getting a new roommate.

"Good luck with him. By the way, you should have the info for his groomer. Caitlin swore by her guy, and she seemed to think he was the only one who could deal with Gimli's fur." Ann dug in her pockets and came up with a crumpled piece of paper and a pen. "I've never seen such a pampered animal, and I know a thing or two about spoiling them."

In the house behind her, the dog slammed his entire body into the window, bounced off and dropped out of sight, and reappeared seconds later to continue barking.

"Thank you," Mallory said. "Actually, I am worried about Caitlin. If you hear anything from her, can you let me know? I told Charlie to tell her I took Gimli, but…"

"Right," said Ann. "Let me give you my number, and you can send me yours. What did you say your name was, again?"

—

Mallory was navigating the curving streets of the oceanside neighborhood when she remembered she hadn't learned anything about the key in the lipstick. Not that she would have asked Charlie. Even before talking to Ann, he was not someone she would trust. But she could have tried to look around the house, maybe gotten into Caitlin's room somehow. As it was, she was no closer to answering her original question. All she had now was more things to worry about and a cat.

She had also gotten herself lost. Not entirely—Mallory knew generally where she was, but she wasn't sure how to get from there to where she was going. The west side of the city had never been the easiest part to navigate, but the damage from the earthquake had made things worse, particularly because the app on Mallory's phone hadn't kept up with the road closures.

She was executing her second consecutive three-point turn when she noticed the other car. She had seen the silver Audi earlier, but only in the general way she was clocking the number of fancy cars around her. But she spotted it again when she was held up by a crew repairing a water line, and by the third time she saw it—turning around behind her at a giant sinkhole—she was sure it was the same car.

Mallory didn't think it was a coincidence. Particularly because the driver in the Audi was wearing large sunglasses and a hoodie and always seemed to be looking away whenever she had them in view.

On the one hand, this could be an opportunity. If she really was being followed by the same person who had broken into her house and tried to take her purse, maybe she could use it to find out more about them, to try to get a better look at their face or at least their license plate. Unlike their previous encounters, Mallory didn't feel so vulnerable here. She was safe in her car, in a busy neighborhood with homes and businesses and probably security cameras that could catch anything that happened.

Then she missed a turn, and Mallory found herself in the Presidio.

The former military base at the northern edge of San Francisco covered more than two of the city's forty-nine square miles, mostly undeveloped. Mallory was on the road that ran along the edge, perched on a cliff that dropped sharply down to the ocean. She had been here before, when the greatest danger was other drivers distracted by the view. But the earthquake had wiped out the shoulder, and now just a small loss of control would send her hundreds of feet down into the crashing waves.

The other car was still behind her, far enough back that she couldn't see the driver anymore but they were still maintaining the distance. There should have been other cars on the road—even after the quake, people were around. It wasn't until Mallory noticed the ROAD CLOSED AHEAD sign that she understood.

She came around a curve and saw why. A rockslide had taken out part of the road, leaving only one lane with cracked and broken asphalt. There was a barrier closing the road in front of the damage, which had been moved partly out of the way.

A smart person would have stopped and turned around. But even the undamaged part of the road was narrow, the silver Audi was getting closer, and there was no one else in sight. The security Mallory had felt earlier was gone—if she went over the cliff here, nobody would ever know anything more than that she had made a mistake driving in the fog.

There was no time to decide. Mallory swerved into the outer lane, passing the barrier with inches to spare. To her left, the edge of the cliff dropped off into the clouds, the ocean invisible below her. The slid-out road was in front of her, and she dodged back to the less damaged side, willing herself not to look down to see if the asphalt crumbled under her tires.

Up ahead, there was an intersection with another road that headed inland. Mallory didn't even look at the sign to see where it went; she just turned, accelerating hard and not looking back.

In all the excitement, Mallory lost track of the other car.

When she did look, she didn't see it, and the new route twisted through overgrown woodland that blocked the view behind her. Eventually she reached a place where the buildings were denser, and the road opened out to a parade ground.

Mallory stepped on the brake, trying to bring her speed and her heart rate down together. There were more cars around here and other traffic. Mallory thought she got another glimpse of the silver Audi, right before a bus pulled in behind her.

There was a parking lot facing the parade ground and buildings all around. Mallory pulled into a space and turned off the car, breathing slowly and trying to decide exactly how stupid she was being.

Another car pulled into the spot next to her, a green SUV. A woman got out, unloaded three corgis from the back, and threw a ball toward the lawn for them to chase. Mallory watched them in wonder, like none of it was real, but she didn't know if she was waking up from a dream or falling into one.

That was what it was like a lot of the time now, even when she hadn't just been through a major scare. Things were normal, but they weren't.

Sometimes, you could fool yourself into thinking nothing had happened. Most of the roads were open, the power and water were back on, people and businesses were returning. The city wasn't quite what it was, but San Francisco had always been a place that changed, and if you didn't know better, you might think this was no different.

But it was. Not just in the damage to the buildings or the

bridge, but to all the lives that had been knocked off their foundations by the quake. Mallory had been lucky—she had family to support her, a place to go, and a job that kept her busy. But how many others had slipped through the cracks? How many people were there like Caitlin, who didn't have anyone close enough, who cared enough, to wonder why they hadn't heard from her and to follow up before six months had passed?

Mallory didn't know if that car had been following her, or if the break-ins had anything to do with anything, or if it was all just a bunch of coincidences. What she did know was that a young woman who loved her cat had left him alone with someone who wouldn't care for him, and more than anything else, that made her sure of what she needed to do next.

On the lawn in front of her, the corgis had moved on and some kids had set up a foam rubber rocket, taking turns jumping on the pump to set it off. Mallory watched them fire and chase it while she waited on hold with the SFPD, tapping through the phone tree to report a missing person.

16

God, it seems like it's been forever." Rachel paused, then laughed. "I know I always say that, but this time I really mean it."

Sonali shook her head. "I know what you mean. I was reading a story about something that happened last Christmas, and I had to remind myself that was less than a year ago."

Mallory started to agree with her but had to stop to dodge out of the way of a man on an electric scooter riding down the middle of the sidewalk.

"Some things haven't changed anyway," she said sourly, once she saved herself from falling into the street. "Why is it never the people you want to get crushed under a collapsing freeway?"

Sonali came back out of the doorway she had stepped into and glared at the man's vanishing back. "I thought they banned those things after all the fires that were started by the batteries?"

"Like a guy like that cares. He probably burned down his whole building and bought a new one with the insurance," Rachel said.

Mallory laughed with the others, but she couldn't help feeling uncomfortable, with herself as much as them. It was something she had noticed since the quake—how easy it was to be angry and how little patience she had for jerks. Not that the sidewalk riders had ever gotten much sympathy from her, but she didn't remember wishing for their violent deaths before.

"Anyway, thanks for getting in touch, Mallory," said Rachel. "I swear, I've been thinking like twice a week I should try to get together with people, but I never did it."

"Me too, but I've gotta say, I was surprised to get your text," Sonali added.

"Why?" asked Mallory, feigning ignorance. The truth was, she knew exactly what her friend was getting at. Honestly, she was surprised no one else had commented.

Sonali remained unimpressed. "Oh, come on. The person who almost skipped her own twenty-first birthday because she didn't get around to inviting anyone is suddenly San Francisco's top social planner? I had to google 'earthquake body swap aliens' before I came here."

"Okay, but would the aliens know you can't resist a gelato?"

They had been walking from the light rail stop where they met and finally reached their destination. Summers in the city might not be scorching, but that didn't deter the local ice cream entrepreneurs. The latest was a pop-up that had appeared in the site of a shuttered bakery, boasting a pedigreed chef at the helm and creative flavors in the tubs.

The three women joined the line that had already formed,

mostly made up of other thirtysomethings in their summer jackets. They almost fit in but not quite—Rachel was overdressed for the crowd, with a designer trench in camel-colored linen over what Mallory could only describe as "fashion shorts," and Sonali stood out the way she always did, with her hair piled on top of her head in an elaborate knot and a bright silk dress under her fleece.

And Mallory, well, Mallory felt like her height made it difficult for her to stand out anywhere.

Mallory was hoping the conversation might turn to what they were going to order, but she should have known better.

"Why were you trying to reach Caitlin?" Rachel asked. "Did you get in touch with her?"

"No, and I'm worried. I went to her house yesterday, and her stepfather hadn't heard from her since the quake. She left her cat with him, and he wasn't taking care of it at all. I ended up taking him home with me. The cat, I mean," Mallory said.

"I didn't think you'd take home her stepdad," Sonali laughed and then looked suddenly serious. "But the cat thing is weird. I didn't get the impression she was someone who would abandon an animal."

"She wouldn't," Rachel confirmed. "Caitlin has always loved her pets more than, well, anything. And she doesn't have a very good relationship with Charlie."

"So what does it mean?" Sonali asked as they inched forward in the line. "Do you think something happened to her?"

"I don't know." Mallory thought for a moment and then decided she might as well tell the whole story at this point.

"Actually, there was another reason I was looking for Caitlin. When we were out that night, before the quake happened, she gave me something. It didn't seem important at the time, and I know you guys will think I'm crazy, but I think someone has been trying to steal it. That's why I wanted to talk to her, to find out what was going on. And then when I found out that no one has seen her..."

Mallory didn't finish that sentence; she didn't want to.

To their credit, neither of the women laughed. Maybe it was knowing that Caitlin was missing, or maybe just the fact that Mallory hadn't made her usual joke out of it, but they both looked serious.

"What was it?" Sonali asked. "The thing she gave you?"

"It looked like a lipstick but inside was some sort of electronics hardware key. I don't know what it's for—there was nothing else."

"What did you do with it?" asked Rachel.

It was the obvious next question, and there was no reason for Mallory not to answer. But she was suddenly aware of all of the people in line with them and the way her pursuer always seemed to be able to find her. Some instinct took over, and the truth got stuck in her throat.

"I mailed it to my aunt in Maryland. If whoever is trying to get it is here, there's no way they'll find it there."

Sonali nodded. "Good thinking. If it was something Caitlin needed urgently, she wouldn't have given it to you. Why do you think she did that?"

"That's one of the things I want to ask her. I hope she isn't in any kind of trouble," Mallory said.

She didn't mention the call she had made to the police missing persons line, or the way she had answered the recorded questions about Caitlin's appearance the last time Mallory had seen her.

They reached the front of the line, and the conversation paused as the three of them squeezed into the tiny shop. Mallory ended up with an ube caramel swirl, and Rachel got the raspberry marzipan, while Sonali went straight for the chocolate.

"Why did you even wait in the whole line if you're just ordering that?" Rachel asked once they were back outside. "How basic can you get?"

"Basic is ordering something you don't want because you think it makes you cool," Sonali said. "If these guys are as good as they say they are, then the chocolate should be exceptional."

There was that tension again, and Mallory could feel it creeping into her shoulders. It was just the aftereffects of the trauma they had all been through, she knew that, but something more felt off here. She took another spoonful of her gelato and tried to defuse the situation.

"I'm just glad we can have things like this again. After the earthquake, everything I read online was that San Francisco was dead and would never come back."

Sonali laughed, the conflict apparently forgotten. "Oh, I know. My grandma called my mom three days after it happened and told her the navy needed to get me out because everything that wasn't on fire was being looted. I tried to explain it wasn't like that, but she was so sure, because she saw it on TV."

"When did you leave?" Rachel asked. "I managed to get on

one of the ferries over to the Oakland Airport after a week. I would have stayed, but I couldn't take the bathroom situation."

"Oh, um. I actually ended up staying down in Palo Alto for a while. They got the power back on pretty early there. So I didn't really have to leave, you know."

"That sounds nice," Mallory said. It also sounded like a completely normal thing to do. Then why did Sonali look so panicked?

Mallory's phone rang, and she glanced down at the screen. An unknown number, so she let it go to voicemail and went on.

"It must have been interesting, staying around here while everything was going on. Were you able to get back up to your apartment at all?"

"No, it wasn't possible," Sonali said. "My building got pretty badly damaged. Anyway, should we be doing anything to find Caitlin?"

The change of subject was so blatant it might as well have come with a siren, but Mallory was still trying to play peacemaker. So before Rachel could jump in with any follow-up questions, she said, "I'd like to, but I don't know what. Charlie said she texted him to say she was going out of town, and if that's true, I don't want to invade her privacy."

"That's a good point," Rachel said, with a knowing look. "But you still went to her house?"

"Well, I didn't know that when I went. And I didn't know about the cat either," said Mallory.

"Did you see her car there?" Sonali asked.

That was something that hadn't occurred to Mallory. "I don't know. I assume her stepfather would have said something if it was. What kind of car does she have?"

"Some kind of luxury brand, I forget," said Rachel. "She would, right?"

"It's an Audi," Sonali said. "I remember, because we parked near each other going to dinner that night, and I was asking her about it on the way into the restaurant. I'd been considering getting one, when I thought I could afford it."

"Do you remember what color hers was?" Mallory asked, her heart in her throat.

"Silver," Sonali said promptly. "She wanted a blue one, but they didn't have any with the sunroof. If I had that kind of money, I'd get exactly the car I wanted, but I guess that's not her style."

"I guess not. I didn't see a car like that at the house, but it could have been in the garage or something."

But it hadn't been in any garage; Mallory was sure of that. Caitlin's silver Audi had been following her through the western side of San Francisco, chasing her for reasons Mallory couldn't begin to imagine. If she had wanted the lipstick back, why hadn't she just asked?

17

They finished their gelatos on a bench in a small neighborhood park. The playground had been closed off with yellow caution tape, but a group of preteens was ignoring it, daring each other to fling themselves higher and higher on the swings. Mallory winced as one boy crashed to the ground, but he immediately got back up and started punching his friends, so she decided he must be okay.

"How did Caitlin's family end up so rich, anyway?" she asked, as the kids chased each other out into the street.

"That was all her mom," Rachel said. "Caitlin's dad left when she was a kid, and her mom hadn't been working. So she got a job at Starbucks or something and went to school for programming at night. It turned out she was really good at it, and she got a job at this little startup called Google. Anyway, you can guess how it went from there."

"Wow, yeah." Mallory had heard about how the early employees had cashed in—even so, it was hard to imagine the turnaround for a single mother going from pouring coffee to a cliff-top mansion.

"When did the stepdad come into the picture?" Mallory asked. She was thinking about what the neighbor had said, about him having an affair. Caitlin's mom might have just been unlucky in love, and Mallory was starting to wonder exactly how unlucky.

"I think they got together about ten years ago, after we graduated. Caitlin and I lost touch after college, but when I moved to San Francisco, we reconnected." Rachel scraped out the last bit of gelato and stared into the empty cup. "She never liked him. Whenever we'd hang out, she always made an excuse not to be at her place, even though she had all that space. That's why I wasn't surprised she left town after the earthquake—I figured she wanted to get away from him."

"I wonder why she stayed there with him at all after her mother died. When I was there, he said the house was Caitlin's responsibility, which made it sound like she must own it," Mallory said.

Rachel nodded. "Everything went to Caitlin in her mother's will. I don't know; I was wondering that too."

"California is a community-property state," Sonali said. "Even if he wasn't in the will and he didn't have anything to do with buying the house, as the widower he would have the rights to continue living there."

"I don't know if anyone is going to be living there for much longer. It looked like the house had been red tagged, and when I got inside, I could see why." Mallory described the cracks she had seen in the laundry room wall, and Sonali recoiled in horror.

"Right on the cliff? And he's still living there? The guy must have a death wish."

"But that could be the reason Caitlin left," Rachel pointed out. "Maybe it isn't such a mystery after all."

—

No cars followed Mallory home from the park. She kept looking around, to the point that the woman sitting across from her on the light rail car watched her warily. But no silver Audi appeared, and the only vehicles she saw on her walk from the stop to her house were a couple of delivery vans and a neighbor pulling into his driveway.

Mallory had gotten in the habit of examining the doors and windows before she went into the apartment, and everything was exactly the way she had left it. She forced her shoulders to relax a fraction as she unlocked the door and the dead bolt. Maybe it was all some crazy misunderstanding and her stalker finally figured out they really wanted a house on the next block. The car that appeared to have been following her might just have been another lost driver, confused by the road closures and hoping Mallory knew where she was going. The fact that it was the same make and color as Caitlin's didn't mean anything; silver Audis were a dime a dozen in San Francisco.

She thought about the tension she had noticed in herself and the others that day. Maybe all of her panicking was another product of the reaction to having her life and home literally shaken out from under her. There were people all over the internet coming up with wild conspiracy theories about the earthquake—how it was caused by a secret government program, or Chinese space lasers, or whatever. Mallory understood that came from the impulse to grab some feeling of control over an uncontrollable situation, but she hadn't considered the possibility for herself. Maybe she just needed to calm down.

Inside the apartment, the scene was anything but calm, but that had nothing to do with any invader—at least not the human kind. Mallory had been trying to keep her cats separate from their new roommate by setting him up with his food and litter box in the bathroom, but she had forgotten that the latch on the door wasn't always reliable.

The cats must have defeated it, and the results were clear across the apartment. Ever since the earthquake, Mallory had avoided keeping breakables out, but the trio had done their best, clearing all her books off the bottom two shelves of the bookcase and somehow managing to wrap the afghan she kept on the couch around the legs of her desk chair. Even the sweater where she had hidden Caitlin's property hadn't been spared, and it was bunched up next to the kitchen door.

That made Mallory pause and wonder if this hadn't just been the cats. But the hardware key was right where she had left it, and the way Mariah was watching her from the top of the bookshelf and Celine was hiding under the TV table, growling steadily, left her with no doubt how they felt about the situation.

Despite that welcome, Gimli seemed to be doing fine. Mallory found him lounging in the middle of her bed, licking his paws.

He purred when Mallory petted him, and she couldn't find any injuries, though she did notice the mats in his fur. She thought about trying to close Gimli back up somewhere, but at this point the damage was done, and everyone seemed okay, so she decided she had other things to worry about.

Like, what was going on here? Ever since she hadn't been able to reach Caitlin, and especially once she found the cat, Mallory had been thinking about worst case scenarios. But she had trouble dismissing the fact that the car that had been following her matched Caitlin's. And now that she thought of it, the person who had tried to grab her bag on the street and the figure in the security camera video could have been Caitlin as well.

Mallory loaded up the video again and tried to get a better look. She realized she had been assuming the housebreaker was a man, but now that she examined the blurry figure, she wasn't so sure. They passed by the light fixture on the side of the house, and they didn't quite line up with the top of it. Mallory knew that the bottom edge of that fixture was just at the level of her forehead, thanks to one unfortunate night on her way home from a birthday party, so she put the person's height at about five foot seven or eight—not as tall as she thought Caitlin was, but short for a man, and she might be missing an inch or two in the angle.

Mallory had opened Caitlin's Instagram to see if she could compare the figures, when she stopped. She wasn't going to prove anything this way—all she could do would be to convince herself of what she already believed. What she needed to do was to find Caitlin and ask her what was going on. And if she couldn't do that, then Mallory needed to come up with some theories of her own that she could test.

Mallory thought back to the question of the car. What if it had been Caitlin following her? She had to know Mallory would give her back her property if she asked, but could there be a reason she didn't feel safe asking? That might have some connection with why she had given Mallory the lipstick case in the first place—that she was being watched at every turn, and it wasn't safe for her to approach directly.

Or, at least, that could be something Caitlin believed. Mallory wasn't an expert on mental illness, but she knew enough about paranoia to see the way it might explain everything. What if Caitlin had been driven to some kind of breakdown by her mother's death, and she had concocted a scenario around the hardware key? She might have thought Mallory was the right person to give it to at dinner that night, then changed her mind and decided Mallory was part of the conspiracy, and broken in to get it back.

The more she thought about it, the more the theory made sense. Caitlin could have been holding it mostly together before the earthquake, only giving into smaller impulses like giving Mallory the key, but the disaster had put her fully over the edge, causing her to even abandon her pet because she thought she wasn't safe. She could be watching her house, and that was how she spotted Mallory to follow her, with some unformed idea of getting the key back.

If that was true, though, then what should Mallory do? At this point, no one was even sure Caitlin was missing, and she didn't think the police were going to listen to her theory about a woman who left on her own but might be having a crisis. A family member would have more pull, but Mallory didn't know where to start with that. Caitlin's stepfather hardly seemed like he would care, and Mallory had no idea if she even had any other family.

Rachel or Kendra might know. They were closer friends with Caitlin, and they were the obvious people to ask and maybe to suggest her theory to and see what they thought of it.

This wasn't the sort of thing you could do over text. Mallory picked up her phone, noticing as she did that she had a new message. That was the unknown call she had ignored earlier—it would probably just be a stretch of silence followed by an automated scammer reciting its pitch. But Mallory hated leaving notifications unread, so she went to clear it before she made her call.

She hit Play expecting to hear that now was the best time to buy solar panels or the IRS wanted her to pay her taxes with gift cards. Instead, a woman's voice came on, brisk and efficient.

"Hi, this call is for Mallory Taylor. This is Dr. Hillary Moran from the San Francisco medical examiner's office. I'm calling about a missing person you reported and a potential body identification?"

Rachel

Where was she? Rachel blinked and rubbed her eyes, trying to find her spot again on the page. She needed to read the document before work on Tuesday, but she couldn't focus.

There was no secret what was bothering her. The get-together with Mallory and Sonali had upset Rachel more than she expected, and she was mad at herself for that. It wasn't like her, or at least it shouldn't be. This sort of thing was going to happen as the city recovered from the disaster and people came back. She needed to learn to deal with it.

Or maybe she just needed to find some new friends. Rachel gave up on trying to read for a while and leaned back, staring at the ceiling. Why did so many people try to hang onto connections they made when they were just teenagers? She had changed; they all had. If it wasn't so hard to meet new people, she would have done it long ago. And now...well, the earthquake had made a lot of things more difficult. She had a lot on her plate right now, but it was something she needed to think about.

Her phone buzzed, and Rachel looked at the message and decided it could wait. Not for long—some things were likely to come back to bite her soon. But she would only make it worse if she acted without thinking. Not this time.

It was funny that they had all had that dinner the night of the earthquake. Rachel had thought at the time that it felt like the end of an era; she had no idea then how right she was.

A truck rumbled down the street, rattling the building. Rachel shuddered, partly at the memories it brought up, and partly at the fact that she was still living in this crappy place, after everything. She had moved to San Francisco with such grand ideas—she was going to make her fortune in the land of the new gold rush. And now here she was, reviewing a marketing document that had probably been spit out by some idiot AI program while the tiny apartment she was spending a fortune on was about to fall down around her. She needed to change that, to change everything about her life. It was what she deserved, and this time nothing was going to stand in her way.

18

Caitlin was dead.

It was dark by the time Mallory got back from the police station, and she fumbled for her keys, blinking spots out of her eyes from the security lights. She thought she might be crying, but no tears came, just a terrible, disconnected feeling of horror.

The trip to the morgue had been a long and confusing process, starting with her returning Dr. Moran's call. The medical examiner had only been able to tell her that they had a body of a young white woman that matched the description Mallory had given, found not long after the earthquake. Mallory had considered trying to say that she wasn't the best person to do the identification, that there were other people who knew Caitlin better, but that didn't seem right. She was the one who thought Caitlin was missing, and dragging in Rachel or Kendra—or trying to convince Caitlin's stepfather—seemed like stepping away from a problem she had created. So she agreed to go, telling herself if she wasn't sure of the identification, she could say so.

But she wasn't unsure. She didn't even get to go into the room with the body, instead sitting outside and looking at a picture of it on a computer screen, but there was no question it was Caitlin. If there had been, it would have been settled when she was shown the woman's clothes—a green double-breasted coatdress, silver tights, and black Prada ankle boots.

"That's what she was wearing the last time I saw her," she had explained to the technician. "It was the night of the earthquake, a couple of hours before it happened."

That, along with Mallory's more tentative identification of the body and the fact that she was able to say that no one she knew had seen Caitlin since the earthquake, seemed to be enough for the police. They asked for Caitlin's full name and the contact information for her family, and Mallory gave them as much as she could and then waited until a police detective could speak to her.

It was a long wait, and Mallory used the time to text her friends with the news. She had a twinge of regret as she sent the messages—she was sure her mother would say it needed at least a phone call. But she didn't trust her voice, and she wasn't even sure if she was supposed to be telling anyone, so cowardice won out. She did send individual messages, at least. Telling people a friend was dead felt wrong for a group chat.

Someone finally came to lead Mallory to a small, sparsely furnished room where an older Black man was waiting. He introduced himself as Detective Murray, and she spent the first ten minutes going over the things she had already said. He gave her more information than she had expected, maybe thinking that

Mallory had been a close friend of Caitlin's. She had died of head injuries—two of them: one at the front of her skull that wasn't severe enough to kill and another at the back that was. The body had been found at the Palace of Fine Arts—an outdoor structure left over from an exhibition over a hundred years ago, now mostly a backdrop for movie scenes and wedding photos.

The palace had been damaged in the earthquake, but Mallory couldn't get a straight answer about whether Caitlin's injuries might have been caused by any of the debris.

The detective did ask her a few times if she had any idea what Caitlin might have been doing so far out on the edge of the city, even describing the spot where the body was found, but Mallory had no answer for him. She tried her best to think back to the end of the dinner, but she hadn't even seen Caitlin leave—all Mallory could remember was when somebody asked and she noticed they were down by one. Certainly, there had been nothing Caitlin had said that suggested she was going to go out adventuring on a cold February night, and the detective confirmed that no coat had been found with the body.

There had also been no form of identification on her, but the detective didn't seem to think that was very telling. The body had been officially found three days after the earthquake—it might have been reported sooner, but the chaos of the disaster meant anyone who was beyond saving was left until there was the capacity to deal with the remains. So there had been plenty of time for the opportunists who had been scouring the city to make off with Caitlin's purse, and there was no knowing when her wallet might have vanished.

Mallory tried to tell the detective about the hardware key, the break-ins, and the car, but he was politely disinterested. Clearly, he thought she was just overexcited, wound up by having seen a friend's body, and looking for drama. The police view on Caitlin's death was that she had gone to the park that night for reasons of her own, and through bad luck, she happened to be under an unstable structure at the time of the earthquake.

After a while, Mallory stopped arguing. She sounded silly, she realized, talking about bad feelings and mysterious cars, and she had no evidence to back up her theories. Ever since the earthquake, the city had been under a microscope, with half the country believing—and frankly hoping—that San Francisco would descend into lawless chaos. It was clear that the main goal of the people Mallory spoke to was to get the particular question of an unidentified young woman's death settled quietly before any news organization picked up on it, and nothing she had to say was significant enough to override that.

The detective did say they would be looking for Caitlin's car, though he also mentioned that a lot of the cars that had been stolen after the earthquake had been moved out of state. Mallory ignored his pessimism—on this point, at least, she thought there was a good chance she would be proved right.

Finally, there were no more questions to ask, no more information Mallory could give. She thanked the officer who led her to the door and asked one last hopeless time to be told if anything came up. Taking his noncommittal answer for what it was worth, she stepped out of the police station, and into the rest of her life.

The entire time she had been talking to the detective, her phone had been buzzing with shocked and horrified reactions from her friends. Once she was on the bus, Mallory spent some time responding to them as best she could, offering what little information she had and agreeing it was terrible and unbelievable.

Kendra seemed to be taking the second part literally, repeatedly questioning Mallory's ability to identify Caitlin when she had known her so little. Mallory tried to explain about the clothes, and that the police were going to follow up with fingerprints and dental records, but Kendra wasn't convinced.

Mallory didn't entirely blame her, and she knew they were all dealing with shock, but with the third text that began with *no offense but*, she lost it and said Kendra should go down to the morgue and look for herself if she wanted to be sure. That was when Mallory realized that Kendra wasn't the only one being overtaken by emotion, and she silenced her phone and focused on not missing her stop.

Back in the apartment, the situation was calm by comparison. A truce must have been reached, because all three cats were in the living room, with Celine and Mariah on either side of the couch and Gimli ignoring them from the desk chair.

Something about seeing him there brought back everything people had said about how much Caitlin had loved him. Mallory had a mental image of Caitlin coming back from that dinner, scooping up her cat and telling him all about her evening while he purred.

And then, for whatever reason, she hadn't changed into

comfortable clothes and stayed at home with him. She had gone back out—probably before the earthquake happened but maybe after—and had ended up in a remote corner of the city, under a hundred-year-old folly that was about to fall down. And that was the last time she had ever seen the pet she had apparently adored.

As though he knew what she was thinking, Gimli jumped down from the chair and sat in front of Mallory, looking up at her questioningly. Over the protestations of the other cats, she picked him up and cuddled him.

"I'm sorry, little guy," Mallory whispered. "She's not coming back."

19

Mallory woke to the sound of the garbage trucks and realized she had forgotten to put out her can. Normally, that would have sent her sprinting for the door, pulling on whatever she could find to cover her pajamas, hoping to wave down the driver. But this time she stayed where she was—fully dressed on the couch where she had fallen asleep—and waited until the rumble faded down the street.

It had been another long night. Going to bed hadn't been an option, not with everything she was feeling and fearing. It didn't seem possible, knowing what she knew and having experienced what she had, that she would shed her protective layer of clothes and lie down to sleep—the very idea of coziness made her feel vulnerable. It wasn't any sort of rational plan of defending herself, more like not sticking a foot out from under the covers, because then the monsters could get it.

She tried to distract herself for a while, first with a streaming drama she had been meaning to catch up on, but she watched a scene three times and didn't know what happened. The voices faded into the background as she ran through her questions for the millionth time.

Why had Caitlin given her the key?

What was it for?

Who wanted it?

Why had Caitlin gone out?

How had she died?

Why had she died?

Finally, Mallory gave in. Around midnight, she took her laptop over to the couch and headed down every internet rabbit hole she could find, looking up everything she could find about Caitlin, her life, and her family.

Now, in the light of day, she reviewed what she had found.

It wasn't much. Caitlin had graduated with honors from their university, though she apparently hadn't learned enough to know to set her Facebook page to private. That was how Mallory learned about the year she had spent volunteering with an ecotourism group in Costa Rica and Caitlin's admission into a philosophy master's program after that. A vague post suggested grad school hadn't worked out, and the rest were almost exclusively cat pictures, with occasional mentions of international travel.

"Must be nice to be rich," Mallory muttered to herself, before she remembered why she was here.

Mallory got up from the couch and stretched, trying to shake off a night of bad sleep. She could hardly remember what she had looked up after digging into Caitlin's social media history, and it was clear that her note-taking had started to suffer around three a.m. She did remember there being something about Caitlin's mother—her LinkedIn page, maybe? Mallory made herself a cup of the strongest coffee she could manage through blurry eyes and moved her computer back to the desk to retrace her virtual steps.

Based on what she had learned, Mallory had some ideas about Caitlin's mother, and her work history bore them out. Deborah Lange had certainly had an impressive career. Her ten years at Google were marked by steady elevations in her role through the levels of software development. Not long after that company went public, she had moved to a senior position at another software startup, which was subsequently sold to her former employer. That cycle repeated itself over the next several years, with Deborah's job titles—and presumably, payouts—increasing. At the time of her death, she listed only advisory roles with a handful of companies, and Mallory could only assume she had enough money that she had decided to enjoy it.

The education section of her page was blank, but she made up for it with other interests. Deborah had been an enthusiastic user of the website's blogging function, for a while posting several times a week. Most of what she wrote was bland corporate boosterism—"exciting innovation" this, "major disruption" that—no different from dozens of other startup founders. But scattered among the essays on cryptocurrency and productivity tips there were digressions into bread baking and music.

Deborah had even posted a video of herself singing in front of a band at a street fair. All the band's members were women in late middle age, and according to the caption, they were performing as The Good Mama Jammers, which gave Mallory an involuntary shudder of secondhand embarrassment.

Their performance of "I'm Still Standing" was capable enough, as far as Mallory could tell through the poor audio of the cell phone recording. Deborah just about had the range for the song, and she threw herself into the lyrics with a vigor that suggested she had thoughts about the subject.

Mallory expanded the video and watched it again, this time focusing more on the person and less on the performance. Deborah, she decided, had been a fun lady. She bounced around the stage in her fringed leather vest and knee-high boots, stopping regularly to brush her long gray hair out of her face. It was clear this was where Caitlin got her height—Deborah must have been at least five foot ten without the boots. Watching it again, Mallory wondered at her joy and her confidence, and felt a wave of regret that she never got to meet this woman.

And how on earth had she ended up with a skeevy guy like Charlie? It seemed unbelievable, but Mallory had known enough women who had blind spots about men, herself included. He could probably be charming when he wanted to, and with all the trouble Mallory was having dating, she couldn't imagine it was easier in your sixties.

Her eyes were starting to get blurry, so Mallory leaned back from the computer and rubbed them, trying to refocus herself at the same time. Why was she doing this? What did she hope to learn from the lives of two dead women?

The problem was, she felt responsible. Not for Caitlin's death, or for Deborah's, but for the fact that no one else seemed to care. It shouldn't have been down to her, barely an acquaintance, to notice that Caitlin was missing, or to identify her body. And if there hadn't been anyone else for those things, who was going to pursue the truth of Caitlin's death? As long as the police could get away with calling it an accident, they weren't going to make trouble for themselves by looking for other explanations.

A college boyfriend had once accused Mallory of taking the things people said to her too seriously. He had been talking about the way she insisted on showing up on time for parties, but the message had stuck with her. It was the sort of thing that made her second-guess herself at times like this, when she was thinking about how Caitlin had been in that restaurant bathroom, ever so casually handing her that lipstick tube across the sinks. Had Caitlin seen something in her then, a person she could trust when she had no one else to reach out to? Or was it just random chance, a joke that had never paid off?

Mallory didn't believe that. Maybe she was being silly or overdramatic, like the police detective had clearly thought, but maybe she wasn't.

Maybe the problem was that no one had been taking Caitlin seriously enough.

20

The second time Mallory woke up that day she was feeling better. Before she had given in and lain down for a nap, she had made the decision that she was going to at least find out enough about Caitlin's death to satisfy her own curiosity. It might not be much, but she hoped if she was able to turn up something solid, she might be able to get the police interested enough to investigate.

The easiest first step was to go to where the body had been found. Mallory didn't know what she would look for there—after six months there wouldn't be any evidence of what had happened. But maybe she could get an idea of what had brought Caitlin to that spot and how, or if, the building really could have killed her.

Because that was another thing that had been on Mallory's mind through her sleepless night. Obviously, a person could be killed by falling rubble in the earthquake—many had been. But those people hadn't just had a family member die, and they hadn't handed off a mysterious object that someone else seemed determined to steal.

Mallory didn't know why someone would have wanted to kill Caitlin, but she didn't know a lot of things. And since no one else was even asking the questions, it was up to her to try to answer them.

—

The Palace of Fine Arts was an oversized replica of an ancient Roman temple, a relic of an exhibition that had been held in the early twentieth century, to show the world how well San Francisco had recovered from the 1906 quake. It had gone through some renovations since, but they hadn't been enough to save it when the earth shifted again, and what had been a fantasy version of a ruin became the real thing.

It was still an attraction, and Mallory found herself dodging tourists as she made her way along the path. There was even a couple in wedding clothes with a photographer, though it wasn't clear if they had a dark sense of humor or if they simply couldn't bring themselves to change their plans.

The structure was still impressive, though not in the way it had been. Enough of the columns that held up the giant domed roof were still standing to give an impression of the shape of it, but most of the dome itself had come down, piling rubble into the reflecting pool. A flock of geese were using it as a ramp, resting on the crumbled chunks of concrete and waddling down to nibble on the weeds growing in the green and muddy water.

There was a path behind the monument, mostly closed off with yellow caution tape. Mallory walked down it as far as she could go. At the edge of the tape, she stopped and examined the damage.

About half of the pillars had fallen down, and the other half looked like they were about to. There was no way of telling what particular piece of masonry might have hit Caitlin—just from where she was standing, Mallory could see dozens that would have done the job.

What she couldn't see was anything that might have brought Caitlin here in the middle of a February night. The posted hours said the park closed at five, and on the broken walls, she could see the security lights that were meant to keep down after-hours activities.

On the other hand, the ruin wasn't the only thing at the site. The palace itself had originally served as a grand entryway to one of the exhibition's pavilions—for fine arts in this case. The first pavilion was long gone, but the building that had replaced it had served many purposes. It had been converted after the earthquake into emergency housing, and before that it was a children's science museum and, most recently, an event space.

Could Caitlin have been going to a late-night show or meeting someone coming from a party? It was as good a reason as any that Mallory could think of for her being there, though she didn't know how she would prove it.

One thing was certain: She wasn't going to make any progress by peering timidly from a distance. Mallory had circled all the way around the park, and now she went back to the ruins, this time with more determination and less concern for the caution tape. When she got to the back of the structure, she stepped over the barrier like she had every right to be there.

There was only one location that matched the description she had gotten, behind the main ruin next to the entrance to the former event space. The path from the parking lot went through a set of pillars, at one time as grand as the ones in the main structure around the lake. But grandeur had done them no good against tectonics, and now half of them lay like boulders across the path.

The area was off-limits for good reason. One of the pillars hadn't completely fallen, and it leaned over the rubble like a drunk, with bare rebar showing through the damaged facade. Mallory gave it a wide berth as she examined the scene, expecting that at any minute a park ranger would scold her away from the area. But they must have been busy somewhere else, and she explored undisturbed.

She didn't know exactly where Caitlin's body had been found, but there were indications that gave Mallory some ideas. Most of the fallen columns had been left where they landed, but there was one section, on the side nearest the building, where several of the smaller pieces looked like they must have been moved from where they had fallen. Mallory knew nothing about police work, but she imagined these were the pieces that had been around, or even on, Caitlin when she was found, and they had been moved to better access the body. With that in mind, she took a closer look.

There would be no chance of finding any stains or marks

on them, not after all this time, but Mallory looked anyway. The smallest of the pieces was about the size of a basketball, and just barely light enough that she could lift it, so she did. A chunk of rebar stuck out of it, like an absurd lollipop stick, and the metal was covered in a reddish-brown crust. Mallory investigated until she was sure it was only rust, and then she moved on, as much relieved as she was disturbed by the way her brain was working.

With nothing more to see on the fragments of masonry, Mallory stepped back to look at the scene. She could see how the police had come up with their conclusions: Here were some heavy objects that had fallen down; there was a person who had been hit on the head and killed. Maybe they thought that Caitlin had dashed into the perceived safety of the pillars, right before they fell on her.

But would she really have done that? Caitlin had lived in California all her life; she would have known this was the worst place to be in an earthquake. It was true that they were taught to shelter in doorways or under furniture, but that was only inside. Outdoors, the sensible and obvious thing was to get as far away from anything that could fall on you as possible. Mallory looked at the wide-open parking lot that was less than ten feet away and wondered.

On the other hand.

The parking lot was right there. The barriers were probably closed at night, but the curbs were low and the land around them was flat, and Mallory had misspent just enough of her youth to know that any car was up for at least that much off-roading. If

Caitlin hadn't died here, and her death hadn't been an accident, this would have been an easy place to dump her body.

After the earthquake, the power had been out across the city. Driving would have been dangerous, but the risk of being seen would have been low, and lower that a car would be remembered. Plus, no power meant no security footage that could be reviewed later.

She thought back to her interaction with Charlie at the house. He had been clear that Caitlin had left of her own accord, and he hadn't seemed very concerned by any of the signs that she might not have.

And what had Sonali said about the rules about who owned the house? Caitlin had inherited everything from her mom, but her stepdad was still living there, apparently with some right to. But what if she had found a way to end that arrangement, or he just got tired of having her around? Or something worse? Maybe it was true that he had an alibi for her mother's death, but that didn't completely let him off being involved. What if Caitlin had known something, and he had taken the opportunity of the earthquake to stop her from exposing him?

Suddenly, Mallory felt like it was a lot more important for her to find out what that hardware key Caitlin had given her was for.

Having gotten all she was going to from this place, Mallory was starting to head home when she got a text. It was from Kendra, and after their last exchange, Mallory was tempted to ignore it. But that only meant it would bother her for longer, so, reluctantly, she opened the message.

To her surprise, it was friendly.

Sorry about yesterday, I was upset. Are you free for lunch?

Typical of Kendra to think she could drop everything to get together on a moment's notice. But the truth was, Mallory was free, and she hadn't eaten. And more than that, she needed to talk to someone, anyone, about what was on her mind.

Kendra

I'm going out for lunch," Kendra called as she picked out her shoes from their cubbyhole.

There was no response, but she didn't expect one. She knew Mark had heard her, and honestly, it wouldn't matter if he hadn't. The chances were slim that he would notice she was gone, and even less that he would care.

Before she left, she stopped at the mirror next to the door, checked her hair, and reapplied her lipstick. Not that Mallory would do as much, obviously. If she had managed anything better than some mascara and a ponytail, Kendra would be shocked.

As the elevator ticked down through the floors in her building, Kendra went back to her phone and looked over the texts again.

Maybe she had come on a little too strong with Mallory. But honestly, who texts to tell you your friend is dead and she saw her body in the morgue? That's psychopath stuff right there. Kendra figured she should know.

Anyway, lunch would give her a chance to straighten it out.

The garage under the building was starting to get fuller these days, after a few blessed months of mostly empty spots. Kendra knew some people were afraid to use it, in case another earthquake came along and trapped them, but she thought that was a far less risky outcome than what was likely to happen to her car if she left it on the street.

It was bad enough just getting out of the garage, she thought as she slammed on the brakes to avoid hitting a man who walked in front of the exit, paying no attention until he turned to scream at her.

"God, I hate this city," Kendra muttered to herself, racing to beat the light so the guy couldn't catch up to her there.

San Francisco wasn't where she belonged, of that Kendra was sure. Her first plan to get out hadn't worked, but Kendra wasn't out of ideas. All she needed right now was one lucky break, and she would be golden.

21

"I guess it really was her."

Kendra had only eaten two bites of her salad, but she was already on her second glass of wine. The six months since the earthquake hadn't changed her much—her blond hair was still past her shoulders, with her roots freshly touched up, and the brand logos made it possible to identify every one of her accessories. The only thing that was different was her weight—Kendra had always been slim, but now she looked practically skeletal.

The restaurant she had chosen was in a hotel in the Financial District, a place that didn't have much to recommend it except that it had been one of the first places to reopen after the quake. Certainly, no one was eating there for the bargains. Mallory picked at her twenty-five-dollar grilled cheese and wondered if she could make a complaint under the postdisaster antigouging laws.

"I know it's hard to believe," she replied, leaving it unsaid that the person Kendra hadn't believed was Mallory. "I just worried, once I saw that she had left her cat. It didn't seem like something she would do."

"Totally not," Kendra agreed. "Oh my god, Cait loved that cat. She would be sending me texts with pics in the middle of the day, like *look how cute he is in the sunbeam* or just a close-up of his toes. And I'm just like, *You've got all this money, and all you can think about is your cat?* I didn't say that to her. Not much, anyway."

Mallory doubted that. Having been on the receiving end of Kendra's constructive criticism, she knew her friend's idea of helping could be thoughtless, to say the least. She could imagine how Kendra would have responded to a string of cat pictures. But there was something else bothering her about that, something that was just out of Mallory's reach in her memory. It would come to her, she was sure.

If she was being honest, "friend" was stretching it. Kendra and Lourdes had been roommates in their respective freshman and sophomore years, after the housing office had lost Lourdes's application. They had all hung out on and off through school, but Mallory hadn't thought of her much until Sonali had a party not long after Kendra had moved to the area and Rachel had invited her along.

They didn't have much in common, and under other circumstances, Mallory might not have bothered to stay in touch. But the further she got from school, the harder she found it to make new friends, and the more she found herself drawn to people who had known her for a long time.

That didn't mean she always liked it.

"Well, she isn't going to send you any more of them," she said.

To her surprise, Kendra actually looked regretful. "I know, and it's awful. Caitlin could be weird, but she was really a nice person. I'm glad you took Gimli. She would have been so sad if something happened to him."

That was enough to make Mallory feel bad about her own attitude, so she softened her tone. "I couldn't leave him there, could I? Not with that awful guy. I didn't know Caitlin very well, but I thought I could do that much for her."

In fact, Mallory was finding herself doing a lot more, starting with the item that was still hidden in the hem of her sweater back home.

"That night at dinner," she began, as Kendra picked at another bite of her salad, "did you think it seemed like there was anything wrong with Caitlin?"

"Other than her leaving without even saying goodbye?" Kendra sniffed, apparently still peeved at the snub. "Yeah, I guess she was kind of down, but her mom died not that long ago, right? So of course she's not going to be all smiles. Actually, there was one other thing. Earlier that week she and I were chatting on WhatsApp, and she said something about how she was worried about what was going to happen to her now. And I asked what she meant, and she said, 'Never mind,' she'd tell me when we met at dinner. I didn't even think of it until we were all texting each other after the earthquake happened, and then it didn't seem like it was very important."

Mallory blinked at the realization, as the memory that had been bothering her before hit. "That's what I forgot. Of *course.*"

"Forgot what?" Kendra asked, but Mallory was already scrolling through her phone.

"Caitlin sent a text too." Mallory found what she was looking for and pointed at the time stamp. "At ten a.m. on Sunday. So either she didn't die in the earthquake, or someone else had her phone and wanted us to think she was alive. Which means that person either killed her or probably knows who did."

"Oh, come on. Don't you think you're being a little dramatic? Lots of people died in the quake; that doesn't mean they were murdered."

"Sure, but those people didn't turn up miles from their homes, in a public park, and then send a text the next day. What are we supposed to believe? That she made it through the earthquake and into the next day, sent the text, and then went out to the Palace of Fine Art just in time for part of it to fall on her?"

"There were aftershocks," Kendra said weakly, but it was clear she wasn't even convincing herself.

"Caitlin didn't die in an aftershock, and you know it," Mallory said. "Even if there had been a big enough one a day later, what was she still doing wearing the same clothes? I saw her house—it was damaged, but it wasn't so bad she would have had to evacuate. She didn't change, because she didn't have a chance." Mallory took a deep breath. "Maybe she never even left her home. Not alive anyway."

Kendra was openly staring at her now. "What are you saying?"

"Like I said, I went to Caitlin's house. I saw her stepfather there, and he wasn't exactly concerned about her being missing. And remember what she said that night, about nightmare stepparents?

Apparently, she inherited everything when her mother died, but he got to stay in the house. What if when the earthquake happened, he saw it as an opportunity to get rid of her and make his life easier?"

Of all the shocking things Mallory had said, she would have thought that would be right up there. But Kendra hardly blinked.

"Yeah, that guy is the worst. I never met him, but Caitlin talked about him a lot. Just a total sleaze, always hitting on other women right in front of her mom and acting like he thought he was God's gift to everyone. And really dumb, too. Caitlin told me one time he got convinced that anything with water in it was bad for him, and eventually they had to take him to the hospital for dehydration."

That wasn't an endorsement of the idea the man could be a murderer, but Mallory was happy to have her impressions confirmed. "Did Caitlin ever say anything about feeling unsafe around him? I mean, stepdads, sometimes the things you hear..."

"I get you, but I don't think so. The thing is, the way the house is laid out, she hardly had to interact with him at all." Kendra picked up the pair of cocktail napkins that had been left under her drinks and arranged them side by side, then put the saltshaker in the middle. "It's like this. You said when you went by, you saw the front living room, plus the kitchen and the laundry. That would all be here"—she pointed to the saltshaker—"in the shared part of the house. But then next to that, you've got the wings, one on each side. Half the house for Deborah, and half for Caitlin, completely separate from each other. The times I went over, I never saw the other part of the house. We'd just go to Caitlin's side and hang out there. She even had her own little kitchenette."

"Wow." Mallory knew the homes of the wealthy were different, but she hadn't been expecting the two-for-one. "Why did she do that? Did she and her mom not get along?"

That wasn't the impression she had gotten so far, and Mallory wondered what else she might have been missing. But Kendra quickly set her straight.

"God, no, they were super close. I can't imagine talking to either of my parents as much as Caitlin talked to her mom. Actually, it was kind of the opposite. Caitlin told me they fixed up the house that way because her mom wanted her to stay there, even when she was an adult, so she set it up so Caitlin would have her own space."

"That's an interesting plan," Mallory said. She wasn't sure she would be onboard with ever sharing a home with family members long term, but she had to admit that the idea of private space did make it more appealing. But…

"It wouldn't be perfect," Mallory said. "Like, if she had something in the house and she didn't want anyone else there to get at it, she still wouldn't want to keep it there long term."

"What are you even talking about?"

Mallory had an idea that Kendra wasn't going to be very interested in the story of Caitlin's lipstick with the surprise inside, but she had already told Sonali and Rachel, so she thought she might as well. As she expected, the further she got into the story, the more incredulous and disdainful Kendra looked, but the other woman held her tongue until Mallory was done talking.

"But why did she give it to *you*?" Kendra sounded offended, and Mallory couldn't blame her. Who would give an item of value to a virtual stranger when two of her friends were right there? It was a question Mallory had been asking herself on and off for the last three days.

"I don't know. That was one of the reasons I started looking for her. The point is, she did, and maybe part of it was that she needed to get it out of the house," Mallory said, and then an idea struck her. "And maybe she wanted to do it in a way that would be harder for someone to guess who had it. Charlie knows you and Rachel are her friends, but he would never have heard of me."

"Mallory, the guy sucks for sure, but isn't that taking it a little far? Caitlin wasn't killed by her stepfather for some mysterious files."

"Well, she was killed by someone for something," Mallory snapped. While they were talking, the waiter had delivered the bill, so she dropped her card and looked around for someone to collect it. "You can think what you want, but I'm going back there to talk to him."

Kendra picked up the card and handed it back to Mallory.

"Okay, fine. Here, I already put it on my account. If we're going out to Sea Cliff, we should try to get across the city before traffic gets bad."

Mallory couldn't hide her surprise. "You want to come?"

Kendra sighed. "I know you think I'm an asshole, but Caitlin was my friend. If something happened to her, I want to know about it. Besides, there's no way you're handling that guy on your own."

22

They didn't quite miss the traffic, so Mallory had plenty of time to think about what she was going to say to Charlie. Easy to offer condolences for Caitlin's death, but then what? Was there any way to convince him to let them up into her room, maybe on the excuse that they would like a memento? Would he even have the right to do it, if it wasn't his house?

"Who do you think is going to inherit, now that Caitlin is gone?" Mallory asked.

"Inherit what? Oh no you don't, you little fucker. Don't even think of trying to cut me off." Kendra had offered to drive, rejecting Mallory's suggestion that they might be better off taking the bus. Her commitment to maximum aggression was impressive; though it made for awkward conversation, they were making more progress than they would have following things like traffic laws.

"The house, and all the money," Mallory said as they won a game of chicken with the delivery truck. "Caitlin got it all when her mom died, right? So where does it go now?"

“That’s a good question.” Kendra swerved into a gap in the next lane to a chorus of honks. “Her father might still be alive, but I don’t think she heard from him after he walked out on them. He never paid any child support, even after her mom took him to court. But I guess he would be Caitlin’s closest relative.”

“That’s so unfair.”

“What isn’t? The whole system is set up for men like him.” Kendra spoke with surprising bitterness, even for her, and Mallory wasn’t sure how to respond. She had an idea that things hadn’t been great with Kendra and Mark recently, but she wasn’t sure she could ask. So she went back to the question at hand.

“Whoever owns that house will have some decisions to make. There was a tag on the building, and from the cracks, I can understand why. I don’t know how the city has let Charlie stay, but at some point, that place is going to need a lot of work, or else it’s going to fall into the ocean.”

“And good luck getting insurance to pay anything. Not that whoever gets that inheritance needs it. Did I tell you—” But whatever the next complaint would have been was cut off by a truck pulling in front of them, and by the time Kendra was done swearing, she had lost the thread of what she was saying.

“Anyway, there’s no point worrying about who gets what,” she eventually finished. “Caitlin is gone, right? No one can do anything for her now.”

Mallory wasn’t sure she agreed with that.

—

It had been only two days since Mallory had last visited Caitlin's house, but changes had come to the neighborhood. A city crew was in the middle of the road, directing traffic around a deep hole where work was being done on some underground pipes. The nearest parking spot they found was three blocks away, and on the walk over, Mallory had more of a chance to observe the damage to the houses.

"It's worse up here than I thought," she said as they passed another caved-in mansion. "I had the impression that most of the damage was in the flats, where everything was built on landfill."

They stopped at an opening between two buildings and looked down to where a team was building a scaffold under a house that had lost its footing.

"Yeah, well how do you think the cliffs here got like that?" Kendra said.

No one was working on Caitlin's house, though it needed it as much as any. The front yard was still overgrown, and the marks were still next to the door, threatening that the building wasn't safe for habitation. For a moment, Mallory wondered if Charlie had finally agreed. As they came up the walk, the house had an abandoned feeling. There was a newspaper on the doorstep, and two packages had been tipped over so they were sitting on their sides in the weeds. It wasn't until they were almost there that she noticed the door.

"It's open," Mallory said.

"What?" Kendra had been trailing behind, looking at the cars parked on the street, and she came up to join her.

"The front door. Look, the dead bolt is turned, but it isn't latched."

Mallory came closer, hesitating before she knocked. The open door wasn't obvious from a distance—it was only ajar, resting on the uncaught dead bolt, and the wood blended seamlessly with the dark room behind it.

That was another thing. It was midafternoon, but the fog gave the day a dim twilit effect, and up and down the street, lights were on in the windows. But the house where Caitlin had lived was dark.

"Maybe he wanted some fresh air. Or he left it open for someone," Kendra said.

"Maybe." Mallory was thinking about the man she had met, who bragged about having a gun to shoot looters. She didn't see him sitting in the dark behind an unlocked door, and she could believe even less that he would have been trusting enough to prop it open and leave.

There was only one way to find out. Mallory rang the doorbell, and when that produced nothing, she knocked.

"Hello? Mr. Williams? Are you there?"

They waited, but nobody answered.

"I guess he's not here," Kendra said and turned to leave.

"Yeah, hang on a minute."

Mallory could have called it instinct, or intuition, or just the fact that she didn't want to get back into the car with Kendra so soon. But the truth was, she was done with not knowing things, with not asking the question, with just walking away. And if that meant she was about to encounter an angry guy hanging out in his underwear or whatever, then that was a risk she was going to have to take, because she wasn't leaving without looking inside that house.

Not that she wasn't going to be careful. He did have a gun, after all. So Mallory opened the door slowly, calling out as she went.

"Mr. Williams? Charlie? It's Mallory and Kendra; we're friends of Caitlin's."

Again, there was no answer. Mallory went further into the building, with Kendra trailing behind her. The front door opened directly into a large living room, which Mallory had seen on her previous visit. It was even more disorderly than she remembered, with beer bottles scattered around and an open pizza box on the couch, its contents half eaten and congealed. The room was dark and cold, and it had the feeling that it had been empty for a while.

"He's obviously not here," Kendra said. "Let's get out before we get in trouble or something. God, it's cold. Did they get their gas turned off or something?"

"You go ahead; I'll catch up. What's through here?" Mallory refused to let herself think about what would happen if someone came in and found them. Something was wrong here; she was surer of that with every step.

Kendra must have either agreed with her or been unwilling to leave her alone, because she stayed with Mallory as she passed through the living room into a hallway that ran along the back of the house. There were closed doors at either end and an archway in the middle with a cold draft coming through it.

"This is the way to the bedroom suites," Kendra said. "That's Caitlin's to the right, and her mom's was on the left. Charlie's now, I guess. Are you going to go in there?" She sounded horrified at the prospect, and even Mallory had to admit that her newfound boldness might not extend that far.

And at least for the moment, it didn't have to.

"Maybe. But let's look over here first," Mallory gestured at the archway, then stopped. "Did you hear something?"

They both stopped to listen, but the only sound was the distant crashing of the waves on the cliff.

"That's funny," Kendra said. "I never noticed the sound of the ocean in here before."

"Does this go outside?" Mallory asked, and Kendra nodded.

"Through the sunroom to the patio. There's an awesome view when it's nice out." She perked up at the memory. "That could explain it. Maybe Charlie went to sit out there, and that's why he hasn't heard us."

"Could be." Mallory didn't say what her gut was telling her about that; she just went through the arched doorway.

It was clear right away where the cold air was coming from. Through the archway, the floors transitioned from wood to tile, covering an area almost as big as the main living room they had come from. It was furnished in the vaguely colonial style of a tropical hotel, complete with a bar and a frozen drink machine. The far wall was entirely lined with folding glass doors, half of which were open. Through them, the fog flowed in on a cold breeze, obscuring what must have been a spectacular view of the ocean.

For a moment, Mallory thought that was all there was to see. She was even about to apologize to Kendra for wasting her time when she noticed the other woman wasn't paying any attention to her. She was focused on a wicker lounge chair that had been set up facing the doors. Mallory had thought at first that the thing draped over the arm was a piece of fabric—a blanket or a forgotten sweater—but looking closer she realized it was a hand.

Nothing about it said that this was someone who was about to jump up and attack, but Mallory still approached cautiously.

"Mr. Williams? Are you all right?"

Caitlin's stepfather was not all right. There was a hole in his left temple, and the back of his head wasn't there at all. A dark stain had turned to crust across the cushions of the sofa, and a gun rested in his other hand.

Kendra started screaming and didn't stop.

"I think we need to call the police," Mallory said dimly, through the fog that seemed to have entered her head.

23

They waited for the police in the front yard, trying to stay out of sight of the neighbors. Mallory had assumed they would be kept out of the house entirely, but the police must not have been as concerned about contamination as she was, because after a long wait—and a harrowing moment when the medical examiner wheeled out the stretcher with the black-wrapped body—she and Kendra were led inside to give their accounts of what happened. Kendra went first.

With the arrival of the police, all pretense of normalcy had gone from the neighborhood. Passersby ogled the house openly, and some people had gathered on the sidewalk, talking among themselves and pointing. Even the utility workers stepped away from their hole in the street to ask the cops what was going on, and when they didn't get any satisfaction, two of them joined the spectators.

At least one person wasn't bothered by the police tape that had been hastily stretched across the front gate. Ann, the neighbor

Mallory had met on her last visit, waited until the cops out front had all been drawn away, then waved Mallory over.

"It's Megan, right? We talked the other day about the cat. What happened?"

"Mallory, actually. And yes, um." Mallory wasn't sure how much she was allowed to say, but no one had told her not to. "I guess, well, Charlie died. My friend and I found him."

She shuddered as she thought of the destroyed skull. In the moment, Mallory had tried to look away, to focus on anything else, and she had settled on the dead man's shoes. Loafers, brown leather, probably expensive. Charlie had been barefoot the last time she had seen him at home; she wondered why he had been wearing them for his death.

"Oh, you poor thing." Ann clicked her tongue and then noticed a policeman approaching. "Come see me when you're done," she said. "I might have something that can help."

Whether the help was for the trauma or the police, or Ann was looking to score some gossip, wasn't clear. And finding out would have to wait, because the officer gestured at the door.

"The detective wants to talk to you," he said to Mallory.

—

Mallory had been hoping it would be the same investigator she had talked to about Caitlin, who might see the connection. But the man waiting for her in the kitchen was someone else, a middle-aged white guy who looked like he spent a lot of money on his haircuts.

"Mallory Taylor?" he asked, and Mallory confirmed that was her. "I'm Detective Oliver. Please tell me how you came to be in this house, and what led you to find the body."

Clearly, there would be no pleasantries here. Mallory laid out the events of the day as well as she could, skipping the parts about suspecting Charlie of killing his stepdaughter and leaving the motivation for their visit at wanting to offer condolences and see if there was anything they could do. She wondered what Kendra had said when she was asked, but there was no way of finding out now, and the detective maintained a poker face throughout her recital.

"When we noticed the cold air coming from the back of the house, we went to look, and that's how we found him," Mallory finished.

"And were you aware that Mr. Williams had a gun?"

"Yes, he mentioned it the last time I was here. The only other time. He said he had it to use against looters. That's why I thought it was strange that the door was open. He didn't seem like he would leave it like that."

The detective made a note, and Mallory wondered if she was still saying too much.

Just answer the question, she reminded herself.

"So this was only the second time you had been here. But you felt comfortable coming into the house uninvited? To look for a man you claim not to have known at all?"

"I knew his stepdaughter. I identified her body." Mallory had assumed the detective would have that information already, but from the surprise in his reaction it was possible he didn't.

"His stepdaughter?" the detective asked. He might have been playing dumb, but there was nothing Mallory could do but answer.

"She died during the earthquake. Everyone thought she had gone away, so there was no missing person report, but I was looking for her recently, and I couldn't find her. That's why I was here before. I ended up taking her cat with me, because Charlie didn't want to care for it." That got a note in the book, though Mallory wasn't sure if she was being recorded as a good friend or a feline avenger. Or possibly just a liar making up a story.

"So you came to talk to him about the death of his stepdaughter?"

"Well, yeah. I had been just looking for her to give her back something of hers I had—I never expected she would be dead. And it was so strange, what happened. I guess I really wanted to know more."

"Uh-huh."

There was a lot more Mallory wanted to add, about Caitlin's text, and the inheritance, and the fact that all three people who had lived in this house had died by some sort of violence over the last year, but the detective's attitude made her cautious. Mallory had heard about not talking to the police—now that she was one of the first people on the scene of finding a dead body, she was starting to understand them.

Oliver went on. "And what did you touch after you came into the house?"

"Nothing, aside from the door." Mallory had already told him that, but the repetition was making her doubt herself.

She was retracing her steps through the house in her mind when the room suddenly got brighter. Mallory looked around to see if someone had come in and turned on a light switch, but no one was there. It was the sky, suddenly visible through the giant picture windows that even lined the kitchen—the wind must have picked up, because the fog cleared away, retreating like it was being chased, and from where she was sitting facing the windows, she suddenly had a complete view of the house's position.

She knew it was at the edge of the land, and the views of the ocean and the bridge would be spectacular, but she hadn't expected the cliff to drop off so sharply, so that the building was cantilevered out into space. In the distance, the bridge stood out starkly against the headlands beyond, looking close enough in the sudden sunshine that Mallory felt like she could almost reach out and join the repair crew.

Captivated, she didn't realize the detective had spoken until he cleared his throat meaningfully.

"I'm sorry," she said, pulling her attention back to him. "Could you repeat the question?"

The detective might have even smiled a bit at that. "I said I think we're done for now. We'll be in touch if there are any further questions. Was there anything else you would like to mention?"

Mallory took a deep breath. She had good reasons for not saying more, to keep her head down and not get into any further trouble. But she also had information, and somebody needed to know it.

"There's one other thing. I mentioned his stepdaughter who

died? She was a friend of mine, and she sent a text message the day after the earthquake. But the way she was found, it was supposed to look like she died in the quake. Something happened to her, and I think someone sent that message to cover it up. And now that Charlie is dead, I think they're related."

"I see." Detective Oliver made another note in his book and then looked Mallory straight in the eye. "I appreciate the information, Ms. Taylor. I think you should keep in mind, though, in a situation like this, people can be under a lot of strain. They do things and they think things that they might not otherwise. We've seen a lot of this since the earthquake happened, and we expect to see more. What I would recommend is that you not get carried away with complicated explanations for simple events. Anyway, have a nice evening."

A uniformed officer had come in, and the detective left before Mallory could think of anything to say. She fumed as she was led to the door, angry at herself for even trying, and at the detective for accusing her of making it all up. Sure, she was probably a little traumatized; who wasn't? But she could still read the time stamp on a text message.

But as she replayed his words, she recognized their actual meaning. Detective Oliver hadn't been talking about her; he had been talking about Charlie. This was going to be another case of going with the simplest, least sensational answer, to save him some work and the city from the specter of widespread violence. Caitlin was killed in an accident; Charlie died by suicide—it was all just the tragic consequences of a natural disaster.

It was a sensible answer, and if anyone would know about the ways and reasons people died, it should be a police detective. But Mallory wasn't convinced.

Technically, she had no reason for her doubts. Charlie had been in his home, with his own gun in his hand. There was no sign she could see that someone had broken in, or that there had been a struggle. The position of the bullet hole in the middle of his forehead seemed like it might be an awkward place for someone to shoot himself, but Mallory didn't know enough about the subject to say for sure. That was something the police would have experts to tell them, and if they didn't think it was suspicious, then who was she to argue?

There was the problem of the number of deaths that had been associated with that household, but even that didn't have to be an issue. In fact, if she wanted to, Mallory could see Charlie's death as putting a bow on the whole thing. He might have killed Caitlin, somehow hoping to use her death to get some or all of Deborah's money, or because Caitlin was asking questions about her mother's death. And then, when her body was discovered after all this time, he might have lost his nerve, thinking he was going to be caught, and took the first way out he could think of.

That made more sense to Mallory than the detective's theory, but she still didn't like it. It was too tidy, too convenient an end to a situation that felt much bigger. If Charlie had been acting alone, how did that account for her own involvement? Even if he somehow knew she had the lipstick tube, how would he have found her apartment? Caitlin didn't have her address, and Charlie didn't strike Mallory as being smart enough to have tracked her down.

What she needed right now was someone else who would listen to her, who at least understood the story as far as she did. Kendra wouldn't have been her first choice to be that person, but they had come here together, and she was the only one available.

At least, that's what Mallory had expected. But when she got to the front yard, Kendra was nowhere to be seen, and looking down the road to where they had parked, she couldn't see the car.

"Are you looking for your friend?" asked the uniformed policeman, who had accompanied her out of the house. "She left a while ago. Said she had an appointment. Do you need a ride somewhere?"

24

Mallory couldn't blame Kendra; after what she had dragged her into, she could understand Kendra not wanting to spend any more time with her. That being said, she wasn't exactly happy about it. Not even a word, a text to say she couldn't wait any longer? Mallory considered sending an angry message of her own to point that out, but she stopped herself. The day had been bad enough without her starting a fight.

At least there was an upside to her abandonment. Mallory would get a rideshare home eventually, but since she didn't have anyone waiting for her, she decided to take the opportunity to visit Caitlin's neighbor, Ann.

The house across the street wasn't quite as grand as Caitlin's, but it was still nicer than anywhere Mallory had ever lived. It looked like it had started as a relatively modest bungalow—probably no bigger than Joan's house before Mallory's basement unit was added. Ann's house had undergone a much more glamorous transformation, adding an entire second floor and an extension on the back that took up almost the entire lot. If the building had been damaged in the earthquake, it had long since been repaired, and the white and tan interiors were nothing but sleek perfection.

"Please ignore the mess," Ann said as she picked a single empty glass off a side table. "It's been quite a week around here. And I guess now it's only going to get worse."

"I'm sorry about that," Mallory said, as though finding the dead man had been an oversight on her part.

"That's okay," Ann said magnanimously. "Someone was bound to come across him eventually. Honestly, he never should have stayed in that house. With all the damage, it can't have been very safe."

Mallory nodded, thinking of the cracks in the exterior walls. "That's true," she said. "But Charlie was shot."

"Was he really? That's interesting. His own gun, I suppose?"

"I think so. It was there when we found him. The police think he shot himself."

Ann snorted. "Not likely. He'd be too worried about what it would do to his hair. Honestly, I'm surprised someone didn't do it sooner."

If Ann was worried about a murderer on the loose in her neighborhood, she didn't show it. She offered Mallory a seat and then crossed the room to a small bar in the corner.

"Can I offer you anything? Some water?"

"Water would be great, thanks." Mallory was starting to wonder why she had been invited here. Surely, if Ann wanted to know in what state Charlie's body had been found, there would be plenty of people to provide her with answers, or at least uninformed speculation.

But Caitlin's neighbor clearly had something more on her mind. She poured a can of lemon sparkling water into two glasses and gave one to Mallory, then sat down facing her and leaned forward.

"I'm glad you came by. I wanted to talk to you again. After you left with the cat, I got to thinking, you know, that whole thing didn't seem right. And then I hear that young Caitlin actually died, back in the earthquake?" Mallory confirmed that, but Ann barely seemed to hear her before she went on. "And now Charlie. Well, like I said, I was thinking. And it didn't seem quite right, what was going on over there."

Three deaths in one household were also something Mallory didn't consider "quite right," but she waited while Ann took a sip of her water.

"We aren't what you'd call a close neighborhood around here," Ann went on. "People mostly keep their business to themselves, and they expect everyone else will, too. You start to think you're not in a city, but of course you are. People are always the same, aren't they?"

"I guess so," said Mallory. She was getting worried that she was about to hear Ann's universal theory of humanity or something, but the conversation went in a different direction.

"I grew up in a small town," Ann said. "Maybe that's why I expect to always be in everyone's business. Anyway, after I talked to you the other day, I started going back over the things that have happened in the last year or so, since Deborah died. Like I said, Charlie was out of town when it happened, but you know how it's always the husband, so I started keeping an eye on him. And he was having female guests around, maybe more than one. But there was definitely at least one who only came by when Caitlin wasn't there. In fact, one time I think Caitlin came home when she wasn't expected—I talked to her the next day, and she said someone had double-booked the room where they were supposed to be doing their improv class, so it was canceled. Anyway, she came home, and all of a sudden, there was all this activity. I'm not sure what went on in the house, but I do know that a girl came out with a shirt or something over her head, and she went down about three blocks before she called a car."

"You followed her?" Mallory had only gotten started in investigating, but here she thought she was in the presence of a master.

"Not exactly. We had a tower room built a few years ago, and you can see quite a ways." She shook her head. "The dark sky people keep trying to get us to get rid of the streetlights, but I say no. How are we supposed to know what's going on if we can't see?"

Ann was completely unembarrassed by the effort she had put into tracking her neighbors. And why should she be? This was more interesting than most of the television shows Mallory watched.

"Did you tell Caitlin what you saw?" she asked.

"Of course. Why wouldn't I? Obviously, her mother was dead at that point, so there was nothing technically wrong with him having someone there, but it was her house, and she had a right to know what was happening in it."

"What did she say?"

Ann paused to remember. "She laughed it off, or at least she tried to. But I got the impression it bothered her more than she let on. It wasn't that long after her mom died, and I can understand her being upset. Not that she ever thought much of Charlie, but when you're mourning someone, I think you want other people to have the same feelings. I could tell while we were still talking, she had a lot to think about."

Mallory was doing some thinking too. "When was this? You said it wasn't long after Deborah's death?"

"Well, it couldn't be, could it? The earthquake was only, what, six months later. Let me see," Ann said, as she counted on her fingers. "Yes, it would have been in January, because we were having that dry spell after all the rain around Christmas, and the reason I was looking out the window in the first place was because I was wondering if we needed to run the sprinklers. Probably the second week of the month, because after that it got cold, and I had to wrap the avocado tree."

That was interesting. About a month before the dinner where Caitlin had given Mallory the lipstick that wasn't, she had learned her stepfather had been seeing someone, who had escaped the house when she came home. There was something bothering Mallory about that, but she didn't have time to interrogate the feeling now, and there was another question on her mind.

"Can you tell me more about Deborah? What was she like? And how did she end up with a guy like Charlie?"

Ann sighed, blowing her breath upward so hard that it ruffled her hair. "That's the question, isn't it? Honestly, if I had a dollar—well, I'd be doing better than Deborah was with her crypto thing, no matter what she said about that. Anyway, you wanted to know what she was like. I didn't know her that well, but I would say that Deb was the eternal optimist. Infuriating, obviously, but you could see how it worked out for her. And, I guess, how it didn't."

"What do you mean?"

"The good thing was, she always believed she could do things. I don't think most people would have done what she did, taking on a new career and succeeding like that. Obviously, she was good at it, but that's never enough. What made her special was she didn't let herself be held back by people saying she couldn't."

Mallory nodded. She had known people like that and envied their certainty. In this case, though, she had an idea of what Ann meant by the way that trait had failed Deborah. "She didn't see the ways she might fail, so she kept going. But when it came to relationships..."

"Right," the older woman agreed. "Optimism is a wonderful thing, but a man like Charlie knows how to use it. I guess I shouldn't blame her, though. She was happy, as far as I know, and if it might have ended badly, she didn't live long enough for that to happen. So why not live for the moment? We never know how many we're going to get."

That was true enough. But Mallory couldn't help wondering if Deborah's blind spot when it came to her man had something to do with how she, and her daughter, had ended up dying.

Sonali

Sonali looked at the clock on her computer and sighed. Four more hours to the end of the day, and she could stop pretending she was able to focus on her work.

It wasn't that she didn't like what she did—people thought corporate accounting sounded like the most boring job in the world, but she found the orderliness of it satisfying. But when things were slow, it didn't offer a lot to focus her imagination, and that was when her thoughts could get away from her.

It would have been better to have a commute to break up the day. But the building her employer was in had been too damaged to reopen, and even with so many companies having left the city, usable office space was at a premium. So she was stuck at a table in her living room, her view the wall of the next building, while she double-checked her spreadsheets and tried to put off thinking about what the upcoming days had in store for her.

Eventually, she was going to have to answer their questions. Sonali knew that; she had made her choices. But she was going to give those answers on her own time, under circumstances she chose. None of that would change the truth, but it would make it easier for her to control the narrative.

What she really didn't need was Mallory bringing up that dinner again.

Of course, Sonali was sad Caitlin was dead, how could she not be? And to say anything else would only make things worse. She just didn't need to go down that particular conversational track right now, was all. But if there was one thing Sonali knew about Mallory, it was that she wouldn't let a thing go.

The next time they saw each other, Sonali decided, they needed to be alone.

25

By the time Mallory got home, she was exhausted. She hadn't encountered death up close before, and now it was all around her. She should have been terrified, but she didn't have the energy. When the invader had been in her home, the fear had been immediate and real—now it seemed to come from everywhere and nowhere at the same time.

What she needed was some time to process and decide what to do next. Up to this point, Mallory had been operating on chance and impulse, and if she was going to find the best way forward, she should spend some quiet time thinking.

The cats had other ideas.

Mallory had made herself some toast and a cup of tea—all she felt like she could manage at this point—and sat down with a blank notepad when she felt a head bump against her leg.

"Not now, Celine," Mallory said automatically, assuming the more demanding of her two cats wanted attention. But a long meow from across the room told her she was wrong. Celine was sitting on the arm of the couch, staring at her and twitching her tail. Just below her, Mariah batted one of her toys under the bookshelf, then looked at Mallory to see what she would do.

It was Gimli who had nudged her and who was staring up at Mallory with a look she took as judgmental.

"What?" Mallory said. "You have water. I just fed you and cleaned your litter box. I don't know what kind of fancy treats Caitlin gave you, but we don't have those. I'm sorry, but your life has taken a turn out of the luxury zone, and you're going to have to learn to deal with it."

Unconvinced, Gimli bumped her again. Mallory sighed and reached down to pet him, noticing as she did that his fur was still full of mats. She had done her best with the brush, and the cat had been more patient than she expected, but it was time to admit defeat. She found the card Ann had given her for Caitlin's groomer and made an appointment through their web portal, cringing at the price. But she didn't know where to find a lower-budget option, and she owed Caitlin at least that much in caring for her pet.

She was taking on a lot for someone she had barely known, but Mallory wasn't bothered by that. The more she dug into Caitlin's life, the more she felt like, despite all her wealth and privilege, this was a young woman who the world had somehow overlooked and left behind. No one deserved that, and if Mallory was the one who was going to prevent it, then that was what she was going to do.

That was her unselfish reason. The other, which she wasn't ashamed to admit, was that until she knew what happened to

Caitlin, she wouldn't be sure she was safe herself. Someone knew she had the hardware key, and Mallory couldn't believe they would give up on trying to get it.

There hadn't been any attempts for the last couple of days, but Mallory could think of theories for that. The most obvious was, with the discovery of Caitlin's body and now Charlie's, the risk had gone up, and what had been a case of minor housebreaking had a better chance of drawing the attention of the police.

There was also the question of what the item actually was—if it led to an account controlled by Caitlin, it might have been easier to get away with accessing it when she wasn't known to be dead.

The other option was that it had been Charlie, and the reason he hadn't tried again was because he was lying in his solarium with a hole in his head.

Fighting that image out of her mind, Mallory tried to refocus on the questions she had a chance of answering. She started with the point at which she had gotten involved: when Caitlin had given her the lipstick tube in the bathroom.

Mallory still didn't know what that was about, but she was sure Caitlin hadn't come to the restaurant with the goal of handing it to her. That wasn't modesty—Mallory had a healthy opinion of herself, but she was aware it wasn't one most of her friends shared. If anyone had asked any of the other women at that table who would be the person you would want to entrust with an item that might be valuable enough to kill over, Mallory, who was best known in that social circle for getting lost three times in the same building on campus, wouldn't be the pick.

So Caitlin had brought the lipstick for another reason, but she had changed her plans. Why? Mallory didn't remember seeing her on her phone, but that didn't mean anything. Everyone had their phones out so much, it wasn't the sort of thing she would notice. It was easy to imagine that Caitlin had gotten a message during the evening, something that made her decide she needed to get the key out of her possession as soon as possible.

Mallory had been the first person to leave the table; she was sure of that. That was as good a reason as any for Caitlin to have chosen her—she might not have wanted to hand over the key in public, and two women going to the bathroom together wasn't suspicious. Really, it was Mallory's bladder that had gotten her into this situation, which surprised her less than it should have.

Was Caitlin planning to go somewhere after the dinner? Mallory remembered how quickly she vanished at the end of the evening—on her way to a meeting or hoping to avoid someone who knew she would be there? If it hadn't been for the earthquake, there might have been a chance of tracking down some information about that—not that Mallory would be able to get it, but the police might have been able to find camera footage from local businesses. But there was no way anything like that would have survived now, even if she could convince someone to go looking for it.

Having exhausted that line of thought, Mallory moved on to her own part in the drama. The key had traveled from Caitlin to her, and since then someone had been trying to get it. The attempts had been bold, to the point of seeming desperate, but not very effective—the best Mallory could say was she didn't think she was up against a professional.

Which was fine, but it didn't narrow things down much. More interesting was the fact that she was targeted at all. How could anyone have known that Mallory would have the lipstick? Caitlin must have died soon after the dinner—close enough that she didn't have time to change out of her going-out clothes. She might have told someone what she had done in that time, but who? And why wouldn't they have come to Mallory directly and asked her for it?

The obvious answer was that the person was Caitlin's killer. Had it been someone Caitlin trusted, who she told her secret in hopes that they would help her keep it safe? And instead they killed her, and then came for Mallory, hoping to steal it before she made the connection.

It was a terrible thought, but Mallory could think of a worse one. In the course of the dinner, she was the only person Caitlin had been alone with. And the only people who knew that were the four other women at the table.

Mallory couldn't believe she was even considering such a thing. Those women were her friends, people she had known for years. It wasn't possible that one of them would steal from her, or worse. It was just one of those crazy thoughts, like when you stepped to the edge of a cliff and something in your brain wanted you to go over.

And yet.

Ann had said a young woman escaped from the house

when Caitlin came home unexpectedly. When they were talking, Mallory had agreed with her theory that it was just embarrassment over the short time after Deborah's death that had made Charlie's date feel the need for secrecy. But what if it was something else? What if the reason the woman had run away with her jacket over her head was because Caitlin would recognize her?

It was a stupid idea. Rude and wrong and overdramatic, and Mallory should have been ashamed of herself. She tried, but she wasn't. Because the more she thought about it, the more it made sense.

Even the fact that someone had broken into Mallory's home. That was one of the things that had bothered her about suspecting Charlie, and it came back to her now. Caitlin didn't know where she lived, even if she had a reason to tell her killer. Mallory didn't own her apartment; there would be no easily accessible public records that said this was her address. It would be possible for someone to track it down, but the first break-in had happened within days of the earthquake. The power had been out across the city, and cellular signal had been spotty at best. And certainly, no one in any city office was around to answer questions about addresses, even if they came with a good cover story. It was hard to believe that someone had been able to do the work it would have taken to connect Mallory's name to the basement door.

Unless they already knew.

Mallory had been petting Gimli for a while, and the other two cats had had enough. They both came over and started winding around her legs and butting against her hands, and finally Mallory gave up and moved over to the couch so she could deal with all of them more efficiently. She welcomed the distraction, because how did you deal with the fact that one of your friends might be a killer?

26

You're lucky I had a cancellation. In the future, just so you know, I usually book about two months out."

Mallory agreed solemnly and followed the man to the back of the shop. In the future, she hoped she would be able to keep Gimli's fur well enough brushed that she wouldn't have to spend the price of two nice dinners on grooming, but she wasn't going to say that.

She couldn't complain about the service, at least. The Cat Place was housed in a storefront in the Marina District, an area that had seen some of the worst damage in the quake. It hadn't been spared—the front windows still had their new stickers on them and their frames exposed, waiting for one of the city's overworked contractors to come back and finish the job. But the interior was dressed in tasteful pastels, warmed up by framed collages of feline clients, and Mallory, who had been expecting to just drop off Gimli and go find herself a coffee, found herself settled in an armchair with a cup of green tea.

The man had introduced himself as Billy, and Mallory had the impression he was the owner and sole employee. He was a Black man, probably about twenty years older than her, with a shaved head and earrings lining both ears. Under his apron (pink and branded with the store name) he wore a matching shirt and shorts in a vibrant tropical print, and his Crocs were decorated with cat-related charms.

Mallory would have described the look as "San Francisco business casual," and it put her more at ease. However expensive his services might be, she didn't think she was going to face any snobbery here.

Once they were sitting, he took the carrier from her and extracted the cat with practiced hands.

"What do we have here? Ooh, some mats are what. Someone hasn't been getting regularly taken care of for the last few months, I'm thinking." He looked up at Mallory, smiling with just a hint of disapproval. "I've been seeing this a lot lately. Everyone had their lives upended, and before you know it, the fur gets out of hand. Did you have to travel with him to a new home? I can tell he's stressed."

"No—I mean, the thing is, he isn't really my cat. At least, he wasn't. I guess maybe he is now."

Billy's expression immediately softened, and he held Gimli closer. "Oh no. Did someone abandon this pretty boy? I always say, the people who do that, when they get to heaven's doors, I hope they find all the animals there waiting to tell on them."

Mallory hadn't planned to get into the whole story, but

she couldn't let Caitlin's memory be maligned that way, even anonymously.

"It wasn't like that," she said. "My friend Caitlin died in—died around the time of the earthquake, but no one knew. I only found her cat the other day, but I don't think she would ever have abandoned him."

"Caitlin? Is this Gimli?" Billy looked horrified, and for a moment, Mallory thought he was going to cry. He lifted the cat up so he could look at its face, and then sadly bumped his nose against Gimli's. "It is him. Oh no. Oh, poor little fellow. Caitlin brought him to me for the first time when he was just a kitten. She had gotten him from a shelter, and she wanted to be sure he got used to being groomed when he was young. And you're right, she would never, never have abandoned him. Oh, that's just terrible."

Billy was as upset as Mallory had seen anyone be about Caitlin's death, and that made her like the man. He was cradling Gimli now, scratching under his chin.

"How did it happen?" Billy asked. "Was her house one of the ones that fell down?"

"No. At least not yet." Mallory hesitated, unsure how much it was wise to share. She couldn't go blabbing her suspicions to everyone she met. But on the other hand, if she didn't say anything, how would anyone know? "Actually, she was found at the Palace of Fine Arts. It looked like some of the rubble had fallen on her."

Billy caught on right away. "'Looked like'? And what was she doing out there in the middle of the night?"

"That's a good question. Unfortunately, the police aren't very interested in asking it."

Billy snorted. "Don't talk to me about the cops. Ask them to do anything tougher than hassling a homeless guy, and it's like their legs are broken. Goddamn shame about that girl, though. She was someone who really cared about animals."

"That's what everyone says," Mallory said. "I'm glad I can take care of Gimli. You think you'll be able to get all the mats out of his fur?"

"Oh, yes, no problem. He may look a little funny for a while, because we're going to have to shave quite a bit, but it'll grow back." Billy hesitated, staring at the cat, then looked up at Mallory. "I only knew Caitlin as a client, but as you can tell, I'm a talker. And the last time she brought this guy in, it was about a week before the quake, and I could tell she was upset about something."

"Did she tell you what it was?"

"Sort of. I asked, of course, and she said all the usual: *it's nothing*, she's just tired, all that. And normally I would have left it, but I'd known her for a while, and I had an idea she wanted me to ask. So I pressed her a bit, and she said it was to do with her mom's death. I guess she had gotten it into her head that it wasn't an accident, and her stepfather had something to do with it."

"But he had an alibi, right?"

"That's what she said. She thought he might have been working with someone else. And I had the sense she was getting some of her suspicions from another person."

That was something Mallory hadn't expected. Her impression

of Caitlin was as someone who was isolated, dealing with everything she was going through with no one to support her. But of course she would have had people in her life—Mallory had met her at a dinner with friends, hadn't she? Still, there was something ominous in the way Billy said "another person."

"What kind of other person? Like a friend or a family member, or..."

"Friend, definitely. I forget what she said exactly, but it was something about how other people could see the things you didn't want to admit to yourself, even when they hurt you. I told her that's not a good friend, but she insisted it was better to know. Said she was done letting things happen and she was making her own plans, but I don't know. She seemed more scared than anything."

Mallory thought about how Caitlin had looked that night in the restaurant. "That was the impression I got, too. The thing is, I didn't even know her that well. I got kind of dragged into this by accident, and it was only because I was trying to figure out what was going on that I found Gimli."

Billy nodded. "You were meant to. Call me crazy, but it was the cats. Like I said about them meeting the bad owners in heaven, they send someone to help the good ones too. Young Caitlin didn't deserve whatever happened to her, and someone up there wants you to make sure it gets found out."

27

Only in San Francisco, Mallory thought as she sipped her latte. She was lucky to have gotten out of there without a tarot reading. Billy had said the grooming would take about an hour, so she had set up camp with her laptop in a nearby café. She had no worries about leaving Gimli with him, at least. If she knew nothing else about the man, he clearly cared a lot about cats.

And he had cared about Caitlin, too. Cared enough to press her when he thought she was upset and to remember what she had told him after all this time. That made Mallory feel like what she was doing wasn't so crazy after all. Mallory didn't believe she had been sent by some sort of feline avatar of justice, but she did want to find out what had happened to Caitlin.

And now she had to deal with the idea that the answer might be closer to her than she liked. Billy hadn't had a name for the friend who had been advising Caitlin, and there was no reason for Mallory to believe that person was anyone she knew or that they had been at the dinner.

Or was there? Wouldn't a friend who had been encouraging Caitlin to suspect her mom had been killed get worried when Caitlin went missing? When she turned up dead? Shouldn't that be the person running around asking questions and calling the police, instead of Mallory?

There were other possibilities for why the person hadn't surfaced. The most obvious was that something had happened to them too. Despite what the news would have the world believe, San Francisco after the earthquake wasn't a sea of dead bodies, but certainly a number of people had been badly injured and killed, in both the quake and the fires that followed.

Or maybe they lost their memory or were abducted by aliens. Mallory could come up with theories all day if she didn't have to bother with reality. There were some things she knew, and those facts pointed to Caitlin having a friend who she told her fears about her mother and that person being involved with her death. And, since she was going on probabilities, the easiest way for that person to know both that Mallory had the key and where to find her was for them to have been at dinner that night.

Sonali. Rachel. Kendra. Lourdes. Four women who Mallory had known for close to half of her life. But did she really know them? They texted, got together for occasional meals, invited each other to their parties. And yes, they all talked about their lives, but there were always things left unsaid.

But were any of those things honestly going to be *By the way, I'm going to kill one of you*? People did change over time, but that was things like their ideas about taxes, not whether or not they were a murderous lunatic.

Mallory shook her head and took another sip of her latte. Right now she was focusing on facts, not her beliefs. And the facts kept leading her back to the people at that table. So setting her feelings aside, where was she?

As far as Mallory knew, Kendra and Rachel had been the closest to Caitlin. They had known her since college, and Kendra had mentioned that they took a trip to Arizona together a couple of years ago. That made them the most likely, at least for the friend who Caitlin would have been confiding in, but Mallory wasn't able to discount the other two yet.

Sonali and Rachel had been roommates for a while after graduation, and it made sense that Sonali would have gotten to know Caitlin then. And of everyone at the dinner that night, Sonali had been the least like herself. It was long enough ago now that Mallory didn't trust her memory, but she was sure she had thought something at the time about Sonali's nervousness.

Then there was Lourdes, who, with her family's and her boyfriend's money, might run in the same circles of wealth as Caitlin, even if they didn't otherwise have much in common. Mallory could imagine them both ending up at a benefit dinner or a movie premiere, or some other rich person thing, and discovering they knew people in common. That would have been enough for Lourdes; she was famously able to make friends from the smallest connection.

And, in a detail Mallory didn't like to remember, there was

one other point about Lourdes. Specifically that in her twenties, she had dated a married man. Mallory had tried her best to hide her judgmental feelings about it, but as always, Lourdes had seen right through her. Far from being ashamed, she had taken every opportunity to bring it up, how great it was to send him home to his wife, how she could keep him on his toes by suggesting date ideas that might get them caught.

It had gone on for almost a year, and then Lourdes abruptly stopped talking about the relationship. Mallory wanted to ask what happened, but she thought it would come across as an I-told-you-so, so she held her tongue. What if it hadn't been a bad experience, though, and Lourdes had decided to try a repeat, with Caitlin's stepfather? The same social circles that could have brought her and Caitlin together would be just as likely to connect her with him.

For Rachel there was no need for that kind of theorizing. She had known Caitlin for years and had made no secret of knowing Charlie as well. That she didn't have anything good to say about him didn't mean much; it was the most obvious thing to do if you were trying to cover for an illicit affair. And Mallory had an idea that Rachel had been the one to suggest the dinner in the first place. She went back through her texts, looking for the start of the thread, but from what she was able to find, it looked like the conversation must have started somewhere else. She could ask the others if they knew, but Mallory couldn't think of a way to bring it up that wouldn't be suspicious.

That was an idea that could work in both directions. Mallory had a secret she was trying to keep, but that was nothing like what the killer had been keeping under wraps. Could anyone really go for so long without making a mistake? It was one thing to hide from the police, but casual conversations between friends had a lot more opportunities to slip up.

Moving on, Kendra was married, but if Mallory was willing to consider her friends to be murderers, then she could hardly stop at imagining one of them to be a cheater. True, Kendra had been the one to drive Mallory to Caitlin's house and find Charlie, but that could have been intentional.

Mallory had no idea if it was true that killers always returned to the scene of the crime, but she did know something about worrying. And if she could go all the way back into the house to check that the stove she hadn't turned on was still off, she could believe that someone who had committed murder would want to get a look around before the police arrived, to make sure they hadn't missed anything.

She was assuming Caitlin's killer had also murdered Charlie, and in this case, Mallory didn't think it was too much of a stretch. Particularly since his death must have come soon after Caitlin's body was identified—it was too much to believe that those things were unrelated. Charlie had been the most obvious suspect for Caitlin's death, and this didn't necessarily change that—he could have had an accomplice who panicked, or he might have been the one losing it and became a liability.

And then there was the third death, or rather the first one. The police had decided that Caitlin's mother had been killed by an accidental fall in her home, but they also thought Caitlin had succumbed to having a chunk of concrete hit her. Two women, mother and daughter, struck in the head—Mallory didn't think you needed a genius detective to make that connection.

Was Deborah the key? Thinking about that led Mallory back to the literal key, the one Caitlin had given her, hidden in a lipstick tube she said belonged to her mother. With little else to go on, Mallory returned to Deborah's LinkedIn page. She didn't think a second pass was going to give her a clue to what kind of secrets the woman might have been holding, but possibly Mallory could find someone in her professional network who could tell her something.

Deborah must have been the sort of person to accept every invitation she got, because she had over a thousand connections. Rather than go through all of them, Mallory turned back to the posts she had looked at earlier, this time paying attention to who had liked and commented on them. She had the beginning of a decent list going when something caught her eye.

It wasn't a post Deborah had written herself, just an article about cryptocurrency she shared from a news site, so Mallory hadn't paid much attention to it before. But there was a thread of comments under it, with Deborah responding to someone named Mike.

Mike: Nice article lol. Easy to make money in crypto when you buy 1000 BTC in 2012, right? Any tips on how the rest of us can get in on it now?

Deborah: Lol. Time machine? Fortune favors the bold. You snooze, you lose.

It wasn't a very dramatic exchange, telling Mallory little more than that Deborah loved clichés and wasn't afraid to mix them. But the information Mike shared, and Deborah appeared to confirm, was a lot more interesting. A quick search brought up that the price of one Bitcoin in 2012 would have been in the thirty-dollar range, which made the purchase a minor investment for how much money Deborah had at the time. But that was over a decade ago, and even with the volatility in the market, that thirty thousand dollars or so would have turned into a significant fortune.

All of which would have been nothing but another data point about the size of Caitlin's inheritance, if it wasn't for something else that Mallory knew. She had dated a guy for a couple of months for whom cryptocurrencies made up about 80 percent of his personality, and she had learned plenty about the technology, whether she had wanted to or not. She didn't remember his last name, but one thing she had taken from that relationship was the knowledge that one of the most secure ways to store the keys that let an owner access their tokens was in something called a "cold wallet," a device that was kept completely separate from the internet, with various security measures to keep anyone from getting unauthorized access.

And one of those measures could be a separate small hardware key.

Lourdes

Was there even going to be a funeral? Lourdes didn't enjoy funerals, but she felt like she was good at them. She could do a sympathetic nod, a well-timed gentle hand press, even improvise a short speech about the dead person on the spot.

And, of course, most of her clothes were black.

Not that any of that mattered. It was a stretch to assume Caitlin's family would have a funeral, not after all this time. And who would hold it? If no one noticed Caitlin was missing, maybe there was no one to care now that she was gone.

Who would have thought it would be Mallory who went to find her?

Lourdes put down her phone and stretched. She had the apartment to herself again. It wasn't so bad—she was getting used to the quiet. And it was nice to have some uninterrupted time to think.

And what she was thinking about was the text from Mallory, the one that said Caitlin's body had been found by the police.

Maybe it wasn't really that surprising, actually, that it was Mallory who had called them. Mallory loved a question, and she never stopped to think about what would happen if she asked it, did she? It wasn't in that girl's vocabulary to leave well enough alone.

28

Hi, Aunt Karen? It's Mallory. I'm fine, thanks. How are you? Oh wow, that's rough. I wouldn't have known that about tomato plants either. Actually, I've been home for about a week now. No, the power is back on pretty much everywhere. I haven't seen any looters, but I'll keep an eye out. Speaking of that, I have kind of a weird request for you. Has anyone gotten in touch to ask about something I sent for you to keep? It's kind of a long story. Anyway, if something like that happens, can you tell them you put it in the bank or something, and then let me know? Sure, or you could just say you hid it. I don't think drawing a treasure map is a good idea… You know what, why not? I promise I'll explain everything soon. Okay, love you. Say hi to Uncle Hugo and the birds for me. Bye."

Mallory ended the call and stared at the phone. Part of her wanted to warn her aunt that her second-favorite niece had implicated her as the holder of an item potentially worth millions of dollars—one that someone might have already killed over. But the difficulty of explaining that was too daunting, and the risk of it spreading around the family was beyond what she was able to handle right now. What's more, Mallory wasn't sure which would be worse—if her aunt believed her, or if she didn't.

That done, Mallory picked up the cardigan and felt the hem again, reassuring herself that the key was still there. The urge to get rid of it was stronger than ever, but so was her desire to see this thing through. How could she not? Was she just going to go on wondering if one of her friends was a killer?

Or more than one of them? If Mallory was going to consider outrageous suspicions, she might as well go all the way. Maybe the person having an affair with Charlie was a red herring, and two or more of them had gotten together and cooked up the whole plan to get rich robbing Caitlin, using her mother's death as the bait. It was an outrageous thing to imagine, but Mallory was in the business of imagining terrible things right now—what was one more?

Caitlin had been tall, and two people could have moved her body more easily than one. But keeping a secret got exponentially more difficult when someone else knew it, and Billy had only mentioned one friend that Caitlin was confiding in. Also, with the communications down after earthquake, coordinating a conspiracy would have been beyond difficult.

Mallory could come up with every practical reason she wanted, but the truth was she simply couldn't bring herself to believe it. Bad enough to imagine she knew one person who was capable of a terrible crime, but two? More? Where would it end?

The answer was that it wouldn't, not until Mallory had some

answers. Until then she would question every interaction, judge every question. And she would always be worried that someone close to her might come for her, whether for the key or to keep her from sharing her information. Mallory knew too much for her own good, but not enough to keep herself safe.

She wondered if that was how Caitlin had felt. She obviously had some idea that she was in danger, or she wouldn't have given Mallory the lipstick tube. But either she wasn't sure, or she didn't think she had enough evidence to tell anyone. So she had done the best she could, and whatever plans she was making had been interrupted by the earthquake.

Mallory was uncomfortably aware that there were similarities between Caitlin's choices and her own. She couldn't change that, not until she knew a lot more than she did now. All she could do was to get to work on finding things out and hope that the Pacific and North American plates had worked out their differences for now.

There was nothing she could do about the second part, but Mallory knew where she had to go to find the answers for the first. She didn't like it, but she knew.

—

Sonali was the first to respond to her text. The surprise was that she was usually slow to respond to plans, but she seemed happy for the suggestion that they get together the next day. Which was a perfectly normal way for a person to be, but at this point, Mallory had lost touch with the idea of normal.

Her plan, if you could call it that, was to meet up with each of the women individually and get them talking about the dinner and about Caitlin. Not that she thought the killer was going to break down and confess, but she hoped she could learn things from the other people who had been at the table, whose memories might be better than hers, or who might know something they weren't aware was relevant. And by seeing each person on her own, Mallory would be able to compare their stories. There was a risk that she might tip her hand too far by saying the wrong thing to the wrong person. But she thought she was better off acting than doing nothing.

While she waited for the rest of the responses, Mallory watched the security camera footage of her home invader again. She had no trouble believing it was a woman—in fact, there was something about the movements that made her think it must be. But was there also something familiar? Part of Mallory thought there might be, but she was wary of being swayed by her preconceptions. It was something you heard all the time about eyewitnesses—if she thought the figure in the video was someone she knew, she might imagine she recognized something about them.

On the other hand…Mallory hit Play again and squinted at the grainy image. What was it about that person that she had seen before?

29

Sonali's apartment was in the block of new buildings that sprouted up around the ballpark over the last few decades, uniform in their tasteful shades of beige and confusing systems for entry. Earthquake damage in this area had been uneven, with some buildings apparently split open while others had only lost some stucco.

The address Mallory had for Sonali was in one of the latter. It was the first time she had been to any of her friends' homes since the disaster, and as she waited at the buzzer, Mallory thought about compromises. Sonali had been very proud of the character of her former apartment, in a 1920s-era building near where Hitchcock had set a scene in *Vertigo*. She had been disdainful of the history-free new builds with their bland sameness and working elevators, though she had (mostly) kept that away from Kendra, who was devoted to all things new.

But people whose buildings had had their facades fall off couldn't be choosers, and if Sonali was unhappy where she had landed, she didn't show any sign of it when Mallory made it to her door, indistinguishable from the others in the vast hallway.

"Good to see you!" Sonali said, greeting her with an awkward hug. "Thanks for coming over. Can I put you on onion duty?"

Mallory had suggested they go for coffee, but Sonali had dinner at her grandparents' house that night, and she had committed to making two dozen samosas. So Mallory took the offered knife and apron and got to work chopping, while Sonali worked on the dough.

It might have been a bad idea to go to the home of someone she allegedly suspected of killing anywhere from one to three people, in order to ask her about it, but Mallory had trouble convincing herself she could be in danger. After all, lots of people might know where she was, her phone would show she had come there, and the building was surrounded by cameras. But however good the rational reasons were for her not to be afraid, they weren't what kept her from making a panicked excuse to leave as soon as she saw the block of knives on the counter. Deep down, Mallory realized, she didn't believe it.

The facts hadn't changed, and she had every reason to think she was right—someone at that dinner was involved in Caitlin's death. But here and now, with the smell of frying spices in the air, a tiny *Star Wars* sweatshirt Sonali was taking for her nephew hanging over the back of a chair in the living room, and a playlist streaming nineties music, she couldn't square those suspicions with reality.

But she had come here for a reason, and if there was nothing to worry about, then there was no reason for her not to raise the subject.

"Caitlin's stepdad? What's even going on?" Sonali said.

"I wish I knew," Mallory said with complete sincerity. "The police think Caitlin's death was an accident and that Charlie killed himself."

"And you found him? With Kendra? What were you guys doing there?"

"Well, we'd been having lunch, and we were talking about Caitlin's death, and there were some questions we came up with that we wanted to ask him. So we went over."

"And you just walked in and found him?"

"Pretty much. The door was open, which was weird. So it seemed like the thing to do, to check. The house is in pretty bad shape, and I thought something might have happened."

It wasn't the exact story, but it was close enough. Mallory didn't really want to go into her entire reasoning—doing so would give too much away or make her sound crazy, or both.

"Did you see anything that looked like someone had broken in?" Sonali asked.

"Not really," said Mallory. "He was sitting on the sofa in a sunroom at the back of the house. It didn't look like he was running away or trying to fight anyone."

"I guess that's why they thought it was suicide. Or I guess it might have been someone he knew." Sonali put the bowl with the dough on top of the refrigerator and took the pot of potatoes off the stove. "It doesn't have to have anything to do with Caitlin, does it? I know there's been a lot of people struggling with their mental health since the quake. And the way Caitlin talked about Charlie, I'm not sure he was the most stable guy."

That was the opening Mallory was waiting for. "Did you know Caitlin well? I'd only met her a couple of times before dinner that night."

Sonali put a potato into a ricer and worked it into a bowl.

"I guess I saw her more than that. She and Kendra were in a book club together a few years ago, and I joined for a while." She must have seen something in Mallory's face, so she added, "The theme of the club was self-help and spiritual books, so that's probably why they didn't ask you."

"Right, of course." Mallory couldn't be offended—her rants about the squishy thinking around wellness and its associated industries were widely known, and barely tolerated, among her friends. "So you hung out with her?"

"Not a lot. The book club met once a month, and a couple of times the three of us would get dinner beforehand. It broke up about six months after I joined, when the person who was hosting moved to Austin. Which was fine, actually. I'd had enough of white ladies explaining yoga to me."

As much as Mallory would have enjoyed seeing how that went down, there were other conversations she was more interested in.

"When you were having these meetings, did Caitlin talk about the things that were concerning her? Like, how the subjects of the books might relate to her own life?"

Sonali had been adding peas to the potato mixture, but she stopped and looked at Mallory.

"Why do you want to know all this? This all happened over three years ago. I get that you're upset about her death, but what's the point of asking about what was on her mind then?"

Those were good questions, and ones that Mallory didn't want to answer.

"I was wondering about how she was found down by the Palace of Fine Arts," she improvised. "Why go there in the middle of the night? But maybe if there was some sort of cult she got into..."

Sonali sighed deeply. "Not every spiritual thing is a cult, Mallory. She was interested in learning how to be more present, to connect with the energy in the universe. There was nothing dangerous about it."

"Yeah, well, that's just what someone in a cult would say." Mallory dodged as Sonali chucked a piece of potato at her head. "But okay, maybe not anything organized like that. But did she have any relationships that seemed weird to you? Like someone might be manipulating her?"

"I really wouldn't know. Like I said, I didn't see her much outside of the book club. Honestly, my impression of her was someone who was smart but didn't have any energy or direction. I guess she didn't need it because of her mother's money. She was looking for something to give her life some meaning, and I don't think she knew what it was. I guess that might have made her vulnerable to someone trying to get at her. One thing I will say, even for that group, she was pretty credulous."

"About what? Like, she believed in Ouija boards, or more of an apple-cider-vinegar-will-solve-all-my-problems sort of thing?"

Sonali laughed as she rolled her eyes. "Closer to the second one, I guess, but not really that either. It was more like she took the things people told her at face value; she never questioned if they were exaggerating, or making things up, or just being polite. It wasn't terrible, just kind of awkward."

"Oh, yeah. I can see that." It made sense with everything else Mallory knew about Caitlin—someone who was possibly too sincere for her own good and assumed the same in others. The sort of person who might not see that they were being led on until it was almost too late.

"Speaking of awkward, did you notice anything strange about Caitlin at dinner that night?" Mallory asked. "Like that she might have been upset or worried about something? At the time, I figured it was because of her mom, but now that we know she died that night, I wonder if there was something going on we could have seen."

"At the dinner? Yeah, um, I don't know. I guess it was like you said, her mom had died, so obviously she wasn't going to be all happy and laughing. But I don't think I really noticed anything."

Was Mallory imagining things? Or was there hesitation in Sonali's answer? She tried again.

"She said something about her stepfather, didn't she? Like she didn't like or trust him?"

"I really don't remember. A lot has happened since then, you know?" Now there was a definite edge to Sonali's voice that

Mallory couldn't understand. Not remembering something from six months ago wasn't strange, even when there hadn't been a disaster. So why was Sonali so defensive?

Normally, Mallory would have assumed she had her reasons and left it alone. But this situation was anything but normal.

"What about after the dinner? I didn't actually see Caitlin leave, did you?"

Sonali was looking away from Mallory, rolling out rounds of the dough, her face hidden behind the curtain of her hair.

"I didn't see her," she said without turning. "I just left. We all just left. Why do you keep asking about that night anyway?"

There was a disdain in her voice, a carelessness Mallory didn't think was genuine. This wasn't the Sonali she knew, and it confused and worried her.

"It was the last time we saw each other before the earthquake, and right after it, Caitlin died," Mallory said. "I want to go over what happened, make sure there isn't something important we're missing."

"Why?" This time Sonali did look at her, and her expression was defiant. "Why do 'we' have to do anything? Can't you just leave the past alone?"

That was about all Mallory could take.

"How far in the past? Am I supposed to forget about the dead body I identified? The one I found? The person who keeps breaking into my house?" Too late, she forgot that she hadn't shared that part yet. She braced herself for Sonali's follow-up questions, but they didn't come.

"God, Mallory, you need to get over yourself. Not everything is about you."

"That's true. For example, I think this is about Caitlin, because she's dead. Doesn't that matter to you at all?"

Sonali took a step back like she had been hit. She bit her lip and looked away for a moment before speaking. "Look, we've all been through a lot. And none of us are thinking straight. Let's just forget about this for now, okay?"

"No, it's not okay. What's wrong with you, Sonali? This doesn't sound like you. Caitlin was your friend, wasn't she? And even if you weren't close, she was still a person who mattered."

"I know that! It's just—" Sonali stopped herself and took a deep breath. "I don't want to talk about that night, okay? There's nothing we can do for Caitlin now. That's up to the police. The best we can do is move forward and try to get on with our lives."

"I can't do that," Mallory said, but as she did, she knew it was hopeless. For whatever reason, she wasn't going to get anything more out of Sonali, and trying would just extend the fight. Instead, she looked at the pan of browning onions on the stove. "But I can't make you do anything either. So, I guess, do these look done to you?"

That broke the tension a little bit. Sonali sighed and rubbed her face, and then came over to look at the pan.

"Those are fine. Look, I think I just need to settle in and get these finished, and it'll be quicker if I do them on my own. Thanks for coming over to help."

"Any time," Mallory said. She took off her borrowed apron,

hung it on a hook, and started to go. But at the kitchen door, she hesitated. Sonali had said enough for Mallory to think she had something to do with Caitlin's death. But if she didn't, and she knew something, she might be in danger herself. There was nothing more to say here, but she had to at least try.

"You know you can tell me stuff, right? If you need someone to talk to?" Mallory said. It was a hopeless impulse, but for a moment she almost thought it paid off. Sonali opened her mouth to speak, but then she shut it again, pressed her lips together, and shook her head.

"There's nothing wrong with me. I just need to get these finished so I can start frying."

30

Back in her car, Mallory expected to be sad or worried she had done or said something wrong. But she wasn't. She was angry.

Angry she was even in this position, suspecting people she thought she knew and could trust of doing a terrible thing for money. And that trying to do what was right only ever seemed to make things worse for her, from being treated as a suspect by the police, to being told by her own friend that she was being dramatic and making it all about herself. But the worst part was the way no one seemed to care, how someone like Caitlin could just vanish and then die, and it was all somebody else's problem. That feeling wasn't just anger, it was helplessness, which only made her angrier.

It wasn't just Sonali; it was everyone. The cops who found Caitlin's body must have asked no questions if they had called it an accident. And even with a second death in the same family, they seemed happy to look the other way. What was the point of talking to the authorities when a cat groomer cared more about the death than they did?

There was always the possibility of going to the media with the story. Mallory started her car and pulled out of the parking spot while she let that idea simmer. On the one hand, a young attractive white girl was exactly the kind of suspicious death that would get coverage. And that attention would probably do more to make the police take it seriously than anything Mallory could say or do.

But almost as soon as she thought of it, Mallory discarded the idea. The coverage of the earthquake and its aftermath had done a lot to erode what little faith she had in the accuracy of national reporting—by the time Mallory had made it to Fresno, the relative she was staying with was convinced she had only barely escaped a Mad Max–style hellscape. She could imagine how that kind of sensationalism would be applied to Caitlin's story, and she didn't see how it would help.

She also wasn't about to subject what few facts she had to some podcast producer's dreams of viral fame. And that was before you even got into what the amateur murder enthusiasts would do once they got their hands on it. As bad as the situation was now, there was no way having a thousand bored people tearing into her and her friends' lives was going to improve it.

No, Mallory thought, if anyone was going to play detective on this case, it would have to be her.

Which meant she was going to have to deal with what had gone on back in that apartment. Mallory had gone in feeling like it was impossible for her to suspect Sonali of having anything to do with Caitlin's death, but she couldn't ignore it now. There might have been other reasons for why she didn't want to talk about what happened at dinner that night—in general or about Caitlin specifically. Mallory could spend all day thinking of them, but she didn't need to do that. What she did need to do was to figure out what happened.

Of course, the fact that Sonali had been so openly against talking about it might be in her favor. It would have been easy to say she didn't notice anything strange, or it had been so long she just couldn't remember. Why would someone trying to avoid suspicion for their crimes make it so obvious that they were hiding something?

It wasn't what a skilled assassin would do, but Mallory wasn't sure that was what she was dealing with. Whoever it was had managed to tip Caitlin off, causing her to spook and give Mallory the key, and had taken wild risks—showing up to search Mallory's apartment while she was there and dragging a dead body to a public place to dump it. If she was right about the sequence of events, the killer was more lucky than good, and luck failed sometimes.

Right now, Mallory was hoping some of that luck had passed on to her. She was going to need it.

—

She had a few hours until her next plans, but it wasn't worth it to go home. Mallory thought about visiting the library to see if she could find any more news stories about Caitlin's mom—with that kind of money, she might have turned up in the society section, or maybe a business publication had covered her death. But she decided to table the idea for now, in favor of another one.

The restaurant where they'd had that last dinner was still there, which was a surprise. Even the businesses whose buildings had escaped with minimal damage had struggled in the aftermath of the earthquake. And while a few new places had opened with the help of insurance money and lowered rents, it was increasingly rare to find something that had survived straight through.

But this one had, and as Mallory perused the menu by the door, she noticed that the dishes hadn't even changed much. The local halibut was off the menu (the stories about dumping sewage weren't entirely false), but the cheesecakes they had shared for dessert were still there.

The restaurant was open, with drink specials until six, so Mallory went in the door and back in time.

Inside, some things had changed. In February the tables had been packed together, close enough that Mallory had to be careful how far she moved her chair. Now the layout was spacious, a change that Mallory suspected had less to do with the comfort of their customers than the downturn in business leaving too many tables empty every night.

There were plenty empty now, but that wasn't surprising for the middle of the afternoon. Even so, the hostess made a show of checking her tablet and looking around the room before leading Mallory to a spot by the window.

She ordered a glass of the same wine she had been drinking that night, hoping it might activate a sensory memory, and also because she felt like she needed it. While she waited for it, she looked around the room and tried to reassemble the events of that evening.

As usual, Mallory had been one of the last to arrive, though she was confident she wasn't actually late. But by the time she got to the restaurant, there had only been two empty seats at the table. Mallory had taken the one between Lourdes and Kendra, and Sonali had arrived last, just behind her.

That was a little unusual itself. Mallory was consistently late because she never allowed enough time for traffic. But Sonali had a reputation of being scrupulously early and the one most likely to give Mallory grief for her poor planning.

At the time, Mallory was glad that for once she wasn't the lone straggler, but now everything took on a potential extra meaning. Something had been going on that Mallory was unaware of, a tension totally separate from the fault-line pressure building under the city. Both disasters had happened that night, but this was the only one she could do anything about.

And to do that, she had to start at the beginning.

The waitress came back with her wine and to take her order, and Mallory took the interruption as an opportunity to reset her thoughts. She was working from the assumption that there had been something going on with Caitlin and another person at the dinner table that night, which had been disrupted, causing Caitlin to give Mallory the key. That fit the facts as she knew them—Caitlin's agitation when they were talking in the bathroom, the handing off of a valuable item to someone she barely knew, the fact that the person who broke into Mallory's house not only knew she would have it, but also where she lived.

Given that, had the dinner been a setup from the beginning, or an opportunity someone had seized? Mallory tried again to remember whose idea it had been in the first place, but her mind came up blank. It definitely wasn't hers, and she was sure it wasn't Caitlin's, because someone had thought to add her later—either Kendra or Rachel, Mallory thought—explaining that they wanted Caitlin to get out more after her mother died.

She was still trying to remember when her food arrived. She had ordered the lunch portion of the pasta dish she had before, in another attempt to Proust her way to a solution, when it occurred to her there were other people who might remember at least some of what had gone on. Setting her phone aside, Mallory smiled at the waitress.

"Thanks, this looks great. I'm glad to see this place is still going. I was actually here with some friends on the night of the earthquake, just a couple of hours before it happened."

The server courteously pretended to be interested. "Oh really? Wow, that's cool. I was on that night, working the bar. Do you remember who your server was?"

Mallory did not and had only a vague idea that it might have been a man. Covering for her embarrassment, she pointed across the rearranged restaurant, to where a cluster of two-tops now stood.

"We were over there, at the big table you used to have. There were six of us."

"Oh right, the girls' night." The waitress stared where Mallory was pointing for a moment, like she was trying to remember. "Yeah, you had Riken. Great guy, really good waiter. He's not here anymore; he moved back to Missouri after the quake."

It was more detail than Mallory had expected anyone at the dinner to have remembered, let alone a waitress who wasn't even working their table. She was suddenly nervous—was there something going on here that she didn't know about?

It was a moment's thought, and Mallory rejected the idea almost as soon as it crossed her mind. She could hardly deflect accusations of being overdramatic if she was going to start suspecting everyone she met. A waitress having a good memory was not so unusual that she needed to start spiraling into paranoia.

"I hope that's what scared him away, and not us," Mallory said, trying to sound normal. "I think we may have gotten a little rowdy a couple of times."

She didn't actually think that at all, but she was interested to know if there had been anything she had missed. But the server was reassuring.

"Oh no, you guys were fine. Seriously, February is so slow, you could have done whatever and we'd have been glad to have you. It's funny, I was just thinking about that night. We got a call a couple months ago, like the day after we reopened, asking about a lost item that had been left here then. I had to tell them sorry, there's no way we could find it. After all this time, plus the earthquake, plus the break-ins, if it was ever here, it's gone."

A group of three people were waiting at the entrance. The

hostess signaled from across the room, and the server acknowledged her and turned to go.

"Anyway, enjoy your meal. Let me know if there's anything else you need," she said and was gone before Mallory could come up with any follow-up questions.

She definitely had some. Like, who had called after all this time to look for an item "lost" in the restaurant? And about those break-ins—had they just been another victim of the spate of thefts that had happened while law enforcement was overstretched? Or was it more targeted, possibly by someone who knew a valuable item had been carried into this place and hadn't left with the person who brought it?

Mallory wasn't sure how she would phrase that last one.

A wave of customers came in, and Mallory didn't see her server for a while. When she came back, she was more hurried, with less time to linger and chat. There was no use trying to subtly try to work around to her questions, so Mallory got to the point.

"I know this is going to sound weird, but when I came here with my friends, I think something happened. And I was just wondering, is there anything you can tell me about that night? Anything you or one of your colleagues might have noticed?"

Mallory was right about one thing; she did sound weird, and the other woman gave her a look of concern. But a person couldn't work in food service in San Francisco and be easily rattled, so she smiled back at Mallory like she wanted to help.

"I'm sorry, I don't think there's anything I can tell you. What is it that you think was going on?"

"Well, one of them died that night, but not in the earthquake." The look of shock on the server's face made Mallory think she might have overshot with the bluntness there. "Nothing to do with the food or anything," she hurried to add. "I'm trying to find out as much as I can about the events that led up to it, and I think the dinner was one of them. It could have to do with that person who called here, and maybe even the break-ins."

"Wow. Um… Well, like I said, there really isn't anything I can tell you. I could ask some of the other people who were here. I'm still connected with Riken on WhatsApp—he's probably your best bet."

Mallory wasn't sure if it was the mention of the death or the phone call that convinced the waitress, but she was suddenly a lot more interested in the story.

"I'm Kate, by the way. You really think our break-ins might be related to you and your friends?"

"Mallory, and yeah. At least, they got into my place and didn't find what they were looking for, so they might have come here. My guess is that's also what they were calling about, to see if someone had found it."

A man at another table was trying to get Kate's attention, and Mallory was aware she was stretching her luck. Fortunately, her new friend seemed to be fully on board.

"I could try to find the number of the person who called. I know it was in the afternoon, and I was on shift. I could probably give you a short list, at least."

"That would be amazing. Can I give you my number or my email?"

Contact information was exchanged, and Mallory paid her bill, leaving a generous tip and briefly wondering if that counted as a bribe.

As she left, she took one look back at the spot where their table had been, all those months ago. Just six young women, having an ordinary dinner at a normal restaurant, none of them having any idea about what was about to happen.

At least, none of them had known about the earthquake. The more she learned, the more Mallory was sure that someone at that table had a very clear idea of how the night was supposed to go.

Kendra

Kendra stepped out of the car with a calmness she didn't feel. It had been a full day now, and she was going to have to make a decision.

Why the hell had she agreed to go with Mallory to that damn house? There had been no reason for it. It's not like she could have done anything there, no matter what had happened. It had been a bad choice, made because she wasn't thinking clearly in the moment. Kendra wasn't going to make that mistake again. That's what she was doing here, with her phone off, thinking clearly and preparing herself before she did anything else.

If only that door hadn't been open. But why did Mallory go in, anyway? Who just walks into a house like that? It was almost like she knew something.

Unbelievable that Mallory had the nerve to text her after all that to ask what had happened. Kendra hadn't responded, and she wasn't going to. This whole thing was Mallory's fault, if she thought about it, and she wasn't going to let that girl interfere with her life for a moment more.

There was a cold breeze blowing off the ocean, carrying more fog with it, and Kendra glared at the incoming clouds like they had been sent particularly to annoy her. That was another thing that was wrong with this place. Beaches should be warm and sunny, not places where you had to pack a sweater and the water turned your toes blue.

None of that was what was really bothering her, of course. Her real problems had nothing to do with the weather, and they would be just as bad anywhere else. Even if she could leave now, and there were lots of reasons why she couldn't, that would be making a choice all by itself. There came a time when even avoiding your problems didn't make them go away.

So the question remained: What was she going to do?

31

When Mallory decided to set up plans with everyone who had been at the dinner, she hadn't thought ahead to what she would do if they all said yes. But Lourdes had replied about five minutes after Sonali, suggesting the same time, and Rachel's response came in less than an hour later. Mallory put Rachel off to the next day but suggested to Lourdes that they meet that evening for drinks. Kendra hadn't replied at all, and Mallory wasn't sure if that was because she was feeling bad for ditching her, or if Kendra had just had enough of her for one week.

Worn out from her encounter with Sonali, she was regretting making plans again so soon, but it was too late to cancel the drinks with Lourdes. Investigating a murder wasn't a leisure activity, Mallory reminded herself.

She had spent longer at the restaurant than she had intended, and even though the bar Lourdes suggested was in the rare part of San Francisco with available parking, Mallory was still late. So she wasn't surprised that Lourdes was already in the bar when she got there. What did surprise her was that she wasn't alone.

"Hey, we saved you a seat. I hope you don't mind—Rachel called right after we were texting, and I invited her along. She said you guys were getting together tomorrow anyway?"

"That's great," Mallory said and tried to make it sound sincere. Part of what she was trying to do was to find out if any of them knew anything about the rest and check their stories against each other. She really needed to be one-on-one for that, but she couldn't say so. So she hugged them both hello and took the offered seat, thinking about how she was going to change her approach.

For the moment, the question was academic. Lourdes and Rachel had been talking when Mallory arrived, and they got right back into their conversation, barely leaving her space to get a word in.

"I know we need to be patient, but it's been six months," Lourdes said. "A normal city would have their garbage service working by now. It's not like the dump fell down."

"On my street we can't put things in front of the buildings anymore. I'm like, *I'm sorry, you want me to drag my bin half a block every week? And then back?* What are we even paying for?" Rachel took another sip of her drink, holding the glass carefully so the condensation on the base wouldn't fall on her lap. Whenever Lourdes had added her to the invitation, it had given Rachel enough time to change. Unlike Mallory, who had come in the same black jeans and T-shirt she had been wearing to help Sonali make samosas, and which now smelled of onions, Rachel was wearing matching gold jewelry and a green jumpsuit, almost the same shade as Caitlin's dress from the night of the dinner. (Mallory reminded herself that didn't mean anything; the color was probably in fashion.) Lourdes's dress was, if anything, a bit much for a weeknight in San Francisco, long and shimmering in gunmetal gray. It was the sort of thing Mallory would love but never buy because she had nowhere to wear it, though now she wondered if that was just a failure of imagination on her part.

Underdressed or not, Mallory hadn't come here to listen to tales of garbage woe.

"I know. I—" Mallory began, but Rachel wasn't done yet.

"And that's not even the worst part. You know how we're supposed to separate our green waste? Well, I've got one neighbor who's appointed herself the trash investigator. She goes through everyone's cans and puts the stuff on top if you have recyclables or vegetables in the wrong one."

Lourdes made a face. "What is it with people who have to get into everyone else's business?"

This didn't bode well for Mallory's plan to get them gossiping about their friends. But they were talking about what had changed since the quake, and that gave her an opening.

"I went back to the restaurant today, the one we had dinner in that night. It's crazy that it's still there."

Rachel was unimpressed. "Everything is reopening now. I thought we might at least get something fresh after what we've been through."

"There's a new club down in SoMa that's supposed to be cool,"

Lourdes said. "A bunch of artist types took over where that bougie bowling alley was and turned it into a performance and dance space."

That sounded interesting, but Mallory wasn't going to be distracted. "Caitlin was really into art, wasn't she? I wish I'd gotten a chance to know her better."

"Why? You hate getting to know people," Lourdes said.

"Lourdes, wow," Rachel admonished her. "Just because it's true doesn't mean you should say it."

They all laughed, including Mallory, who mostly meant it.

"But seriously," she said. "She really did seem like a nice person. Just kind of lost, you know? I don't know if that had to do with losing her mom."

"Yes and no," Rachel said, thoughtfully. "That messed her up, of course, but ever since we graduated, she's always been, like, trying to find herself. Which is crazy, right? If I had her kind of money, I'd find myself in Ibiza with an Italian count feeding me champagne."

Lourdes rolled her eyes. "Money doesn't solve as many problems as you think."

"Maybe you just need more of it," Rachel retorted. "All I know is it would solve most of mine."

"Well, it didn't keep Caitlin alive. Her or her mom," Mallory said. "Actually, I'm starting to wonder if it's what killed them both."

The drink must have gone straight to her head—she hadn't meant to show her hand like that. She was having the same problem she had with Sonali—her theories about a friend being involved in Caitlin's death had been clear enough when she was alone in her apartment, but now that she was here, talking to them, she had trouble squaring her ideas with reality.

Of course, there were other reasons not to tell your friends that you thought someone you all knew might have been murdered for her money. For example, they were likely to look at you like you had lost your mind.

"You aren't serious," Rachel said. "I feel bad that none of us realized she was missing, too, but I don't think we need to start making up crazy things."

"Is it really that crazy? Saturday night we all go to dinner, and she's acting weird. She leaves without saying goodbye to anyone. Less than three hours later, she's dead, still wearing the same clothes we saw her in, miles from her home. I think it's crazier not to consider that someone might have killed her."

"There was an earthquake, Mallory. A lot of people died," said Lourdes.

"But most of them were in their homes or their cars. What was she doing at the Palace of Fine Arts in the middle of the night? Are you really going to tell me she was the kind of person who would hop a fence to go for a midnight stroll? In February?"

"It was an accident. I don't know why it happened, but it did." Lourdes's tone was slow and measured, in a way that suggested she was losing her patience.

Mallory had none left. "And her mom's death was an accident, too? And her stepfather just happened to kill himself in the same time period? That's a lot of dead people in one family all at once."

"Coincidences happen," said Rachel. "I know it sounds wild when you say it like that, but is it really less likely than some big conspiracy? Ever since the earthquake, all bets are off about what's normal."

Lourdes was nodding along, and Mallory felt control of the conversation slipping away from her. She didn't want to bring up the hardware key and her own break-ins again—that would only risk sounding like she was making it about herself. Instead, she went with something neither of them could deny.

Mallory took a deep breath. "Okay, fine. Now explain how she sent us all a text the next morning saying she was okay."

That stopped them. First Lourdes then Rachel went for their phones, and Mallory waited as they scrolled back through the messages and looked at the date stamps.

"Maybe she scheduled it to send from earlier?" Lourdes said when she was finally convinced.

"Before the earthquake? She just happened to schedule a text for the next morning saying she was okay?"

"You said she seemed weird at dinner," Rachel pointed out. "And she did leave without saying goodbye. Maybe she wanted to let us all know she was all right, but she didn't want to wake us up."

"Oh, come on. And you were saying my ideas were improbable? Why can't you at least accept the possibility that all of this doesn't add up?" Mallory said.

Lourdes took another sip of her drink and sighed. "What if we do believe it? What's the point? It was six months ago, and there was an earthquake. If the police don't think there's enough to investigate, what are you going to do? There are a lot of injustices in the world, Mallory. You've got to let go of this idea you can do anything about them."

"No," said Mallory.

"No?" Rachel asked. "No what?"

"No, I don't have to give up. Somebody in this goddamn world has to care about something."

32

Lourdes and Mallory stared at each other, neither willing to look away. Lourdes was trying to affect a superior attitude, but Mallory wasn't fooled. She had known her friend for too long, and if Lourdes actually didn't care about something, she would have just made a remark about people who took things too seriously and moved on. Instead she was trying to use the force of her personality to get Mallory to back down from asking questions about another woman's death.

It had worked before, about other things. But not this time, Mallory thought. She'd had enough. Enough of people telling her to give up, of being ignored and dismissed. If Lourdes, or anyone else, wanted to stop her at this point, it was going to take a lot more than a mean look and a hair flip.

Rachel was saying something about not making it weird, but they both ignored her. To banish the thoughts of what her friends were thinking about her, Mallory focused on her memories of Caitlin's face, the way it had looked in that mirror in the restaurant bathroom, and then the next time she had seen it, on the medical examiner's table. Caitlin thought she had a friend, didn't she? But more and more, Mallory was sure Caitlin had been wrong about that. Well, maybe she had been wrong too. What kind of friend would have such strong feelings about her looking into another person's death?

There was one obvious answer to that. The possibility that someone at this table was the killer made Mallory think she should at least pretend to back off when Lourdes broke her gaze and rolled her eyes.

"Fine. If you're going to have delusions of heroism, that's your business. I was just trying to keep you from embarrassing yourself, running around playing Batman."

"I appreciate your concern," Mallory snarked. "We all know how important my high-society reputation is."

"Okay, you two, enough," said Rachel. "Mallory, we're all upset about Caitlin's death. I knew her since we were teenagers; we went through a lot together. She was the one who picked me up from the airport when Spencer dumped me when we were leaving for Hawaii. Yesterday I came across a cat rescue having an adoption event at the grocery store, and I was about to text her pictures when I realized I couldn't. I mean, I could, but she wouldn't see them. That was when it really hit me, that Caitlin was never going to be able to look at kitten pictures again." Her voice caught, and she looked away for a moment, then back at Mallory. "Of course I care that she died. I just don't know what you think we can do about it."

"I don't know either," Mallory said. "But I can't not try. And we were the last people to see her that night. Are you sure she didn't say anything? About being afraid of someone, or something?"

Somehow, their glasses had all emptied while they were arguing, and the bartender came around to collect them.

"Another round?" he asked, and Lourdes nodded.

"Put it on my tab. I think we could all use it."

Mallory wasn't going to disagree.

The drinks arrived, and in the meantime, Lourdes seemed to have made a decision of her own.

"For the record, I still think this is ridiculous. But if we've got to talk about that dinner, fine. I didn't know Caitlin well, but I did think she didn't want to be there. It wasn't surprising; she was obviously still grieving her mom. Honestly, I don't know why she came at all. Why not just stay home? There'd be chances to go out later."

Mallory thought about that house on the cliffside and the unpleasant man Caitlin had been sharing it with. "Maybe staying in was worse. I don't think Caitlin liked her stepfather very much. I sure didn't, and I only met him once."

"Are you sure you should be talking like that?" Rachel said. "You did find his body."

Mallory shrugged. "Do you really think if I was killing obnoxious men, I'd start with him? He wouldn't even be on the first page of the list. Rachel, you must have met him. What did you think of Charlie?"

"I don't know. He sucked but he wasn't, like, a monster." Rachel balanced the perilously full martini glass in her fingertips.

"Caitlin wouldn't have liked anyone her mom married. And Charlie didn't like having her around either. I think he figured she would eventually move out, and he and Deborah would have the place to themselves. It's an amazing house, right?"

It was, but Mallory didn't think that was the main point. "Then why did he stay after Deborah died? I get that he had the right, under the law, but the house belonged to Caitlin; he was never going to own it."

"That is weird," Lourdes agreed. "I don't know why Caitlin didn't offer him some money to leave. That's what I would have done."

"Maybe she did, and he didn't take it. Or maybe they were still negotiating. Who knows?" Rachel said. "The guy needed somewhere to live; she had this giant house. Why not just share? It wasn't going to be for the long term. And obviously no one knew about the earthquake."

"I don't think anyone is going to be living there for a while," Mallory added. "The building was tagged, and from what I saw inside, it was for good reason. It'll cost a fortune to make it livable again."

"Worth it," Lourdes said with authority. "No one could build anything new out there now. For those views, someone will pay what it takes."

What if someone already did? Mallory thought.

Aloud, she said, "I guess that'll be up to Caitlin's dad, then. Unless she has some other close relatives or a will, he'll inherit it from her, right? Do you know anything about him, Rachel?"

"Not really," Rachel said. "I know she hated him after he abandoned her and her mom. And he showed up again when they had money, asking for payments, even though he had skipped out on child support for years. If it all really does go to him, she'd hate that."

"It's a good thing she isn't around to see it, then," said Lourdes. "Seriously, though, if Mallory is going to stick to this idea that someone killed her and her mom, he's the obvious one, right? Mom's money goes to Caitlin, Caitlin's young and she doesn't have a will, so he gets it as her closest relative. Do it now before she gets married or has kids, and he's golden."

Lourdes leaned against the skinny back of her barstool, her shimmering dress draped over her long crossed legs. She looked like an advertisement for something—expensive vodka or watches for people who didn't care what time it was.

"Sure, but how would he have gotten to her?" Rachel asked. "When I said Caitlin hated her dad, I wasn't kidding. She would never have let him into the house."

That wasn't the problem Mallory had with the theory, but without mentioning the hardware key or the fact that someone involved knew her address, she couldn't bring them up. She decided to play along.

"What if he and Charlie were working together? Maybe after Deborah died, or even before. Charlie had the opportunity but not the motive, and her dad had the motive but not the opportunity. So Charlie makes sure the dad gets all the money, and he's supposed to cut Charlie in, but instead he shoots him so he can keep it all."

"And gets rid of the only witness at the same time?" Lourdes said, and then she laughed. "Okay, I know it was my idea, but none of us actually believe any of this, right? I mean, I've heard of crazier things, but only because I watch a lot of K-dramas."

She finished her drink and picked up the bill the bartender had left. "Anyway, I've had enough of this. I say we go see what this club is like. I'm sick to death of sitting around like old people, gossiping and acting like there isn't a whole city out there."

"Sounds good to me," Rachel said as she took out a compact and touched up her lipstick. "If we're going to spend all this money to live in the city, we might as well get something out of it."

Sitting around like an old person was one of Mallory's favorite things to do, and she hadn't brought any makeup. But this whole outing had been her idea in the first place, and she wasn't going to get anywhere staying in her apartment with the cats.

Nothing about this day had gone the way she had planned, but what else was new? She had set off on this investigation with no idea about what she was doing except that she needed to know more than she did, and talking to people seemed like the best way to get there. She wasn't sure she had made any progress in that direction—if anything, seeing her friends again face-to-face had only made her more confused. But she had fought through it this far, still hoping that eventually she would turn something up.

And it looked like the next round was starting.

Rachel

It was a relief to get out of that place. Rachel liked a high-end bar as much as the next civilized person, but something about that place was starting to feel claustrophobic. The club would be much more interesting, she thought. And if she had to deal with art, there should at least be some partying involved.

Also, clubs were loud. That meant Mallory wouldn't be able to bring up her questions about Caitlin again, unless she wanted to shout them over the music. Rachel had enough of talking about that for one night.

She thought she had handled herself well with Mallory there, though she hadn't expected to get so emotional. It was understandable, she supposed. They hadn't been as close as they once were, but Caitlin had been a part of her life for a long time. Knowing that someone like that wasn't there anymore, that would take some adjusting to.

But she didn't need to get into any more details about it tonight, which was why she took the lead as they left the bar, keeping Lourdes between her and Mallory. God, that girl was weird. What kind of person thinks that much about death? And she hadn't even known Caitlin that well. Of all of them... There was no point worrying about that. The past was the past, and that was it.

Now was the time for Rachel to be thinking about the future.

33

It was only three blocks from the bar to the club, so Rachel's suggestion that they get an Uber was vetoed in favor of walking. A Giants game had just finished, and even though the stadium was still under repair and the team playing miles away in Sacramento, fans in orange and black streamed out of the bars around the shuttered ballpark. The team was having a terrible season, but that didn't matter—the post-disaster surge of local pride meant that every hit was treated like a World Series win.

The game must have ended in a loss, because the crowd that passed the women was more subdued than jubilant, and Mallory only had to dodge one drunk bro trying to hug her.

"Some things never change, I guess," she said when they were safely out of earshot of the man and his friends. "I keep hearing that someday I'm going to be old enough to be invisible to guys like that, and I can't wait."

"It's because you're so small," Rachel said. "Guys think they can pick you up. Like, literally."

She actually sounded a little put out, and Mallory internally rolled her eyes at the thought that Rachel could be annoyed that she hadn't been the one drawing the unwanted attention.

Lourdes laughed and said, "You really are too portable, Mal. You should get one of those vests like my aunt has for her chihuahua so it doesn't get carried off by a hawk."

They had reached the four-story building that housed the club, and a line was winding out the door. So there was plenty of time for looking up pictures of tiny dogs in vests with multicolored plastic spikes and for the other two to do some speculating on what size Mallory would require. They even got the bouncer into the conversation when they were closer to the door, which Mallory found embarrassing, but it got them inside.

The club was like no venue she had ever been to before. Not in every way—there was the same pulsing music, anonymous house beats that ran together from every direction. And the bar looked familiar enough: the same assortment of bottles behind the taps, being served by the same over-it bartenders working their way through the crowd of people fighting for their attention.

But beyond that, the creators of the place had decided to stretch the definition of what constituted a "club."

For one thing, there was nothing that could be recognizably called a dance floor. People danced wherever they felt like it, weaving in and out of the rest of the crowd. Some were responding to the closest source of music, others wearing headphones playing them a party of their own. If there were human DJs controlling any of it, they were nowhere to be seen. The music came through speakers that had been attached to anything that would hold them, and as Mallory ventured deeper into the building, one song gave way to another without anything to announce the change. Around all of it, art was crammed into the space with no regard for curation or composition.

Or safety codes, Mallory thought as a headphone wearer grooved their way across her path, sending her into the many arms of a human-octopus statue. It was made of something like papier-mâché, and Mallory's shirt got caught on its chicken wire structure. By the time she got herself free, she had lost sight of Lourdes and Rachel in the surging crowd.

Unsure of what else to do, Mallory forged deeper into the building. She had a vague hope of finding a more open area where she might be able to spot her friends—Lourdes, at least, should have been easy to pick out in her silver dress.

That was before she passed three people in metallics, as well as one man who looked like he had made his own space suit out of aluminum foil and a woman wearing nothing but silver body paint and a matching thong. At that point, Mallory gave up on reconnecting with the people who had brought her and allowed the flow of people to carry her along.

Eventually, she found herself on a balcony on the third level, overlooking a large open area on the floor below. From this vantage point, she could see where the bowling lanes used to be, from when the space had served corporate outings and yuppie birthday parties. The pits along the back wall had been boarded up, and the gutters had been covered with new flooring that almost matched what was there. But the shadows where the lane markers had been were visible in the way the lights reflected off them. And if the floor had been refinished, the work hadn't been thorough, because partiers were regularly sliding on the lanes, running into each other and falling down.

It happened often enough that the people standing next to Mallory started a drinking game based on type and severity of the falls. Put off by their giggles at a man's head bouncing off the floor, Mallory edged her way back through the crowd and started looking for an exit. She hadn't spotted either Lourdes or Rachel since they came inside, and by now, she didn't think she was going to. And if she did, what then? Was she going to shout questions about Caitlin at them over the music, hoping to hear them answer?

She had to admit, this entire day had been a waste. Her plan to talk to the other people who had been at the dinner had failed, possibly because she didn't ask the right questions. Sonali was mad at her, Lourdes and Rachel thought she was being dramatic, and after their adventure at Caitlin's house, Kendra had completely vanished. Even the waiter had moved to Missouri.

Maybe she shouldn't be doing this at all. No, scratch that. Mallory knew she shouldn't be doing it. She had no special skills, no knowledge. Someone else absolutely should have been working on investigating Caitlin's death and keeping Mallory safe from whoever was trying to steal her property. The problem was, there was no one else. There was only Mallory, and it was becoming increasingly clear to her that she wasn't going to be enough.

Lost in her recriminations, it took Mallory a minute to realize she was also simply lost. She had been following exit signs, but she must have missed one, because she had ended up in a corner between a leering demon made of construction debris and a tinfoil vagina. There was a door in the wall, but it was labeled NOT AN EXIT and locked for good measure.

The crowd surged around her, and Mallory let herself be carried along to another area she hadn't seen before. A smoke machine was belching out sickly sweet fumes that represented fog or smoke over a model of the damaged city, which shook every few minutes. It was an area she would have preferred to avoid, but through the mist she spotted the distinctive green light of an exit sign.

Mallory fought her way toward it, squinting and coughing. The crowd was thinner in this part of the room at least—she must not have been the only one who didn't appreciate the special effects. She had a vague sense of someone passing behind her, but her eyes were watering ferociously, and it was all she could do to keep them focused on the light over the door.

That wasn't an illusion, at least. The door was unlocked, and Mallory opened it to a rush of cold air that pushed it out of her hands and slammed it into the wall behind her. The stairwell it opened into was badly lit, but half a flight down, a window had been propped open, letting in the real fog of the summer night. Still coughing, Mallory stopped in front of it and leaned on the sill, breathing deeply and blinking until her eyes cleared. She was just thinking she was lucky to have found these stairs that no one else in the crowded club seemed to be using when she felt the hand on her back.

At first, Mallory thought it was just someone trying to get past her, possibly drunk and losing their balance. But the force behind the shove increased, and the other hand that gripped the waistband of her pants and lifted her through the window left no doubt about what they were trying to do.

Mallory fought as hard as she could, yelling at the top of her voice and kicking with all the force she could manage. She connected a couple of times, and she felt her attacker falter behind her when Mallory's sneaker found their shin. But it wasn't enough, she really was too small, and as soon as her fingers were pried off the window frame, there was nothing more to stop Mallory from tumbling out into the darkness.

34

In a way, it was the art that saved her.

The building stood on a narrow canal that connected to the bay, draining the filled-in land the neighborhood was built on. The drop from the window should have been a sheer three stories onto the rocks at the edge of the water, for a quick and certain death. But part of the wall had been decorated with a twisting sculpture of a dragon, and by some miracle, Mallory was able to grab it and stop her fall.

She waited to see if her attacker was going to check on their work, to see why her screams had stopped so abruptly. But no face appeared in the opening, and as the seconds ticked past, Mallory decided they must have thought it was more important to get away from the scene.

That was the good news. The bad news was that there was no way Mallory could get back to that window, and her fingers were already starting to hurt. She tried shouting for help, but she could feel the beat of the music pounding through the walls, and the industrial buildings across the narrow stretch of water were dark. There was no one nearby to hear her, not even if she shouted herself hoarse. Help wouldn't be coming, so Mallory tried to figure out how to get out of this.

There weren't a lot of options. The sculpture felt strong enough, but it only went down another ten feet or so—not enough for her to get safely to the ground. But there was another window near the end of it, and it was open. If she could make it there, she might have a chance.

Mallory inched her way down to the end of the dragon, where it was supported by a bracket. At this end, the piece moved under her weight and creaked ominously.

The window was farther away than it had looked—at least four feet and slightly up. Mallory tried shouting again, in case someone might be there. But her voice vanished into the fog, and no shocked face appeared. So Mallory squinted her eyes shut, and then she opened them and judged the distance.

It was nearly the length of both her arms from where she was to the window, and once she let go with one hand, she wasn't sure she was going to be able to get it back. She had one shot to reach her goal, and she wasn't sure what was going to happen after that.

One chance is better than none, Mallory reminded herself.

She shifted herself back as far as she could, to get a head start on swinging. Letting her weight carry her forward, she let go with her right hand and reached. She was almost as surprised as relieved when her fingers caught on the frame, and in her shock, she nearly lost it. But with a last, terrified burst of strength, she pushed herself up with her toes on the wall and was able to get her hand all the way around the rough and splintered wood.

Her relief was short-lived. Mallory grasped at the window ledge, but she could only get enough purchase to hold herself steady—at this angle there was no way she could support her weight with one hand. She pressed her body against the masonry and tried to control her breath. Whatever she was going to do next, she needed to be calm.

The water didn't look any better than it had before, but Mallory didn't think she had any other options. She was steeling herself to try and jump out as far as possible, in hopes of hitting a deeper part, when a strong hand gripped her wrist.

"Hang on, honey. I've got you."

All Mallory could see of her rescuer was some long painted nails and an armload of bangles, but it looked like salvation to her. Supported by her right hand, she reached over with her left, which was grabbed by another pair. Together, they hoisted her through the window like she was as light as air and deposited her, trembling, on the floor.

"Okay, folks, give her some space. Honey, what happened? Are you okay?"

Mallory wanted to answer—she even thought of a snappy comeback. (*Oh, just hanging around.*) But all the panic she had been holding in since she felt that hand on her back came rushing over her, and her mouth wouldn't make the words. All she could do was to crouch on the ground, staring at the scraped and worn floorboards and willing the world to stop spinning around her.

A hand rested on her shoulder and patted it gently. "Take your time, hon. You were in some kind of trouble there, weren't you?"

The understatement was hilarious to Mallory, and her laugh came out as a strangled hiccup. But it was enough to shake her out of her shock and back to reality, and eventually her breathing became slower and more even, and she was able to raise her head.

"Thank you," she said. "Thank you for saving me. I don't know what I would have done if you hadn't been there."

"Of course, hon. That's what we're here for. Are you hurt?"

Slowly, Mallory's vision cleared, and she was able to get a better look at the people in the room. Her rescuer was a drag queen in full dress, with her face painted bone white, Kabuki-style lipstick, and eyebrows drawn in high black arches. She was dressed in a long sequined blue gown, and her wig was an improbably high pile of curls in a matching shade, adorned with a sailing ship on top.

Next to her, presumably the other person who had helped Mallory through the window, was another queen, shorter and not quite so resplendent, with her makeup partly done and her hair wrapped in a scarf. Behind them, two people dressed in coveralls who had been working on some sort of structure made out of old party supplies stopped to stare at her.

"I think I'm okay, actually," Mallory said. "Just a little shaken up. Or a lot, actually."

"That's not surprising." Her second savior came over to pat her shoulder and unsubtly checked her eyes in the light. "How did you end up out there? That's a hell of a wrong turn to take."

Mallory hesitated. Was she really going to tell these nice

people that she was investigating her friends for the murder of another one, and that she suspected they had just tried to kill her too? They already thought there might be something wrong with her, and she didn't blame them. But the last thing she wanted right now was to be taken to the police, to be released to the people she had come with.

"There was a guy," she said. "He was trying to talk to me out in the street, and when I turned him down, he followed me in here. I don't think he takes rejection well."

The queens gave each other knowing looks.

"*Men,*" said the first one, and that seemed to be all that needed to be said.

"Should I call security?" asked one of the artists.

Mallory was ready, and she shook her head. "I'd rather not, if that's okay? I just want this all to be over."

"I understand," her rescuer said. "The security guys here aren't that bad, but they're still the type, you know? Why don't you just rest up for a minute, and then we'll see about getting you home. I'm Donna VerSoChic, by the way. You can call me Donna. This is Bling Crosby," she said, indicating the other queen. "And our artistic friends are Sal and Noel."

She held out her hand, and Mallory shook it.

"Nice to meet you, Donna. I'm, um, Caitlin."

"My pleasure, Um Caitlin." Donna smiled, and it occurred to Mallory that she had better not press her luck with any more untruths.

35

Hoping to distract them from the question of her name, Mallory tried to figure out where she was. The room was smaller than any other space she had seen in the building, and though the music was still pounding through the walls, it was clear this was a place for preparation and creation. A salvaged mirror hung on one wall over a table laid with makeup and hairstyling tools, and the rest of the room was filled with art supplies, loosely defined. The air smelled of hair spray and hot glue.

"I didn't know this was here," she said. "Do you guys make the art in the club?"

"Some of it," said one of the overall-wearing people. "We take submissions from artists all over the city. And other places too. There's a really cool metal sculptors' collective in Vallejo and an artist in Alameda who does crazy dioramas."

Mallory thought of the smoke machine that had incapacitated her earlier. "Did they do the city scene on the third floor? Because the earthquake effect was cool, but the stuff that was being used for the fog…"

She didn't know how exactly to explain the problem without blaming the art for what happened to her, but it turned out she didn't need to.

"Oh god, that smoke machine," Donna said. "I swear, I don't care how pissy Craig gets; he's going to have to find something else."

"That might be a good idea," Mallory agreed.

It didn't escape her how surreal this situation was—discussing art with a group of strangers mere minutes after she had narrowly escaped certain death. In a way, the strangeness made it easier. Mallory wasn't sure if she could have navigated a "normal" social interaction at this moment, and her new friends had an approach to life that allowed for a lot of leeway in what they would accept without question.

But, speaking of friends, the longer she stayed in this building, the more danger she was likely to be in. Mallory tried standing up and found that though her legs were shaky, they would support her.

"I really appreciate what you all did, saving me," she said. "I really need to get out of here. I just, I think I've had enough for one night, you know?"

That last part was true. The way Mallory was feeling, she had had enough for at least a year. And she must have been convincing, because instead of insisting on the police or some other normal course of action, everyone just nodded in agreement.

"There's a private staircase just through here," Bling Crosby said. She got up from where she had been crouched next to Mallory, went over to the door, and looked out. "The coast is clear. This opens out on the other side of the building from the main entrance, so you should be fine."

It was the first time Mallory had tried to sneak out of a nightclub, but clearly she was among experts here.

"Do you have someone who can come pick you up?" Donna asked.

Mallory thought about that. Did she? Her immediate friend group was out, for obvious reasons. There were people she could think of asking in an emergency, like her coworkers or landlord, but even that felt risky. Plus, the obvious thing would be for them to take her home, and she couldn't do that. What Mallory needed was to disappear, at least for the rest of the night. In the morning, she would figure out her next steps, but right now she could only manage one thing at a time.

And that thing was to get as far as possible from the people who knew she was there.

So she said, "Not really. Since the earthquake, I've lost touch with everyone. I'm wondering if I should have come back at all."

"I get why you're saying that, but you're wrong." It was one of the people in artist coveralls, who had been silent until that point, speaking with urgency and determination.

"We have to come back," they went on. "The people are the city. Otherwise it's just a bunch of buildings. Corporations turning it into a tourist theme park. We've got to stay here, be weird, be whatever we are. Otherwise, what's the point?"

They had a glue gun in their hand and had been waving it for emphasis. Suddenly aware of what they were doing, they lowered it and looked sheepish.

"Anyway, that's what I think. I can walk you down to the street if you want. I probably need some fresh air. I think the glue fumes are getting to me." They went to the door and checked outside again before looking back to Mallory. "Are you sure you're okay to go now?"

"I think so." Mallory's legs were steadier, though her mind was still spinning. But someone in this building wanted to kill her, and that was the best reason to leave a party she ever had.

"I don't like just sending you out there," Donna said thoughtfully. "I know you don't want to talk to the cops, but we should at least change how you look a bit."

"Oh, god, Donna, not another one of your disguises," said Bling. "Remember what happened with the guy from the ferry?"

Donna looked mildly offended. "Well, why not? We have your old wigs here. What else are we going to do with them? And how was I supposed to know he was allergic to glue?"

In the end, they decided on a gray hoodie, which had been being used to prop up a paint palette. It smelled like weed and turpentine, and came down almost to Mallory's knees, but there was no denying that once she had it on with the hood up, she was unlikely to be recognized at a distance.

She turned to the queens and held out her hand. "Thank you again for saving me. I'd kiss you, but I don't want to ruin your makeup."

"Clever girl," said Donna, who took her hand and shook it, her rings pressing into Mallory's fingers. "I'd say you're welcome around here anytime, but I don't imagine you'll want to come back. Still, we'll keep an eye out for you."

"Thanks. I'm glad someone is."

—

The artist—Mallory was pretty sure it was Sal—led her down a set of stairs that looked like the ones she had recently left so dramatically. This one had no windows, though, for which Mallory was grateful.

"Have you been involved with the club for a long time?" she asked as they passed under flickering fluorescent lights.

"Since just after the earthquake, yeah. I had been working in a studio in the Mission, but our building was totally flattened. I don't have a lot of space for my art where I live, so I was really lucky that the collective here took me on." Somewhere deep in the building a sound system started playing "Gangnam Style," and Sal shrugged. "The club part was how they decided to fund it. We were having parties for our friends, but people kept showing up and wanting to get in, so it was like, these paints aren't free, you know? But it's kind of a thing now, and the crowd has gotten less cool. No offense."

"None taken. I think I met one of the least cool people on those other stairs."

Sal laughed and then shook their head. "Yeah, the dudebros have been a real problem. Up to now they've mostly just been wrecking the art, but some of us have been worried about violence for a while. It'll probably get brought up with the committee, but I don't know if they're going to do anything. I think they've gotten to like the money. Honestly, I don't like what it's done to the place we had. There's still good things, but if we're going to put up with stuff like that, what are we? I almost wish the whole thing had been a flop."

"Money is like that," Mallory agreed, thinking about the hardware key still hidden in the hem of her sweater. "You want it, but not what it can do to people. It brings out things you'd never have believed were possible."

Like pushing you out of a window, just to give a random example.

They came out into an alley next to the building and followed it to a major road, away from the front entrance. If anyone was looking for her, they wouldn't expect to see her here, and her disguise, as simple as it was, would be enough to keep her from being spotted by a casual observer. But the key was to get away as fast as possible, and that presented its own problems.

Her companion must have been thinking along the same lines.

"If you're going to call a rideshare, you probably want to go out a couple of blocks," Sal said. "There's always a crowd out front, and people get mixed up and take each other's rides."

Mallory looked around at the busy street, considering her options until a pair of headlights in the distance gave her an idea.

"The thing is, I'd really rather not hang out that long. I can catch the streetcar here and take it to somewhere I'll be safer. As long as there are a lot of people around, I should be okay."

It wasn't much of a plan, and Sal's face showed what they thought of it. But Mallory didn't give them any time to object—the streetcar was approaching the stop, and a large group dressed for a bachelorette party had gathered on the platform. So she thanked her new friend again and made a dash for it, slipping onto the car between two very drunk women in towering shoes and a put-upon looking guy carrying a blow-up doll.

Safely screened, she made it into a seat near the middle. The temptation to look back was great—to see if Sal had seen her go or to check the area for anyone she knew, but Mallory resisted. The last thing she wanted was to expose her face in the brightly lit windows.

She did sneak a look around at the other riders, enough to be sure she hadn't stumbled into a car with anyone who might recognize her. But her luck held out—none of the other passengers looked at all familiar or were paying her any attention. Perched on the edge of her seat, Mallory pulled the edges of her borrowed hoodie around her face. As she did, she noticed that her fingernails were cracked and torn, and the skin had been scraped off the tips of her fingers.

Her face was damp where she had touched it, and Mallory thought at first she was bleeding. But the truth was worse: She was crying.

36

Mallory fought to get herself under control, but it was hopeless. Fortunately, a crying woman on Muni at eleven p.m. wasn't something anyone paid attention to. So Mallory gave up and let go, wiping her filthy face with someone else's sweatshirt, until whatever was passing through her let go and moved on.

When she could finally think clearly, she tried to take in her situation. There was no avoiding it now—one of her friends had tried to kill her. Mallory didn't waste any time on alternate theories—she was done with trying to find comfort in lying to herself. She had pushed too hard, asked too many questions, and someone close to her had decided their life was going to be better if she wasn't around anymore.

Her first thought was that she had narrowed her four suspects down to two—Lourdes and Rachel. They were the ones who had been with her at the club, and either of them could have ensured she was left on her own and vulnerable and then followed her until they had an opportunity to strike. Logically, it made sense. But could she really eliminate the other two?

It would be easy enough for someone to text Lourdes and Rachel, or both, and ask what they were doing this evening—maybe even suggest meeting up at some point. She also knew that some of them had shared their locations from their phones with each other, something Mallory was too security conscious to do, even with her best friends.

She got that one right, at least.

And if it was more than one person working together, then the whole setup at the club could have been a trap. The truth was, it wasn't worth the risk to trust any of them. And maybe not worth it to trust anyone, period, until she had some more information and a plan. For now, that meant she was going to have to keep herself out of sight.

The streetcar she was on ran around the edge of the city, along the road that bordered the bay and went past the waterfront tourist traps. Unlike the iconic cable cars, which were still out of order, the route was mostly flat and had been repaired since the earthquake.

Not everything was back to normal, though. The progress of the streetcar was much slower than Mallory remembered, and the interior was covered with signs detailing route disruptions and schedule changes. Studying them, it was clear she was going to have trouble getting to any other part of the city at this time of night.

The bachelorette party got off at a waterfront hotel, and with them gone, the car was almost empty. Mallory knew if she hadn't been spotted by now, there was little chance she would be, but she didn't like the feeling of exposure. She pulled the hood closer around her face and leaned forward, staring at her hands.

By some miracle, her phone had survived her adventure. Mallory had turned off the location services as soon as she got on the streetcar—not that she thought anyone looking for her would have the technical knowledge to attack it, but she wasn't taking any chances. She didn't love the idea of having a device on her that tracked her every movement at the best of times, and right now it seemed like an unnecessary risk.

The obvious thing to do would be to get off and call a rideshare to take her home. But precisely because it was obvious, Mallory didn't want to do that. Right now, the thing that was keeping her the safest was that the person who pushed her out the window presumably didn't know she had survived, and as soon as she turned up somewhere she was expected to be, that would put her back in danger. But she also couldn't keep riding around on streetcars all night, and she didn't want to.

Inspiration came in the form of a lightbulb. Actually several hundred of them, making up the sign for the last tourist attraction on the route. Ghirardelli Square might have had its origins as a factory, but it had long ago been converted to stores and restaurants that no one who lived in the city went to. The one exception was the chocolate shop and ice cream parlor itself, which Mallory had visited several times, always when she had a visitor from out of town.

But as she remembered, it was open surprisingly late. And she couldn't think of anywhere she would be less likely to run into someone she knew.

Mallory had gotten off the streetcar and started up the steps to the shops before it occurred to her the hours might have changed or the place closed entirely since the earthquake. She was ready to feel dumb, but she had underestimated the power of the tourist economy. The ice cream parlor wasn't only open; there was a line at the register, where teenagers in brand-new San Francisco sweatshirts were comparing notes on their day and complaining about the summer cold.

That early supper had been a long time ago, so Mallory ordered a full-sized sundae. It came piled with whipped cream and nuts, topped with the traditional cherry of unnatural brightness. Mallory ate the first few bites without really tasting them, just let the sugar hit her system and waited for her brain to start working again.

Eventually her mind began to clear.

That wasn't entirely a good thing, because all Mallory could think about was which of her friends had just tried to kill her. While Rachel and Lourdes were the most obvious suspects, but they weren't the only ones. Mallory still had no idea why Sonali had reacted so strongly to her questions about Caitlin and what had happened at that dinner, and she hadn't heard anything at all from Kendra since they had found Charlie's body together. Either of them might have found out the plans for that evening, and tracked Mallory until they had a chance to put her out of the way.

It was an outrageous thing to think while eating ice cream, but her fall from the window had erased Mallory's ability to give anyone the benefit of the doubt. One of her friends was a murderer: What had been a terrible suspicion had become a certainty. And until she knew which one, she was going to be in danger.

37

Mallory had selected a table near the back where she could see most of the shop. Next to her, the display of chocolate-making equipment sat idle, and plywood stood in for several of the windows. The place had been designed with large crowds in mind, with multiple seating areas and a roped-off space where the line could wind past displays of chocolates. But between the late hour and the downturn in tourism, there were only a scattering of customers present that night.

That wasn't the only sign of the times. A whole section of the building had been closed off where the brick walls were perilously cracked, and Mallory noticed that one of their menu items, the Quake Shake, had been discontinued.

She was halfway done with her sundae before Mallory considered her next steps. She had already decided she wasn't going home that night, which meant a hotel was in her future. The places closest to where she was were a mix of outrageously expensive and sketchy (sometimes both), but there were plenty of them, and it wasn't hard to find one that could take a reservation at eleven o'clock for that same night.

She hesitated putting it on her credit card but reminded herself that it wasn't the CIA who was after her. Of all her friends, Mallory was probably the most technically capable and the one who shared the least of her personal information online. Still, she hated that she was leaving digital footprints everywhere she went.

She would have to go back to her apartment in the morning, if only to feed the cats. And unless her plan was to vanish entirely, she had to accept that her friends would find out soon that she was still alive. So it would be very helpful if she had some idea which of them she needed to be worried about.

There was one upside to the attack on her. If she was assuming it was related to Caitlin's death (and she was), then the person she was looking for was at the dinner before the earthquake, in her apartment two days later, and at the club tonight. As far as she knew, Lourdes and Rachel could fill all three of the requirements. But what about Kendra and Sonali?

Mallory had been worried about other people using her internet presence to find out where she was. Now, it was time for her to turn that around.

For now, Mallory decided to set aside the idea of a collaboration and tackle each of them individually. She started with the easy stuff. Kendra and Sonali were both active on social media, mainly Instagram for Sonali, while Kendra favored TikTok. Mallory already had a fake Instagram account she used to follow the reality TV stars she didn't want anyone to know about, so she started there.

It looked like Sonali had been telling the truth about dinner at her grandparents' house. Pictures had been posted less than an hour ago, showing her family all gathered around the table, with the samosas they had been making prominently displayed. Others had her nieces and nephews playing Wiffle ball in the yard, and there was a short video of a dog wearing a hat.

But the one Mallory was the most interested in was the final entry, a reel shot outside in the darkness. The camera pointed briefly at the sky, then back at Sonali's youngest nephew, wearing the sweatshirt Mallory had seen that afternoon in the apartment. He was pointing up excitedly and saying something Mallory couldn't quite make out. According to the caption, they were watching a meteor shower, and when she went back and expanded the image of the sky, she could see faint lines streaking across the darkness.

That was something she could work with. Mallory's sundae melted in its glass as she hunted for information. There had indeed been a meteor shower tonight, visible from Northern California starting at ten and going until moonrise at midnight.

Mallory sat back in the bent wood chair, almost dizzy with relief. Sonali's family lived in Tracy, a small city at the edge of one of the inland valleys. It was a place that had clear skies when San Francisco was socked in with fog, but more importantly than that, even with good traffic, it was more than an hour's drive away. Mallory didn't know the exact time she had been pushed out of the window, but she had looked at her watch soon after she was rescued, and it was just after ten thirty. There was no way Sonali could have gotten to the city, found the club, and tracked down Mallory in that time.

It was the most encouraging information she had learned all week, but Mallory wasn't going to act on it yet. She still thought her best chance was to not let anyone know she was safe, and even if Sonali wasn't a direct threat, there was still a risk that any information she had might reach someone who was.

As if to drive home the point, at that moment a text came through from Lourdes. Cursing herself for not having at least put her phone in airplane mode, Mallory left it unread and hoped that would be good enough. It would be possible to see that her phone was still on and receiving, but as long as she didn't open it, she didn't think she would give away that she was still alive, just that her phone was.

But she wasn't taking any more chances. Abandoning what was left of her melted ice cream, Mallory bussed her table and headed for the door. The ice cream parlor was about to close anyway, and she didn't want to make herself memorable by being the person they had to shoo out at midnight. Before she left, she double-checked the location of the hotel she had booked, then shut off all the connectivity functions on her phone.

It wasn't paranoia if someone was trying to kill you.

38

The hotel wasn't as bad as Mallory had been afraid it would be. The room was tiny and wildly overpriced, but it was clean, the hot water plentiful, and the Wi-Fi free and fast.

It was after midnight by the time Mallory checked in and got herself settled, but she wasn't ready to sleep. Having given herself some comfort about Sonali, her next task was checking Kendra's movements.

There, she didn't have any luck. There was no activity for the last two days on any of Kendra's accounts. Not just no posts, but no likes or comments either.

That didn't necessarily mean anything—Mallory had stayed offline for longer than that, for reasons that were no more sinister than needing to give her psyche some recovery time.

But it was worrying. Mallory reminded herself that Kendra had a husband, and he would be there if anything happened to her. And maybe Kendra's safety wasn't what she should be concerned about. There were other reasons why she might be staying out of touch right now, like if she was busy trying to find ways to get Mallory to stop investigating.

She had ended up on Facebook, a site she almost never visited, and while she was there, she checked on the others. None of her friends were Facebook users, and their pages offered little more than some long-ago Wordle scores for Lourdes and a picture Rachel had been tagged in at a work Christmas party. There was nothing since the quake, at least that Mallory could find without logging in.

There was no sign that Sonali had been on the site herself either, but her relatives didn't seem to mind that. They wrote regularly on her page, with all their posts set to public, sharing details of their lives and asking about hers. Mallory mostly regarded it with amusement, until she found a comment from a week after the earthquake.

She recognized the name as being one of Sonali's many aunts—not one of the ones who lived locally, Mallory thought. She had shared a drawing of a large-eyed child hugging a teddy bear with bandages around its head, and underneath it she had written "Thinking of YOU!! Get well soon!!!" That was followed up three days later with another comment: "We tried to call the hospital about you, but they wouldn't talk to us. Please call soon!!!!!"

Mallory set her phone down on the bed and lay back against the pillows. Sonali had been in the hospital? How had she not known?

There was nothing more on Sonali's page, and the rest of

her aunt's posts on her own page were focused on falling for various copy-and-paste hoaxes and wishing people happy birthday.

The screen blurred in front of Mallory's eyes. She hadn't slept well in a week, and she knew she needed to be rested for whatever would come next. But she just wanted to look at one more thing before she went to sleep.

It was something that had occurred to Mallory while she was riding the bus away from the club, listening to the bachelorette partiers drunkenly talking about their night. One of them had been talking about how she found out her boyfriend was cheating when she looked at his friend's Instagram and saw her boyfriend at a party with someone who wasn't her. Mallory didn't think she would get that lucky, but it did occur to her that the one person she hadn't really looked into so far was Charlie. However he had died, it seemed like he must have been connected to the other crimes in some way.

Plus, if there was one person she didn't have to worry about seeing her searches, it was him.

Twenty minutes later, her phone battery was down to 18 percent, and Mallory didn't know anything more than she had, except that her instincts had been right, and she should trust them more. Charlie had maintained a website, two Instagram profiles, and at least three TikTok accounts that she could find, all ostensibly focused on supporting his DJ career.

How well they did was an open question, with follower counts in the low double digits across all the platforms, but based on his activity (all public), there was no question where his real interests lay. Aspiring and famous singers and models, random twentysomethings selling skin care routines, obvious pornbots: If the profile picture was young, female, and attractive, Charlie could be counted on to like it and leave an admiring comment.

Mallory hardly needed to check to know the behavior went back to well before Deborah's death, though in a more low-key way. She supposed having a rich wife might make a man want to be more careful about how he was presenting himself online, but clearly, old habits died hard.

Even the earthquake hadn't dampened his enthusiasms. If anything, his flirting had gotten more obvious (and less welcome, if his complaints of being blocked by women he had DMed were to be believed). It was as if whatever he had been fearing was no longer relevant, and he felt free to behave however he wanted. That could have been a consequence of believing the police had too much to do after a disaster to bother with a death that had already been ruled accidental. But Mallory wondered if there was more to it, like he knew his stepdaughter wouldn't be around to press the case.

Uncomfortable, but no better informed, Mallory was about to log off when one of the comments caught her eye. She noticed it because it was one of the few male profiles Charlie had responded to. Unlike his other comments, there were no heart eyes or vegetable emojis, just a single question posted under a video by someone who called himself a "personal finance influencer."

> I have a question for you about tenancy rights. How do you know what items in a house belong to you if you have the right to live there? Does a judge have to decide if it's valuable?

There were no follow up questions, and no response from the influencer. Mallory drifted off to sleep wondering what it meant.

39

Morning brought its own problems. Mallory's fingers ached from where they had gripped the sculpture, her head was swimming with confusion and exhaustion, and her phone was almost out of battery.

And somewhere out there, one of her friends wanted her dead.

Mallory had left her car in a parking lot near the first bar, but even though it was probably in danger of being ticketed and towed, she wasn't going back to get it now. That left her with public transit and rideshares as her options, and she opted for the former. Not only because she was already thinking about how much it was going to cost her when she eventually did need to get her car back but, rational or not, she felt like she wanted to stay in busy public places for now. Mallory had always enjoyed the anonymity of a crowd; now she craved it.

The next question was where to go. After some thought, and serious misgivings, Mallory decided that she did just need to head home. It would be the end of the illusion that the attempt to kill her had been successful, but there was no way she was going to be able to maintain that for very long. And someone needed to feed the cats.

Not wanting to waste precious battery life looking up bus routes, Mallory tried to plan by memory, which was how she ended up going by the longest possible route. She was changing buses for the second time when she realized she was only two blocks from Sonali's old apartment. Curious, she interrupted her trip and crossed the street. She had heard about the destruction from Sonali, but she hadn't seen it for herself, and the question of the hospital stay was fresh in her mind.

It only took one look at the building where Sonali had been living to wipe out any doubts that her friend might have been badly injured. The block was made up of a row of attached apartment buildings, each with its own design. The entire front facade of the building next to Sonali's had collapsed, taking part of the fronts of each of its neighbors with it. There had been bay windows on either side of the facade—Mallory thought Sonali's apartment had been on the top floor on the left, which looked intact, but its matching pair on the right side had been wiped away, as had the ones on the lower level. The stairway that led to the front door was still barely passable, but rubble had tumbled down to block more than half of it.

And this was the state of it when renovations had already begun. At least, Mallory presumed they had—scaffolding covered the front of the building, and plastic tarps were draped over the holes, but if any repairs were underway, they weren't visible yet.

Mallory was trying to get a peek under the tarps when she realized she had company.

"Morning," said the old man. "See anything interesting?"

He had a paper coffee cup in one hand and was holding the leash for an elderly dog with the other, and his tone was conversational. Still, Mallory had a sudden urge to flee, as though she had thought she was invisible and had suddenly found herself seen.

Shrugging off her embarrassment, she smiled back at him. "My friend was living in this building when the earthquake happened. Do you think they're going to get it repaired? I think she'd like to move back, if she can."

"I don't blame her, this is a great little neighborhood," the man said. "But I don't think it's likely to be fixed soon. It doesn't look so bad from out here, but I heard there's a bunch of structural stuff they have to do inside. If it wasn't for the historic committees, this whole part of the block would probably be a teardown. I live across the street there, so you know, I'm hoping they get it opened sometime, however they do it. It's not the same around here with so many people gone. Which unit was your friend in?"

"The top one over there," Mallory said, pointing. "Her name is Sonali—did you know her?"

"The Indian girl? Sure, she'd always stop and give Dahlia a scratch if we ever met her out on a walk. I'm amazed she'd want to come back here after what happened. Poor kid, how's she recovering?"

Mallory swallowed hard. "She's doing really well, actually. If you didn't know, you'd never guess anything happened."

"That's good to hear. She gave all of us quite a scare, for sure."

"Can you tell me what actually happened? She doesn't like to talk about it."

"I can imagine. You see those stairs there?" He pointed to the partially blocked entry to the building. "That didn't happen right away. It was after the earthquake, with everyone evacuating the building, when there was an aftershock and a whole chunk of the wall came down. And your friend was the unlucky one who was coming out the door right then. A bunch of us saw it, and we got her out, which was good because the ambulance wasn't coming for anything. Finally, her friend came with her car and said she would take her to the hospital, and that's the last we saw of them. I'm glad it worked out okay."

"Me too," said Mallory, her head spinning. How had she not known? Sonali must have called someone—who was the friend who picked her up? And now that Mallory thought of it, how had she called? Phone service had been out for hours after the quake; it was days before it was possible to make a voice call. Sonali must have gotten lucky with a text that went through, but who had she sent it to?

It wasn't until she had said goodbye to the neighbor and found her next bus that another thought occurred to Mallory. If Sonali had been as badly hurt as he said, then there was no way she could have gotten to Caitlin, killed her, and dumped the body. Mallory had already been sure Sonali couldn't be the person who pushed her out of the window; now she had an alibi for the other key time.

As far as Mallory was concerned, that put Sonali out of the

running for being the person she was looking for. Which just left the question of why she had reacted so strongly to the idea of discussing what had happened at the dinner, but now Mallory was less afraid to ask directly.

Still, she hesitated. She had already considered the possibility that more than one of her friends was involved or that the killer could be working with a confederate. That would mean that even the most airtight alibi wasn't a guarantee of safety, and if she really believed it, she should stick to her approach of staying away from all of them, no matter what.

But did she really think that was what was going on? Every encounter she had with the presumed killer had been only one person, even when two might have been more effective (like the attempted bag snatching or any of the break-ins). Billy, the cat groomer, had remembered Caitlin talking about being advised by a friend, singular, and there was still the problem of how the coconspirators were supposed to have arranged all this through a total communications blackout—which would only have been harder if one of them was in the hospital.

And there was the general problem of having two friends who were willing to kill for money, not just one. And then where did Charlie come in? Would he have been having affairs with both of them? It would certainly explain why he was dead, but the theory stretched even her belief.

Balanced against that, Mallory had her current situation. She was alone, exhausted, and desperately short on information. Her most recent plan, to learn more by talking to each of her friends, had failed spectacularly, and she had no next step she could think of. Unless it was to take a chance and use the information she had to reach out to someone who might be able to help her.

Trusting anyone at this point was a risk. But it was an even bigger one to think she could keep going on her own.

She got off the bus at the next stop and caught one going the other direction, back to Sonali's apartment.

40

"Mallory? What are you doing here? Oh my god, you look terrible. What happened?"

It wasn't the best greeting, but understandable in the circumstances.

"Lots of things, actually," Mallory said. "Can I come in?"

"Um." Sonali was holding the door partway open, blocking it with her body, and she seemed reluctant to move. Mallory was starting to second-guess her confidence that she wasn't in danger here when another voice came from inside.

"Babe? What's going on? Who's here?"

Mallory had similar questions. But she didn't ask, just waited while Sonali went through an internal struggle and finally opened the door the rest of the way.

"Okay, you might as well come in. Isn't that what you were wearing yesterday? What is even going on with you?"

"You aren't going to believe me, but I think I need to explain."

Sonali gave her a funny look, but she led Mallory into the

living room, where a woman was sitting on the sofa, a spoon in her hand and a bowl balanced on her knee.

"Mallory, this is Kate. Kate, Mallory."

"We've met," said Mallory. "Nice to see you again, Kate."

What the waitress from the restaurant where they had met for dinner was doing in Sonali's living room at nine in the morning, Mallory couldn't quite understand. She could come up with a few guesses, of course, but all of them required some adjustments in her thinking.

Kate, at least, seemed more amused than uncomfortable.

"Nice to see you too." She cast an appraising eye over Mallory's distressed appearance. "Do you guys need to talk about something private? I can find somewhere else to be for a bit."

Mallory shook her head. "You might as well hang around. It'll save Sonali time telling you later about how one of her friends went crazy. Plus, you've already heard some of it."

Sonali had been looking back and forth between them with increasing confusion. "How do you guys know each other? Did someone tell you about us?"

"Mallory came into the restaurant yesterday," Kate said. "She had some questions about the dinner you all had there the night of the earthquake. Nothing about us, though."

And that settled one of the things Mallory was wondering, though it was low enough on the list that she was happy to leave it aside for the time being.

"Yes and yes. I'll get to all of that in a second, but one quick question first—has anyone gotten in touch to ask if you've seen me?"

"Asking me?" asked Sonali. "No, why?"

"Long story. Anyway, if you get any calls, just pretend you never met me, okay?"

"Mallory, what the hell is going on?" Sonali turned to Kate, looking apologetic. "Seriously, this is not usually how things are with me."

"That's true; she's very undramatic," Mallory offered. "This is a real outlier."

Kate laughed. "Are you kidding? I'm loving it all. Come on, you've teased us long enough. Get to the good stuff. What's the big mystery about that dinner? Why is everyone looking for something that's supposed to be in the restaurant?"

Mallory took a deep breath. "Because at the current price of Bitcoin, it's worth around six million dollars, give or take. And it's not in the restaurant. I've got it."

Mallory had never stunned a room into silence before. She took a second to enjoy the sensation before continuing.

"Bear with me. It all started that night at dinner, my part of it at least."

She told them about talking with Caitlin in the bathroom, the lipstick and how she forgot about it, the break-ins at her apartment after the earthquake, and the attempted robbery on the street. When she got to the part where she opened the lipstick and found the hardware key, Sonali interrupted her.

"Was that the thing you told us about? The one you sent to your aunt?"

"Right, that was it." Mallory was as sure as she could be at this point that Sonali wasn't a danger to her, but some secrets were best kept. "I didn't know what it was at the time, but later when I was looking into Caitlin's mom's life, I found out she bought a lot of Bitcoin early on. Those can be stored in electronic wallets that use a key like the one I found, so my guess is that's what it was. Someone has the rest of the wallet, but without that key, they can't get to the money. And it would be a lot of money."

"Why do you think your friend gave it to you? Did she know she was in danger?" Kate asked.

"I don't know. She may have started to suspect something, and I was the first person she found. She must have had it with her that night for a reason. I think she was going to give it to someone at that table, someone who convinced her they were on her side. But during the dinner, Caitlin realized that wasn't true. She needed to get the key away, so she handed it to me. I can only guess at her plans for after that, but whatever they were, the earthquake must have disrupted them."

"Wait a minute," Sonali said. "Are you saying one of our friends was...was involved in what happened to Caitlin?"

She couldn't bring herself to say "murder," and Mallory didn't blame her. It had taken her a long time to get around it too.

"What other reason would she have to change her mind in the middle of the dinner? And how else would someone know to break into my house to look for the key? It would have to be someone who was there, who knew I was the only person who had been alone with her."

"That's completely wild," said Kate. "So you think that's what the person who called asking if anything had been left at the restaurant was about?"

"And possibly the break-in too. After all, they wouldn't know for sure I had it. Caitlin might have hidden it somewhere and planned to come back for it. They committed at least one murder for that money; they would be bound to try everything to find it."

"At least one?" Kate asked. Sonali hadn't spoken for the last few minutes and looked confused and lost in thought. Mallory could understand that.

"Caitlin's mother died last year," she explained. "It was ruled an accident, but with everything that's happened since..."

"Got it. Wow. So this friend of hers kills her mom, steals part of the money thing, and then kills her to get the other part. Except you had it, so they went looking. That's all pretty crazy." Kate sounded impressed but less skeptical than Mallory would have expected. She wondered if the life of a waitress made someone more willing to accept the strangeness of people.

"There were six people at that table, right?" she went on. "Two of you are here, and one is dead. So that leaves the other three."

"Kendra, Lourdes, and Rachel," Sonali said automatically, like someone coming out of a dream. "But somehow you know it wasn't me—why?"

"I didn't for a while, and you really made it hard the way you were acting. By the way, when were you planning to tell people about how you ended up in the hospital?"

"What? How did you find out?"

"Never mind that; are you okay? And, I mean, what the hell?"

Sonali looked at Kate, then back at Mallory, then down to the floor.

"I guess it's time for me to do some storytelling too. So, um, Kate and I had just started dating that week. And when we decided on the restaurant, I didn't realize it was the place where she worked. So I was kind of freaking out about that, and I didn't handle it very well. Then the earthquake happened, and I got hurt and, well..." Sonali glanced at Kate, and Mallory thought she was starting to get the picture.

"Your neighbor mentioned a 'friend' who took you to the hospital. Is that why you didn't tell us about it? Because you didn't want us to know you were dating someone?"

Mallory almost said *know you were dating a woman*, but she bit her tongue. As far as she knew, Sonali's dating history had been exclusively with men. But she wasn't sure how much Kate knew, and she didn't want to be the one to say it.

Apparently, she needn't have worried.

"I know it was the wrong thing to do," said Sonali. "I was going to tell you all at dinner, but with Kate being there, it was too weird. Then she was coming over later, and I was thinking about how to try and explain to her, when I had the accident. And after that, it was all so terrible, trying to go to the hospital and seeing the people who were there, I didn't want to talk about it at all. But the longer it went, the weirder it all got. That's why I was so mad at you yesterday, when you kept wanting to talk about dinner. I didn't know how to tell you anything without telling everything."

"And you have to understand how that looked to me, when I'm thinking there are four people at that table who could have killed Caitlin. It wasn't until I found out about you getting hurt that I knew it wasn't you, which is why I'm here. Actually, there was one more thing, which I'll get to in a minute. But you have to see how I was suspicious."

Kate shook her head in disbelief. "Did you seriously freak out so much about us that one of your friends thought you were a murderer? I knew you were having some issues coming out, but that's a new one for me."

Sonali squirmed and looked to Mallory for help, but she had none to offer.

"I'm sorry," Sonali said, addressing both of them. "I thought I had a handle on everything, but stuff kept happening, and it all spiraled out of control. But I told my family last night, and they were better about it than I thought they would be. I guess I need to learn to trust people more."

"That's okay," said Mallory. "Lately I've been thinking about trusting less. As much as I was convinced it had to be one of us who killed Caitlin, I never really believed it, and that's what got me in trouble last night."

"Was that the other thing you mentioned? About why you knew it wasn't me?"

"Yes, it was." Mallory took a deep breath. "I went out with Lourdes and Rachel last night. We were at a nightclub in SoMa, and we got separated. And then somebody pushed me out of a window. I saw that you were at your grandma's house when it happened, so that gives you a double alibi."

"Wait, what? Who pushed you?" Sonali had been sitting on the sofa next to Kate, and she got up to come over to Mallory's chair to examine her hands. "Is that how this happened? Your nails are completely wrecked."

"You ever hear someone say they're hanging on by their fingertips? That was pretty much me. I can tell you the whole story another time, so let's just say I had some good luck. But I didn't see who pushed me. I think they must have just shoved and ran. Which is why I asked you not to tell anyone that I'm here."

Sonali let go of her hand and looked Mallory in the eye. "I know it's how you're coping, but you need to stop making jokes about this. What you're telling us is crazy and terrible, and if I'm going to take it seriously, then I need to get it from you."

Mallory's instinct was to argue, but she stopped herself. "You're right, I'm sorry. I don't want any of this to be real, but it is. I've been trying to find the person who killed Caitlin for her sake, but after what happened last night, I think I must be getting too close for someone's comfort."

"And it was one of those two people you were with who did it?" Kate said.

"It could have been. But I also haven't heard anything from Kendra for a couple of days. Not since we found Charlie's body together. She left while I was talking to the police, and that was the last I saw of her."

This time it was Kate who broke out laughing.

"I'm sorry. I know we just said this wasn't a joke," she said when she had gathered herself. "It's just, you wouldn't believe how many times Sonali has told me how ordinary and boring her friends are, and then here you turn up with murders all over the place, and falling out of windows, and missing millions, and it's just, like, Sunday morning. If this is boring, I don't want to know what exciting is like."

"I don't either," said Sonali. "I'm still trying to get my head around it. Going back to the beginning—why did Caitlin have the key in the lipstick with her in the first place?"

"I don't know, but I think the killer might have convinced her she had something to fear from her stepfather." Mallory told them about what she had learned from the cat groomer, about how Caitlin had a friend who was advising her about something important. "If the other part of the hardware wallet was already missing, Caitlin might have been convinced she had to get the key out of the house so Charlie couldn't steal it too. I just wish she had told someone who was giving her the advice."

"Too bad she didn't have a diary. I kept one when I was a teenager, and that's exactly the sort of thing I would have written in it," Kate said.

Sonali turned to her, her eyes wide with surprise. "But she did! I can't believe I forgot that. I'm not sure how many people even knew about it. I only found out because our book club went on a retreat, and she and I were driving together, and we had to go back because she had left it under her mattress. I guess that was where she always kept it at home, so she did it out of force of habit, then forgot it when she was packing. She said she had been keeping it since she was a kid. It was something she picked up from her mother. It seemed like it was pretty important to her."

41

Mallory didn't stay long at Sonali's apartment. She could have—it would almost certainly have been safer than what she was going to do next. But she had done what she had needed to, which was to make sure that someone else knew the whole story of what had happened since the earthquake. She was sure enough now that Sonali didn't have anything to do with it, and even more confident about Kate. If her plans didn't work out, she was going to need someone who was able and willing to tell the story to the police, no matter how unlikely it sounded.

Because at this point, Mallory saw three options. She could pack up the cats, leave the key on the kitchen table, run away, and hope whoever took it didn't use their millions to hunt her down. She could try to keep going about her normal life and hope that if she stopped being a threat, she would be left alone, and so would her aunt, the key's fictional custodian. Or she could keep going, taking what she did know about her opponent and finding out more, until one or the other of them had their luck run out.

They weren't great choices, but it wasn't really a question. Mallory had already made her decision.

Her first stop was back at her apartment. It wasn't the safest place Mallory could be—in some ways it might have been the most dangerous. Her attacker must have known by now that no body had been found behind the club, and this was the first place they would expect her to turn up. There was no one obviously watching as she walked from the bus stop to her gate, but they wouldn't need to be. Between the cars parked on both sides of the street, the sheltered stairways to the empty buildings, and the debris of ongoing construction, Mallory could have searched for an hour and not found every possible hiding spot.

Or there might have been no one there at all. Either way, it didn't matter. Until and unless her plans worked out, Mallory would be in danger; the exact degree and direction it came from was unimportant.

The apartment was exactly as Mallory had left it, with the exception of some damage that could only have been done by very angry cats. She gathered up the ornaments that had been knocked off the top of the bookshelf and threw some paper towels over the puddle in the middle of the living room before going to fill the empty food bowls and distributing a peace offering of treats. She tried to pick up Celine and hold her in her lap for a minute, but the cat had no interest in sentiment and meowed until Mallory released her to go back to sharpening her claws on the scratching post.

"Yeah, well, you'll be sorry if I don't come back," Mallory said, and she was oddly comforted by knowing that wasn't true.

Her next task was to find an appropriate outfit for what she was planning. That wasn't hard—most of Mallory's wardrobe would have fit the bill. She settled on a not-too-new oxford shirt and some faded khakis and supplemented them with the gardening gloves she had bought when she thought she was going to get into houseplants. She could have used some other accessories, but this would have to do for now.

She was just coming out of the bedroom when there was a knock on her door. Mallory froze. She had locked the gate behind her and double-checked the new hinges for signs of damage or manipulation. If anyone had gotten in, they only could have done it if they had gotten her key.

"Mal? Are you home? I thought I heard you running the water."

Or if they were her landlady, coming down the back stairs from her own home. Mallory stuffed the gloves into her pocket and went to answer the door.

"Hi, Joan. What's up?"

"Oh, not much. I hadn't seen you around for a bit so I thought I'd check in. Also, one of your friends stopped by, wanting to see you."

"Oh, really? Who was it?" Mallory tried to sound casual, but there was a hitch in her voice. It didn't necessarily mean anything—someone who was genuinely worried about her might have contacted her landlady when Mallory vanished from a nightclub and stopped answering her phone.

But in fact, it was none of the above.

"Harry, that guy from across the street. He said he found some more camera footage to show you and asked me to tell you to drop by anytime if you want to see it. By the way, if you need any help filing a police report, just let me know. I'm not exactly friends with the cops around here, but I think they take you more seriously if you're a homeowner."

"Thanks, I appreciate that." Mariah came to wind herself around their ankles, and it suddenly occurred to Mallory that she hadn't mentioned to Joan that she'd added a third cat to her household. Between that, and the fact that she was acutely aware of the mess on the floor that she still hadn't cleaned up, she tried to steer the conversation to a conclusion.

"I should go see him and find out what it's about. Did he say if he got a good look at their face?"

"No, but what good would that do anyway? Unless—do you think you could use one of those AI tools that can find a person anywhere? I've been worried about those myself. There are probably some pictures around that I wouldn't want to be seen in!"

She laughed and Mallory joined in. There was no point in saying she expected to be able to identify the perpetrator the old-fashioned way: by having it be someone she knew.

—

"Hi, is Harry here? I'm Mallory, from across the street."

Harry's mother had answered the door, and Mallory felt like she was going over to a friend's house, asking if he could play. An oddly childish image, considering what she was here for.

The woman, who introduced herself as Lianne, left Mallory in the exquisitely clean living room and went to find her son. He was there within minutes, before Mallory even had a chance to sneak a look at more than a couple of the vinyl records on the shelf (Bartók and Garth Brooks, for variety).

"Thanks for coming by. I tried to leave you a message, but I couldn't get through."

"Yeah, my phone's been having trouble lately. What's up? Did you get a better image of my home invader?"

"Not exactly. But I did find something else I thought was interesting." Harry had come in with a laptop tucked under his arm, which he set up on a sideboard and opened the video player.

"I've been looking for other people in the neighborhood who have cameras that might have caught something. Haven't found any that were working that soon after the earthquake, but I was talking to the people in the house on the opposite corner from you a couple of weeks ago, and they said they were getting one. Then this morning I heard from them, and look what they found."

He hit Play, and the screen blinked on with the familiar sight of Mallory's block. The camera was pointed at the sidewalk, but the side of Joan's house and the door to the back garden were clearly visible in the background. Based on the time stamp, it was early in the morning, and the street was empty. Then a car drove up, parking right in front of the camera, and someone got out.

This time, there was no problem seeing the person's face. It was Kendra, looking tired and worried, her hair limp and damp, like she had just stepped out of the shower and gotten into the car without drying it. She didn't appear to notice the camera, just crossed the street directly to Mallory's gate.

Kendra rang the bell, waited for a few minutes, then rang it again. Then she fished around in her bag, pulled out a pen and a piece of paper, and quickly wrote something before folding it and slipping it under the gate. She rang the bell one more time, and looked up and down the street, before crossing back to her car and driving away.

"That's really interesting," Mallory said. "I didn't see anything when I came in. I should go back and look."

"Wait, that's not all," said Harry. He hit the Fast-Forward button, skipping ahead five or ten minutes in the recording before going back to regular speed. "Now watch what happens next."

At first, it was nothing. A car passed, and a bird fluttered down to the curb before flying away. Then a person came into view on the other side of the street, walking with an exaggerated casualness. Unlike Kendra, their face was obscured, hidden behind a sweatshirt hood and sunglasses that were out of place in the foggy morning light.

The new person didn't look around but acted like they had dropped something in front of Mallory's gate. When they stood up, Mallory could see them tucking something white into their pocket.

She hoped to get a glimpse of the person's face when they turned around, but they kept walking and vanished from the frame without looking back.

Harry stopped the recording and looked at Mallory.

"You're right," she said. "That was interesting."

"What do you think it was about?" Harry asked.

"I don't know," Mallory said slowly, but she was starting to have some ideas. "I was away with my phone off last night, so the first person might have left the note when they couldn't reach me."

"And the second person?"

"I guess they wanted to see what was in the note."

Mallory looked at her watch. The security camera footage was from just after five a.m.; it was almost eleven now. If anything was going to have happened as a result of what she had seen, it already would have. All she could do at this point was to stick to her original plan and hope it turned up the information she needed.

She turned to Harry. "Thanks a lot for sharing this with me. If you come up with anything else, can you let me know? I can stop by again later, but right now I need to get going."

"Going where?"

Mallory hesitated. At this point, was there any real reason not to tell? And if something went wrong… "All these break-ins and stuff, I think they have to do with a friend of mine who died during the earthquake. I need to go to her house and search for something. If I'm lucky it'll have the key to all of what's been going on."

"Are you sure that's safe?" Harry asked.

"Not at all. But look at this." Mallory gestured at the screen. "People are coming here, to where I live. Nothing is going to be safe until I put this whole thing to bed."

She expected him to respond with protests and dire warnings, but Harry just nodded thoughtfully.

“Hang on a sec,” he said. “I’ve got something that might help.”

He was only gone for a couple of minutes, and when he came back, he was carrying a plastic case and a belt bag. He set the case down on the table and opened it. Inside was a chunky black and yellow device that looked like a ray gun from a retro sci-fi movie.

“It’s a Taser,” Harry explained. “I bought it after the quake, when my grandma insisted on going across the city to do her shopping. She said it was too heavy, and she wouldn’t carry it, so it’s still all charged up. I practiced with it a little; it’s not hard to use. You just really want to make sure you aren’t touching the probes when you pull the trigger.”

He showed her how to pack it away in the carrier, which Mallory looped over her shoulder. It was hardly subtle, but she felt better knowing she wouldn’t be facing whatever was to come unarmed.

“Thanks,” she said. “I’ll try to bring it back in good shape.”

“Don’t worry about it. These things are meant to be used, right? I just wish there was more I could do to help,” Harry said.

Mallory thought for a moment. “Actually, there is. When you were out after the quake, you had a vest and a hard hat, right? Would it be okay if I borrowed them too?”

42

Mallory had planned to leave directly after her visit with Harry, but what he had shown her threw her plans into question. She went back and checked the area around the gate, just in case there was something the second visitor had missed. There was nothing, and she was left with a choice. Did she continue with what she was going to do, or look for Kendra and try to find out what was in that note?

There were a couple of problems with the second course of action. To start with, she wasn't sure where to find Kendra if she wasn't at her home. And what would happen if she did? There were three people left who could have pushed Mallory out of the window, and Kendra was one of them. It was unlikely she would have expected Mallory to see her on the security footage, but if the note had reached her, that wouldn't have been necessary.

Mallory was inclined to see the second intruder as malicious, but what if it was the other way around? The note could have been meant to draw her into a trap, and they might have stolen it to keep her from falling into it.

The truth was, she had no way of knowing. But she couldn't let it go at that. If it had been genuine, what had Kendra wanted to tell her that was so important? And what did it mean that someone else had gotten to that note before Mallory did?

Mallory wasn't going to be able to find it out on her own. Fortunately, she didn't have to do everything on her own.

"Hi, Sonali? Listen, I need to ask you a favor. Can you check in on Kendra for me? Don't tell her I asked; just find out if she's okay. Maybe see if she wants to do brunch or something? She loves brunch. Anyway, maybe it's nothing, but I'm worried. Yeah, if you can't reach her, I'd go over. Her husband might know what she's up to. Thanks. I'll explain later. I've got to go."

—

Her car was still racking up time in a downtown parking garage, and the bus options to Caitlin's neighborhood weren't great, so Mallory took the chance of turning the location back on on her phone and called a rideshare. She gave it an address a block away from her destination and spent the ride going over what she was planning.

She put on the vest and hard hat before she got out of the car, and let the driver think whatever he wanted about that.

It was the middle of a summer Sunday, but the neighborhood sat silent, like the people who lived here paid too much to put up with noise. Even given that, Caitlin's house was noticeably vacant, with construction debris in the overgrown front yard, new plywood covering one of the front windows, and a fresh warning notice stuck to the door.

Mallory had a moment of fear that her planned entrance point would have been closed off, but she willed herself to approach with confidence. With the hat and vest and a clipboard she had dug out of her closet, her hope was that she looked like another city employee, here to survey a damaged house. The last thing she wanted right now was one of the neighbors calling the police to report a vagrant breaking in.

Well, maybe not the last thing.

Unlike her previous visits, Mallory didn't approach the front door. That was unlikely to work now, and it was too exposed to the street. But she remembered noticing some damage to the doors in the room where Charlie had died. That was her destination, and she hoped they hadn't been fixed yet.

She was in luck. Whoever was doing the work on the house must not have been very thorough, because the only repairs to the door were a sheet of plastic taped over the broken panes of glass and two screws angled in on either side of the broken latch. Mallory made short work of those with the screwdriver she had tucked into the pocket in her vest, and the door was open.

The room looked like it had the last time she had been in it, minus one body. Mallory tried not to look at the sofa where he had been lying, but she didn't manage to avoid seeing the dark pool, now completely dry, that spread across the floor. She moved quickly past it; there was little chance that what she was looking for was in this room.

She skipped the kitchen and the living room as well. None of the public spaces in the house seemed like good places for Caitlin to hide her diary, and that was what Mallory was looking for.

It was a long shot, of course. Caitlin had been dead for over six months now, and her stepfather had had the run of the house since then, and possibly her killer as well. If there was anything to find here, they probably would have found it, and Mallory was taking this risk for nothing. But Sonali saying Caitlin treated her diary like a secret gave her hope, and that was enough. A diary would almost certainly have information about who had convinced Caitlin to hand off the key—if not a name, at least enough information that Mallory would be able to figure it out.

If that diary was here, she was determined to find it.

Her first stop would be Caitlin's bedroom. Sonali had said Caitlin kept her diary under her mattress, so that was the obvious place to look.

There were two staircases leading up, one on either side of the door to the sunroom. The one on the right had more obvious damage, and thinking of the cracks in the kitchen wall, which was directly below it, Mallory chose the stairs on the left.

It was clear pretty quickly that she had chosen wrong, at least as far as finding Caitlin's bedroom went. Mallory remembered what Kendra had said, about the house being divided into two wings, and there was no question this one had belonged to Deborah.

It had been a while since Caitlin's mom had been there, obviously, and Charlie had taken over the space in the meantime. A large flat-screen television had been set up in the middle of the room, with a chair in front of it and video game paraphernalia around it, and men's clothes were draped over every surface. (Mallory did a quick check—if Charlie had any female guests while he was living alone, they hadn't kept anything here.) The bed was unmade, and without looking too closely, Mallory didn't think the sheets had been washed recently.

But Mallory didn't imagine Charlie had anything to do with the Persian rugs on the floor or the packed bookshelves that lined the walls. The furniture also had a distinctly feminine feeling to it—all curved blond wood and soft cushions, in contrast to the black-leather functionality of the gaming chair.

This room wasn't her intended destination, but Mallory lingered, looking around. She had spent the last week examining Deborah's life from the outside, but now here she was, in the heart of her home. There was a cushioned seat in a window nook surrounded by bookshelves—exactly the sort of thing Mallory would have had in her room if she was able to design whatever she wanted.

The view out of the window was of the Golden Gate Bridge, of course. Mallory took a moment to admire it, and then her gaze strayed to the floor where she was standing. There was a line between her feet, and after staring at it for a minute, she realized it was where something had been covering the hardwood and then been removed, leaving a border between the faded and new finish on floor. There had been an area rug here, Mallory realized.

There were three doors in the bedroom: the one she had come through from the hallway, a folding set to a walk-in closet, and a grand pair that opened to a huge slate-tiled bathroom. Inside was a shower with three different heads, a sleek black tub with a dizzying array of nozzles and a panel on the side for temperature settings, double sinks with lights around the mirrors, and a separate toilet cubicle that was almost as big as Mallory's entire bathroom. Here, again, there were signs of Deborah's taste and Charlie's occupancy, with the tub used for storage of empty shampoo bottles and a selection of body sprays on the marble and gold vanity.

Mallory checked the drawers, in case there was another lipstick tube like the one that had made its way to her, but there were none, only drawers with the residual scents of perfume and powder. The only thing in any of them was an old charger with a style of connector that Mallory didn't recognize, large, flat, and awkward.

Looking for the lipstick gave Mallory another idea. Sonali had said Caitlin got the idea to keep a journal from her mother. What if that was still here?

It was even more of a long shot than the chance of finding Caitlin's diary—Deborah had been dead for almost a year, and her belongings had obviously been cleared out. But there was a chance that it might have been hidden or overlooked, and right now Mallory was trying whatever she could.

Back at the bookshelves, Mallory considered the possibilities. She had chosen this as the first place to look, on the theory that the best place to hide a leaf was in a forest, and also because Charlie didn't strike her as a big reader. The shelves were built into the walls, and from the way they coordinated with the furniture,

Mallory assumed they had been a custom job. That left open the possibility of secret compartments, which was where she started, running her fingers under the shelves and along the sides.

On the third shelf she tried, she hit a tiny lever, which popped open a drawer. But it was empty, and from the stiff way it opened, Mallory wasn't sure it had ever been used.

She went on, but something about the approach felt wrong. A diary was something you wrote in every day—the fussiness of constantly opening a compartment to store it would get old fast. Plus, the odds of someone seeing you access it grew with every use.

Mallory had never met Deborah, but in a strange way, she felt like she knew her. Caitlin's mother might have had these shelves built with the idea she would hide things in them, but the impracticality of it would have become clear.

Forcing herself to look past her doubts, Mallory leaned into her instincts. What else did she know about Deborah? That she had been a software engineer, someone who came to the profession later in life and had achieved great success. Someone who was enthusiastic about new technologies, and probably pretty pleased with herself for her good bet on those Bitcoins. And someone who had wanted to record her life but wanted to keep her thoughts under her control.

And, based on the name of her band, someone with a fairly simple sense of humor.

Mallory stepped back and looked at the bookshelves. There was an ominous creaking noise from downstairs, but she ignored it. The house had stayed standing for this long; surely it could handle another day.

"Since when have I had any bad luck?" she murmured to herself, as her gaze settled on a book on the bottom shelf.

Maybe it was the title, or the way the binding didn't look quite right. But when Mallory took the copy of *Bridget Jones's Diary* off the bottom shelf and opened it, she wasn't surprised that the pages inside had been cut away, creating a hollow where an old PalmPilot had been hidden.

The ancient technology seemed like an odd choice at first, but as Mallory tucked it into her pocket, she thought she saw the reasoning. After all, you couldn't hack something that had no connection to the internet. It was the same thinking that would have been behind Deborah storing her funds in the cold wallet. The woman was nothing if not consistent.

Mallory would have loved to go through the contents of the device, but she had already been here for half an hour, and she hadn't even started to look for what she came for.

So she went back down to the living room and to the second staircase. She had just started up it when she heard footsteps. Assuming she had been caught, Mallory turned to face the music. At least if she got arrested, she would be safe.

But there was no wall of angry police waiting for her at the base of the stairs. Just one familiar face.

"Oh, hi, Rachel. What are you doing here?"

Rachel laughed, easy and relaxed. "I was about to ask you the same thing."

Caitlin

When she woke up, the house was dark, and her head was throbbing. Caitlin tried to stand, but dizziness and nausea washed over her, and she crumpled back on the floor. Where was she? What happened? She opened her eyes again and realized she was lying on one of the area rugs in her mother's bedroom, the one by the window. Why had she come in here? How had she fallen down?

Slowly, bits of the evening came back to her. She had gone out somewhere, and something had happened. Looking down, she noticed she was wearing her green coatdress and boots. She must have been home for a while—why hadn't she changed her clothes?

Caitlin had a sense there was something urgent she needed to do, but she couldn't remember what.

After a little more time, she was able to pull herself up and onto the window seat. The night was clear, but there was something wrong with the view, and it took her a minute to figure out what it was. The bridge should have had its lights on, but it was dark. Everything was dark—the houses on either side of her, the buildings on the peninsula across the bay. Caitlin realized she could hear sirens, and there was a smell of gas in the air.

She found her phone in her pocket and tried to look up what was going on, but she had no signal, and the Wi-Fi was down. It wasn't clear how long that had been—the last text Caitlin had was from one of the girls at the dinner saying she was running late.

Dinner. That was important. What had happened at dinner?

Something kept telling her she needed to leave, but standing was still too hard. She sank back on the window seat, her pulse pounding in her ears, and tried her phone again. Going through the texts about the dinner, details began coming back. There had been five of them, plus her. Kendra, Rachel, Sonali, Lourdes, and Mallory. The list of names pinged something in her memory, but she couldn't quite grasp it.

Nothing in the messages gave her a clue. Just some back and forth about times and restaurants, a joke between Mallory and Lourdes about cilantro. Caitlin remembered that—she had been relieved that she wasn't the only one who didn't like the stuff. She didn't know Mallory very well, but that had made her want to like her. Was that what it was, a new friend? There was something there, but that wasn't quite it.

Her heartbeat was so loud that Caitlin felt like she could barely hear anything else. Sometimes it sounded like the house shifting; other times she thought she heard footsteps approaching. She sat back and took deep breaths like her therapist taught her, trying to get herself to a calm place. Right now what was important was that she had a head injury and needed to get help. Whatever she was trying to remember could wait.

There was another sound, and this time Caitlin was sure it really was footsteps. A cloud had moved across the moon, cutting off her only source of light, but it drifted on, and she was able to see a figure on the other side of the room.

"Who's there?" Caitlin asked. "Charlie, if that's you, this isn't funny."

"It's not Charlie," said the person. "I just wanted to see if you were okay."

"Rachel? What are you doing here?"

Rachel came forward, crossing the bedroom until she was visible in the moonlight.

"I wanted to see if you were okay," she repeated. "There was an earthquake. Are you hurt?"

"I fell. I think I hit my head." Something was wrong here; Caitlin was sure of it. But her memory was so fuzzy—she needed time to think. "Was it a big earthquake?" she asked.

"Pretty big. The power is out all over the city. I think a lot of buildings fell down."

"Oh, wow." That made some things make sense to Caitlin, but not others. "But why are you here? It's the middle of the night."

"Actually, I was on my way over already. I wanted to talk to you. What happened at dinner?"

Caitlin scrunched up her forehead in concentration. That was what she had been trying to remember. But for some reason she didn't want to tell Rachel that.

"I don't know. Everything's kind of fuzzy," she said.

"You were going to give me the key, remember? Do you still have it?"

"No, I—" And suddenly Caitlin did remember. Not everything, but enough. Enough to know why she had felt the need to get away, and why she wasn't happy to have her friend in the room with her.

"I don't have it anymore. I think I, um, I must have left it at the restaurant."

Rachel advanced toward her, smiling and holding the heavy brass Buddha statue from the table by the door. "That was a really careless thing to do with something so valuable. Why would you do that?"

"I don't know," she replied. It seemed like the safest thing to say. Caitlin was in danger now, she was sure, and she needed to get out of here. But Rachel was between her and the door, and Caitlin was too weak to fight past her. Her best chance was to get into the bathroom—she could lock herself in there and hope her phone would get signal soon.

"I think I'm going to throw up," Caitlin said.

She jumped up to run across the room, but something—concussion or an aftershock, she would never know—made her lose her footing, and she tumbled to the floor. Desperately, Caitlin tried to pull herself back to her feet, but her arms and legs wouldn't obey her, and she could hear Rachel's footsteps getting closer.

There was a crash of pain at the back of Caitlin's skull, and then nothing.

43

Where did you go last night? We were looking for you," Rachel asked.

"I had to leave the club in a hurry," Mallory said. "Did you come here looking for me?"

"Well, you did seem like you were pretty obsessed with Caitlin. I thought maybe you were going to do something crazy."

Mallory didn't think that tracked, to put it mildly. There were a lot of places someone could have looked for her, like at her home, but the only person Joan had mentioned coming by was Harry.

She didn't say so, though.

Instead, she replied, "I wouldn't say obsessed, exactly, but I do think it's important. I thought I might be able to find something in Caitlin's bedroom, but I took a wrong turn. I was just taking a look around, but we should probably get going. We aren't supposed to be here, obviously."

"Obviously."

Rachel was on the stairs below Mallory, blocking the exit.

Above her, Mallory stood with one hand on the railing and the other on the bag with the Taser. She didn't believe for a minute that Rachel had come here innocently looking for her. The question was, what was she going to do about it? What she needed was something more than a suspicion, some fact she could hang her fears on and act.

Mallory thought about the room she had just been in, with its window seat over the ocean and the double doors open to the gleaming bathroom. And that's when she remembered.

"Have you been in Deborah's part of the house before?" Mallory asked.

"No, never. I didn't come over much—I don't think Caitlin liked people to see that she lived with her mom. But when I did, we only spent time in her room. She even had a little kitchen area. We should look there next. If there's anything here that can tell us what happened to Caitlin, it makes sense it would be in her room."

"I don't know," said Mallory. "I don't think this part of the building is very stable."

"It'll be fine. And you want to find out, right? I don't think you're going to get another chance."

Mallory didn't want to go further into the building with Rachel, and her mind was racing as she tried to come up with a way out. She knew now that she was in danger, and what it was that had made Caitlin panic at dinner that night. What she didn't know was how she would prove any of it.

The PalmPilot in her jeans pocket pressed against her leg, reminding Mallory of another thing she didn't want Rachel to know about. Would there be enough information on there to settle the question? Deborah had died months before her daughter, but she might have written something in her diary that would lead to the answer.

Even if it did, that wasn't going to help her much now. The Taser, on the other hand, might do the job. As they continued up the stairs to Caitlin's room, Mallory began to form her plan. She didn't know how long a person would be down after they had been tasered, but she guessed it would be harder to make it back down an uneven set of stairs. If she hit Rachel when they got to the room, she would probably have enough time to make it out of the house. If she was lucky, Ann might be home across the street, and Mallory could convince her to help.

What would happen after that was an open question. At the moment, Mallory only cared that, for her, there *was* an after.

Unlike the other staircase, which had gone straight up and ended at the bedroom, this one had a right turn halfway up, at a landing with a window that caught another glimpse of the view. Mallory was grateful for it, not because she wanted to admire the scenery, but for the light it let in. She had appreciated the darkness when she thought she had been in the house alone, for the cover it gave her from being spotted from the outside. But now it felt more like a shadowy trap.

Mallory paused on the landing, like she was taking a moment to catch her breath, and waved Rachel around to pass her. That didn't work, and Rachel stopped next to her, looking out the window.

"Aren't the views in this place amazing? Caitlin told me once it was one of the last houses that was allowed to be built this far out on the cliffs. I'm not surprised it was so damaged in the quake." Her tone was light and cheerful, but Mallory thought she detected a tremble in Rachel's voice. Could someone who killed two people really be nervous about trying for the third time? Mallory didn't know, but she was glad the window was too small and too high up to be pushed through.

The steps after the landing were wider and shallower, leading to a closed door at the top of the staircase. The smell of gas was stronger here, which would have made Mallory nervous if she didn't have so many other things to worry about. She didn't think she was the only one of them who had plans for what she was going to do when they got to Caitlin's room, and she would have given a lot to know what Rachel had in mind.

The only thing she had for encouragement was that the crimes so far had been uncomplicated and opportunistic. Caitlin had been hit on the back of the head, Charlie shot with his own gun. Even the attempt on Mallory relied on her being alone and unsuspecting next to an open window. How would Rachel respond to someone who was aware and ready for her?

Mallory was afraid she was about to find out.

44

There was a dead bolt on the door at the top of the stairs, and Mallory thought for a moment they were both going to have to recalculate. But it wasn't engaged, and the door opened easily.

The gas smell inside was so strong that Mallory gagged. She realized immediately, whatever she had in mind, it was less important than the risk of staying in that room.

Mallory turned to Rachel. "We have to get out of here; this is dangerous."

"Yeah, no kidding." Rachel grabbed Mallory by the shoulders and shoved her into the room. "You think I didn't check here first? Your bad luck that you always had a terrible sense of direction."

She tried to push Mallory further in and close her inside, but Mallory was ready for her. Bracing herself on the doorknob, she jammed the back of her shoe under the door. The helmet that had been part of her disguise slid down over her eyes, which gave her an idea. As Rachel grabbed her shoulders to try and move her into the room, Mallory head-butted her, landing the crown of the helmet on Rachel's nose.

"Ow! God dammit, you little bitch."

Rachel reeled back, grabbing the helmet off Mallory's head and throwing it across the room. Taking advantage of her temporary freedom, Mallory pulled the Taser out of its bag and aimed it at Rachel. She was about to pull the trigger when her brain kicked in and stopped her from setting off a spark in a room full of gas.

Mallory barely had time to finish that thought when Rachel was on her again, grabbing at the Taser. She swung her arm wildly, managing to hit Rachel in the face but losing her grip on the weapon in the process. It tumbled to the floor, and Rachel pounced on it, giving Mallory time to unwedge her shoe and lunge out to the stairs.

She stumbled and fell, sliding down and landing with her feet three steps up from her head. Above her, Rachel was still in the room fumbling with the Taser.

"No, don't!" Mallory shouted, trying to warn her. But Rachel must have misunderstood, because she smiled, pointed the weapon at Mallory, and pulled the trigger.

The fireball that blossomed around Rachel's body filled the room and shook the building. Mallory flung her arms over her head as she felt the rush of searing heat. But there must not have been enough gas in the stairway to ignite, and coughing and squinting, Mallory was able to pull herself to her feet.

Behind her the room was a wall of flame. There was no way Rachel could have survived in there, so Mallory spent no time looking for her. It was enough to get herself out, and as the smoke built up and the structure shifted under her, Mallory wasn't sure she was going to make it.

By the time she reached the bottom of the stairs, the fire had spread to the kitchen. Mallory looked over to see the damaged wall break away and fall, taking half the countertop and cabinets with it.

The rush of air that came in fed the fire with fresh oxygen, causing a burst of smoke to swirl around Mallory. Coughing and half blinded, she tried to remember the way to the front door. But she lost her bearings in the darkness, stumbling into a wall and then a small table that fell in front of her and got tangled in her feet.

Mallory tried to remember the lessons from her grade school safety courses, pulling her shirt over her mouth and dropping to her knees to crawl in what she hoped was the right direction. She ran into another wall, and something hot fell on her leg, causing her to yelp and inhale a mouthful of smoke.

The coughing was so violent that Mallory couldn't even crawl forward. She wasn't even sure forward was the way to go—she was so turned around, she might have been going back into the fire. She tried feeling her way along the floor, looking for a part that felt less hot, but it was all the same. So she chose at random and started crawling again, hoping for once in her life her sense of direction hadn't failed her.

She had gone less than a foot when a hand landed on her shoulder and pulled her back the way she had come.

"I've got her! I think it's Mal!" shouted a muffled voice as a light shone in her face. "Come on, we have to get out of here."

Mallory clung to her rescuer as another pair of hands grabbed her other shoulder. Together, they ran forward through the smoky passage, toward a rectangle of light. As they got closer, Mallory could see it was the front door, with another figure standing in it, waving their arms.

"Come on! Come on!" a familiar voice was yelling. "Don't stop—let's get her all the way back to the car."

They came out of the door together, Mallory barely able to keep up as her feet kept failing under her. Out of the house, the light was bright and clear, but her eyes were still watering too much from the smoke to see more than the path under her feet.

Out on the sidewalk, she had the sense of other people around, but the little group didn't stop until they were halfway down the block. They came to rest next to a car, and Mallory was finally able to wipe her eyes and catch her breath.

"Give her some space," said the person closest to her. "Mal, are you okay? What the hell happened?"

It was Lourdes, her eyes rimmed with red and a scarf looped around her neck. On the other side of Mallory, still holding her arm, was Kendra, and Sonali stood back eyeing the curious onlookers.

Mallory tried to take a deep breath to start to explain, but she was interrupted by a bout of coughing.

"I came here to look for something. But Rachel—" She stopped, overwhelmed by explaining what she knew. That the woman who had been friend to all of them had killed at least two, possibly three people, and had just died trying to kill her too. All for money. A lot of money, but that was it. Nothing big or meaningful. How would anyone respond to hearing a story like that? Who would even believe her?

"Rachel murdered Caitlin," Kendra finished helpfully for her. "We put it together just now. Sonali's girlfriend got the phone number of the person who called the restaurant asking for anything Caitlin left behind, and it was Rachel's. And Lourdes had her location shared on her phone, so we knew she had come here. Did she make it out?"

Mallory shook her head, struggling to take it all in. "No, she—no. There was no way."

Her vision had cleared now, and she was able to look more closely at her friends. She had a lot of questions, at least as many as they probably had for her, but in the moment, she could only think of one.

"How did you find me in all the smoke?"

"Luck, mostly. Also, it helped that you were wearing this." Lourdes tugged on the shoulder of Mallory's borrowed high-visibility vest. "It's a good look for you. I think you should go with it."

There was the rising sound of sirens in the distance. For Mallory, hearing them was a relief, and then a source of anxiety. What was going to happen now? What would she say? What kind of prison sentence did you get if they decided you committed arson that killed a person?

"Are you girls okay?" It was Ann, Caitlin's neighbor from across the street, who had come over to check on them. She glanced down at Mallory in her soot-covered outfit and raised her eyebrows. "You do get up to things, don't you? Come into the house and we can talk until the fire department gets here."

45

The doorbell rang, and Mallory jumped. It would be a while before she was comfortable again in her apartment, even though the danger was over. But she would get there, eventually. Suppressing the urge to lock herself in the bedroom again, she got up to open the gate for Lourdes.

"Watch the door as we're going through—Celine has been trying to escape lately."

"Not a fan of her new roommate? I can relate."

Lourdes followed Mallory into the apartment, carefully squeezing through the barely open door.

"It could be that," Mallory said. "But also there's a squirrel that's been coming by and antagonizing her, and I think she's out for revenge."

"Don't do it," Lourdes said to the cat, who was making a liar out of Mallory by sitting calmly on the sofa. "Seeking revenge means you dig two graves, or something."

"That must be what she's been doing in the litter box. Can I get you something to drink? I've got tea, coffee, wine—"

"Wine? Mallory, it's eleven a.m."

Mallory grinned. "White or red?"

They settled on sparkling water, with an option to get into the wine later, and took their glasses to the picnic table in the backyard. It was September, and the warm weather had finally returned, even to Mallory's foggy corner of the city, and she was relishing every moment.

"You didn't have to come all the way out here," she said as Lourdes adjusted her hat to shade her face from the sun. "I could have met you somewhere downtown."

Lourdes shook her head. "I think you've done enough for now. Let someone else do the work for a change. Besides, you know we would scare people talking about what happened."

"Okay, fair. With my luck we'd probably have a cop eavesdropping on us."

That would be a problem, because the four of them, with the help of Ann, had recently spent some time lying to the police.

It hadn't been a major lie, anyway. Ann had been out in her yard when Sonali, Lourdes, and Kendra arrived, and she had seen them go in after the fire started. If she remembered four women going to the house to find their friend and coming away together, that wasn't much of a difference.

The story Lourdes composed, and the rest of them stuck to, was that Rachel had come to the house for reasons none of them knew, and they had come to look for her. It helped that when the police searched Rachel's apartment, they found Caitlin's phone and clothes with Charlie's blood on them. The final public statement about the case had been one short press release, saying that a local DJ was believed to have been killed by an acquaintance, who subsequently died in an accident. The impression Mallory had from her last talk with the detective was that Rachel was assumed to have been back at the house to destroy evidence and hadn't realized how dangerous it was to ignite gas.

"Why do you think she killed Charlie?" Lourdes asked, after they went over it all again. "They were lovers, right?"

"It looks that way. My best guess is he didn't know about the murder, and Rachel was the one who told him Caitlin had left on her own. Then, when Caitlin's body turned up, he started asking questions, and she decided he had to be put out of the way. Plus, if he wasn't going to inherit the house or any of the money, he wasn't much use to her. That would explain why she went all out to get the key I had. That money was the only thing she could take free and clear."

"Speaking of that, I have something for you." Lourdes reached into her oversized purse and pulled out a small black rectangle. "Do you have any idea what this is?"

Mallory turned it over in her hands. It was metal and surprisingly heavy, and there was a sequence of numbers on it that looked familiar. "I can't say for sure, but it looks like a hardware wallet. Where did you find it?"

"In Rachel's apartment. I had a key, from the time she asked me to take care of her plants while she was on vacation. So I waited until it looked like the police were done, and I went in and had a look around."

"The police didn't take it?"

"They didn't know where to look. Years ago, Rachel told me of this clever hiding place she had thought of, at the bottom of a box of tampons. Her idea was that men would be too embarrassed to look there, so that's half the people who might be robbing her. She must not have had a new idea since then, because that's where I found it. Do you think it's Caitlin's?"

"There's one way to find out."

Mallory got up and went into the apartment and fished the hardware key out of its hiding place. As she did, she had another rush of fear, to be exposing this secret she had worked so hard to keep. That money had tempted one of her friends to murder—could it happen twice?

Lourdes was waiting for her outside, and Mallory could feel herself starting to panic. Was it always going to be like this now? Afraid of everyone she knew in case they turned out to be dangerous?

She took a deep breath and loosened her grip on the key. Staring at the little piece of plastic and metal in her hand, she made a decision. Rachel wasn't everybody; she wasn't even most people. Mallory was going to live her life like that was true and take her chances. Sometimes you had to accept that there would always be risks and do what you can to be smart about it, but not let it stop you from existing in the world. After all, she still lived on the fault, didn't she?

"You must have had that thing pretty well hidden," Lourdes said when Mallory finally made it back outside. "I was starting to worry."

"Yes, well, let's just say I don't reveal my secrets."

"Smart girl. So are we going to see if this thing works?"

Mallory picked up the key and the wallet and weighed them in her hands.

"I guess we might as well."

46

I just can't get into cottage cheese. It's not even really cheese; it's cheese's annoying cousin."

Mallory took a sip of her mimosa. "Anyway, I'm done with the food influencers. I saw one who wanted us all to spend a day every week eating nothing but bean broth. No thank you."

"Yuck," Sonali agreed as she unwound another bite of her cinnamon bun. Then the busboy finished refilling their water glasses and she leaned in to the table. "Okay, so you got the lipstick open, and you found the key thing. Then what?"

"Well, that was about the time I figured it had to be someone who was at the dinner. Because who else would have known that Caitlin could have given it to me?"

It wasn't the first time she had told them this story in the two weeks since the fire, but there always seemed to be more questions. Mallory even had some of her own. So when Sonali had suggested they all meet up for brunch, it hadn't taken long for the topic to come up again.

"And you had to suspect all of us," Kendra said. She sounded a little sour about it, and Mallory didn't blame her.

Lourdes was taking it much more in stride. "Of course she did; she'd be stupid not to. Would you have known it was Rachel right away? Because I wouldn't."

"She could be really mean about things, though," said Sonali. "Remember that time someone took her laundry out of the dryer, and she dumped all their clothes in the storm drain? If someone crossed her, she never took it well."

"But that's a long way from murder," Mallory pointed out. "I didn't feel good about it, but after what happened at the club, I couldn't risk trusting anyone. At least not until I figured out that Sonali had alibis for the earthquake and the attack on me. So I figured I could talk to her, at least."

"And it's a good thing you did," Lourdes said. "Because if she hadn't called Kendra, and they both hadn't called me, we never would have found you in time."

"And I wouldn't be here now," Mallory finished. The four of them were sitting on a restaurant patio in the bright September sunshine, already on their second round of mimosas. In this place, surrounded by chatting brunchers and flowering shrubs, it was easy to feel like nothing had ever happened.

"Of course," she went on. "If Kendra had told me about Rachel and Charlie right away, it might not have been a problem."

Everyone else turned to Kendra, but she remained defiant. "And would you have believed me if you suspected me too? Anyway, I didn't even know who he was until we found his body.

I just knew I'd seen Rachel out with some older guy who was all over her a couple of months ago, and when I asked if she was seeing someone, she said she wasn't. So I figured, none of my business. But then we found him dead, and I realized that was Caitlin's stepdad, and..." She trailed off, then shrugged. "It was a lot to take in. I had to think about it for a bit. Eventually I did decide I needed to tell you, but I couldn't get you on the phone, and I didn't want to say it in a voicemail, so I decided to leave a note."

"Which Rachel stole, because she was watching my house," said Mallory. "At that point, I'm not sure which of us was in more danger."

"That was something else I forgot to tell you guys about. When Sonali called me, I had just gotten a message from someone in Half Moon Bay who said they had a package for me that was misdelivered and I could come get it that night. I thought it was weird, but there was some paperwork that I had been waiting for, so I was going to go down there and see. I never heard from them again, and my stuff came the next day, so I didn't think anything more about it. But I wonder if that might have been Rachel."

Sonali shook her head. "Unbelievable. How long did she think she was going to get away with having everyone around her die?"

"If she got the money? Forever, probably," Mallory said. "You can buy a lot of innocence with six million bucks."

"So you never got Kendra's note. How did you know Rachel was trouble when you met her in the house?" asked Lourdes.

Mallory added a few strawberries to her plate, to balance out the beignets, and had some more mimosa. "Well, the fact that she showed up there at all was kind of a giveaway. But the real thing was when she said she had never been in Caitlin's mom's room before. Remember how we were talking at that dinner about the things we would want in our dream houses? Rachel said she would like a fancy Japanese bathtub with temperature controls. Not exactly a standard item, but one Caitlin's mom happened to have. That was what tipped Caitlin off that Rachel knew more than she was telling. So she panicked and gave me the hardware key, and well, here we are."

"And there she is," Sonali finished. "I'm just glad the police bought the story your friend told them. How did you get to know that lady, anyway?"

"Ann? She knew Caitlin and her family from living across the street from them for so long. I think she was pretty upset that the police didn't do more about Deborah's or Caitlin's deaths, so she wanted to help. We were lucky she did. Someone like that is the sort of person cops listen to, you know?"

Mallory kept her voice low, still worried about being overheard, but however good the donuts were, they must not have been the kind that drew in law enforcement, because none of the people at the other tables paid any attention to them.

"Speaking of rich ladies, did you ever manage to crack the code in that diary you found?" Kendra asked. "Not that you could give it to the police now, I guess."

"No, that would probably raise some questions," Mallory agreed. "But I did get in. It turned out to be pretty simple, just a file that wouldn't open unless the device was plugged in. The hardest part was finding a vintage charging cable."

"Was there anything on it?" Lourdes asked.

"Sort of. Obviously, she died before any of this happened. But she did know Rachel and Charlie were having an affair. She even wrote she didn't want to make a big deal out of it because Caitlin had trouble making friends. But she did say she was going to confront him and kick him out. That was one of the last entries."

"Wow," said Sonali. No one else had anything to add, and the four of them sat in silence for a while, working through their thoughts. Finally, Kendra said the thing that was on everyone's minds.

"So do we think Rachel killed her?"

"I don't think there's any way to know," Mallory said.

"But if I was in a betting mood, I'd put at least a grand on it," said Lourdes. "God, I can't believe I could know someone for so long and never realize she was a total psycho. I had to take 'empath' out of my Instagram bio."

Mallory turned to Sonali. "What does Kate think of all this? I'm sorry it's how she got introduced to us."

Sonali laughed. "She thinks it's completely nuts, but she's been cool about it. She was glad to be able to help with getting that phone number. She said it made her feel like waitressing was her superpower. She's sorry she couldn't come today, but she had to work. We thought next weekend we could do a picnic, maybe Saturday afternoon?"

"Oh, um, next Saturday isn't good for me," Mallory said. "Can we do the week after?"

"Sure, but why?" Sonali looked at her curiously, and Mallory could feel her face getting red.

"Well, my neighbor—the one who loaned me the Taser—when I went to give him the new one I bought, he asked me if I wanted to go to a street fair in Japantown. We're going to see a drum group some of his friends are in."

"Mal!" Lourdes laughed and wagged a finger at her. "Dating the boy next door? Who would have thought."

"Across the street, but yeah. He seems cool. I just hope it doesn't get weird, you know? I'd hate to have to find a new place."

"On that topic, I have some news." Kendra pushed her plate away and looked awkwardly around the table. "Mark is quitting his job at the hospital. He and some colleagues are going to start their own practice in Sacramento. So we're moving there at the end of the month."

"*Sacramento*?" said Sonali, expressing the shock they were all feeling. "Kendra, you won't go east of Alcatraz. Are you serious?"

Kendra was defensive. "It's not that bad. They've got a lot of nice restaurants there now. The *New York Times* did a whole piece on it."

"They also have cows," Mallory pointed out. "You hate cows."

"It's not like they wander around downtown. Anyway, there was no way they were going to be able to afford the rent on the kind of space they needed around here. I've got a job at an insurance company there, and they're even going to pay our relocation costs. And do you know what else they don't have there? A fault line. So the next time this city falls down, you can all come visit me in my nice air-conditioned house and tell me what a good decision I made."

She sounded defiant, and she was smiling, but Mallory thought she detected a tremble in Kendra's voice. Still, she wasn't worried.

"I think it's great for you. I've always thought you'd find your true form as the evil queen of the suburbs."

Kendra narrowed her eyes at her, still smiling. "Bitch," she said.

"See? Perfect. Those drugstore blonds won't know what hit them."

Everyone laughed, and Kendra raised her glass at Mallory in tribute. "And if one of them tries to take me out, I know who I can turn to. When are you starting your security service?"

"Around about the twelfth of never," Mallory said. "Mallory Taylor Investigations is officially out of business. From now on I'm going to devote my life to becoming a crazy cat lady. Excitement is for other people."

"Yeah, well, I might have to come to you for tips on the cat lady thing." Lourdes had been quiet while Kendra had told her story, and now she was playing with her coffee cup. "Emil and I just broke up. He's staying in a hotel downtown while we figure out what to do about the lease."

This time there was shock again, but without the amusement.

"Oh damn, Lourdes. I'm so sorry," Mallory said. "What happened?"

"What didn't? I'd known for a while that some of the other guys at the law firm had gotten him into drugs, but I thought it was just at a recreational level. Which I guess it was, if your idea of fun is blowing through ten grand in a weekend. And apparently his other idea of fun was to screw his dealer's girlfriend, who also turned out to be an expensive habit."

"Oh no, Lourdes, that's terrible," Sonali said. "Do you think it was because of the quake? I know a lot of people have trouble with dealing with the trauma of a disaster like that."

Lourdes shook her head. "I wish I could blame the earthquake, but it all started months before that. I think the real problem is that he's just an asshole."

"That's pretty common too," Mallory offered. "I'm sorry, that really sucks."

"It all came to a head about a month ago, when the dealer stopped by my work to say Emil was behind on his bills, and if I didn't take care of it, he was going to tell my boss that Emil had given me the girlfriend's syphilis. He hadn't, but I paid anyway. And I've been spending the rest of the time locking down my finances and getting my life in order so I could get out."

There was another chorus of sympathy, but Lourdes waved it off and turned to Mallory.

"That was why I couldn't take it when you started talking about how someone killed Caitlin. I know it's not fair, but you were asking questions and saying we should do something, and I was just like, *I cannot add another thing right now*. I meant to apologize to you when I came over the other day, but then we got distracted with the crypto wallet thing, and I lost my nerve. Anyway, I'm sorry."

"It's okay," Mallory said. "You were going through a lot."

"I was going through a lot? You got thrown out a window! Look, it's an explanation, not an excuse. But now I'm going to focus on being single for a while and only give my attention to the people who deserve it."

"I'll drink to that," said Kendra, raising her mimosa. They all toasted, and then she looked at Mallory. "So you've got all the crypto now? What are you going to do? Turn it over to the police?"

"Or maybe just throw it into the bay," Lourdes said. "Something like that is never going to stop causing trouble."

Mallory shook her head. In fact, she had been carrying the wallet with her wherever she went, too afraid to leave it at home and not wanting to commit to any long-term storage.

"I don't know. There's no way I can keep it. And I can't go to the police. I just wish I could do something for Caitlin with it. It's bad enough to think of everything going to her deadbeat dad. I don't know what she would have wanted, but I'm sure it's not that."

"Didn't you hear?" Sonali said. "A lawyer came forward the other day with the will Caitlin had him draw up for her. She left everything to a no-kill shelter on Valencia. They're going to build a new wing and name it after her."

"Did she?" Mallory brightened, and then she took the hardware wallet and key out of her purse and set them on the table. "In that case, I think we have an anonymous donation to make."

Mallory

Another February, and Mallory found herself back at the bayfront park where she had stopped after her mad drive across the Presidio. She still had no idea what Rachel had been trying to accomplish by chasing her there. (She was sure now that it had been Rachel following her, in Caitlin's car.) Harry's theory was that it was an attempt at tracking her movements that had gone hopelessly wrong, but that was one of the many things Mallory would never know for sure.

More information about Rachel had come out in the six months since her death. Stories of money going missing from employers, neighbors' vanishing pets, cruel rumors started about exes—it was hard to say what was true and what was exaggerated with the benefit of hindsight, once Charlie's murder had hit the news.

There had even been a true crime documentary about it, with some added speculation about Caitlin and Deborah's deaths. A producer had contacted Mallory, because she was on the record as having identified Caitlin's body, but she told them nothing and blocked their number. They had still found a photo of her to add to the show, and the day after it aired, Mallory had received a fruit basket, addressed to "Caitlin" (complete with quotation marks) and signed "Donna VerSoChic & Co."

But that was as far as her notoricty had gone, and Mallory found she was able to live her life as unnoticed as ever. Certainly, no one in the crowd around her paid any attention as she got an empanada from one of the food trucks and found a spot on the edge of the lawn where she had a good view.

The Golden Gate Bridge was finally reopening, almost a year to the day since the earthquake, and it seemed like everyone in the city had come out to see it. The main party was out at the observation area near the toll plaza, but Mallory hadn't wanted to brave that crowd. So she had chosen this park, with its more distant vantage point, to mark the moment.

Someone nearby was playing the radio coverage of the event, and as Mallory listened to the tinny voices of politicians talking about resilience and rebirth, her mind drifted back to everything that had happened over the last year. That amount of time never seemed right—sometimes it was like it had been ten years, other times just a couple of weeks. The one thing that was consistent was the feeling of life being divided into a distinct before and after, a past that wasn't just a foreign country but another planet.

That was, for the people who got to have an after. While she waited for the bridge to open, Mallory turned and looked the other way, where the ruined roof of the Palace of Fine Arts was just visible across the buildings of the old military base. The shelter that had been Caitlin's beneficiary had given her a nice funeral and memorial in a cemetery in Colma, but Mallory would always think of that monument as her real grave, chosen for her by someone she thought she could trust. Mallory wished there was some way Caitlin could have known that she hadn't left this world without anyone caring about her or at least that her cat was okay. But she didn't think that was possible, so she had to comfort herself with the fact that she knew it.

A cheer went up from the crowd, and Mallory turned back around just in time to see the lights from the line of fire trucks making their ceremonial first crossing of the bridge. Someone started playing "(I Left My Heart) In San Francisco," and Mallory joined the sing-along, though she knew none of the words outside of the chorus. Nobody seemed to mind that, or the fact that everyone was singing in their own personal key and none of them sounded much like Tony Bennett. All that mattered was that they were here, strangers together in a city that kept surviving against the odds.

Reading Group Guide

1. What does your dream home look like? Where would it be located, and what would it contain?

2. Are you prepared for emergency situations in your area? Do you have a plan should something like the earthquake from the novel happen?

3. How have you seen communities support each other during and after a disaster? What about difficult times allows for complete strangers to come together?

4. If you needed to leave your home with no guarantee of returning, what would you be sure to take with you?

5. How do natural disasters such as earthquakes, floods, and hurricanes continue to affect communities long after the media attention has left them? Which groups of people tend to be most impacted by such disasters?

6. If you were in Mallory's situation, what would you have done? Would you have tossed the lipstick? Continued the investigation? Gone so far as to investigate your friends?

7. Are you still friends with the people you knew in high school or college? What is it that keeps (or doesn't keep) people connected from childhood to adulthood?

8. How close are you with your neighbors? Are you interested in the affairs of your neighbors, or do you prefer to keep to yourself?

9. Mallory is told time and time again that she needs to stop taking things so seriously and learn when to leave something alone. What do you think of these accusations against her? Why does she keep going despite those who want her to stop?

10. How do you think having great amounts of money can affect a person? Is that effect always negative? Does it make a difference if you are born to wealth versus if you gained it through your own work?

11. Did you realize who was behind the attacks and murders before it was revealed? Why or why not?

12. What would you have done with the crypto wallet money if you were in Mallory's position?

A Conversation with the Author

Where did the inspiration for this novel come from?

Oddly enough, my original idea was to have the disruption that comes after the first chapter be COVID, not an earthquake. But I think it's a little too soon to be telling that story, and when I stepped back and thought about what other things could separate people for a period of time and disrupt their lives, an earthquake seemed like the obvious choice. I've lived in California all my life, and the threat of "the big one" has been present for as long as I can remember, so it's something I've spent a lot of time thinking about, long before I started to write this book.

What went into the decision to write a few sections from each woman's perspective? What was that like?

Overall, *She Had Enough* is Mallory's story, but I wanted to get the other points of view in there to show the ways the earthquake and Caitlin's death were affecting all of them differently. I also found that it helped me to think through the characters and their motivations, why each of them acted the ways they did when Mallory confronted them.

Do you have a favorite character from the book?

I love them all! (Except for the ones I hate…) But if I had to choose, it would probably be Donna VerSoChic, Mallory's unexpected savior. She was great fun to write, and even though she only appears in one scene, I think she makes a big impact.

There's an emphasis on animals and the love and care for them throughout the book. Does this come from somewhere specific?

Really just my own love of animals, I think. Both Mallory and Caitlin are somewhat on their own, so their pets stand in for human connections for them in different ways.

What would you like readers to take away from the story?

I would like for readers to take away a sense that it's important to care about things, even if it seems futile. The world can be a big, ugly place, and the incentives to only care about what affects you personally are strong. But community matters and so does caring for its own sake.

Acknowledgments

Congratulations! You've read a whole book and made it to the part where I admit I have no idea how this thing got made and thank the people who did it. (Unless you skipped to here, in which case, not how I would do it, but okay. FYI, there's a minor spoiler below.)

As ever and always, thanks to my agent, Abby Saul, for reading, supporting, encouraging, and advocating in all the best ways. Thank you also to Anna Michels for her excellent editorial suggestions and work on all parts of the book.

And thanks to the copy editors, cover designers, book designers, publicists, audiobook producers, and everyone else at Poisoned Pen Press and Sourcebooks for everything they do to make these books come to life.

Then there's my writing community, without whom this all might be possible, but it would never be as fun. Thanks to Karen, Karen, Mariella, and Michelle for encouragement, advice, and general merriment, sometimes all at the same time. And thanks to the Larkies for being the group chat I need but do not always deserve. In the last book I told you all to never change, and I'm delighted you all took my advice.

Special thanks to Jason Powell for his advice about electrical sparks, gas leaks, and the dangerous combination thereof. If there is any technical accuracy about those things in this book, it is due to him; any mistakes are entirely my own.

Thanks to Mom and Dad for supporting me all these years and for always having questions at my events.

Most of all, thank you to Cameron for loving and believing in me and my crazy dreams.

Finally, thank you to everyone out in the world, fighting against injustice and fascism, even when the people around you say to give up and be quiet. There is nothing more radical than to be a source of caring in a world that is determined to make you hopeless.

About the Author

© Andrea Sher

Stacie Grey is an author and fan of mysteries who lives in Alameda, California, with her husband and dog. In what passes for normal life, she works in biotech research. She mostly posts to Instagram and Mastodon and occasionally writes a newsletter.